SLAMMER

NEW YORK TIMES & USA TODAY BESTSELLING AUTHOR

TABATHA VARGO

Slammer/ Tabatha Vargo/RD Douglas
Cover Art by Mae I Design/Regina Wamba
Book design by Inkstain Interior Book Designing
Text set in Cochin LT.

PRINT
ISBN-13: 978-1516967261
ISBN-10: 1516967267

EBOOK
ISBN-10:0986117323
ISBN-13:978-0-9861173-2-9

"Monsters are real, and ghosts are real too. They live inside us, and sometimes, they win."

STEPHEN KING

SLAMMER

PROLOGUE

A SLITHER OF sunlight peeked in through the curtains hanging from the single window in the room, blinding me when I opened my crust-filled eyes. Pain radiated through my brain, splintering across my synapses. Groaning from the severe headache, I slammed my eyes closed and prayed that I wouldn't throw up all over myself.

My head ached with the beat of my heart, a sledgehammer landing against my forehead with each pump of my blood. I rubbed at my sore temples in hopes of making the pain lessen, but there was only the mind-numbing ache.

The stale remnants of beer lathered my dry tongue like flavored cotton. Smacking my lips together, I swallowed the sandpaper that glazed my tight throat. Cravings for water rolled through my stomach as I prayed for moisture in my mouth and a pain-free mind.

Again, I opened my eyes, my blurry vision landing on the ripped curtain flowing from the window like a silky waterfall. It swayed in a breeze I didn't feel, directing my attention to the ceiling fan above me. I stared as the blades cut through the musty air, making dust particles dance in the slice of light from outside.

In the distance, the sound of a clock teased the pain hammering through my brain, making my dark lashes flutter in agony.

Tick-tock, tick-tock.

It was almost too much to handle.

I moved to sit up, but fire shot down my spine, making me gasp. The pain was hot and blazed through my body like fire-tipped daggers. Trying to cry out was futile. Only broken, hushed noises pushed past my cracked lips. I licked them, thick, dried blood tingeing my taste buds and filling my mouth with the metallic flavor of life.

That was when the smell hit me—the acrid scent of death. It was unlike anything I'd ever smelled before—like the end of someone—like dark cries in the night and rotting flesh. Topping it off was the overwhelming scent of blood. It hovered over me, suffocating me. Someone had bled out near me. There had to be more somewhere, and it was considerably more than the tiny bit that seeped from my chapped lips.

I tried to remember the night before, but there was nothing but a few flashes of color—tiny moments of memory that included blonde hair and red, luscious lips—Sarah. I'd been with her. She'd wrapped her sweet lips around my cock and showed me a night I would never forget, but that was all I remembered.

I wasn't sure where I was or how I'd gotten there. Actually, any memories I had of the last few days of my life were gone, except for a few flashes every now and again. Any others were swiped clean from my mind and replaced with nothingness—the equivalent of a TV with no signal—a gray mass of fuzziness.

Wherever I was, I knew I needed to get the hell out of there and get home. My mom would be waiting for me. I wasn't a baby, but even at nineteen, I still checked in. Being an only child meant my mother was very protective of me.

I was a respectful young man. After living with an abusive husband for most of her adult life, my mom taught me well. Since my father's death, it had only been us, and I wasn't about to have her sitting home worried for longer than she needed to be.

Rolling onto my side proved to be harder than it should've been, but I managed. I gasped at the pain and stiffness in my body. I was on a hardwood floor, and there was no telling how long I'd been lying there. If the pain in my young body was any kind of indication, I'd say days.

I rolled over completely and paused. Breath rushed from my lungs, leaving them deflated and still. Cold, lifeless eyes stared back at me—eyes of death—eyes of the end.

It was an unfamiliar guy with light hair and blue eyes. However, a cloudy fog had formed over his eyes, leaving them looking gray instead. His mouth was gaped open, revealing a row of perfect white teeth. It was as if he'd screamed his final breath— screams that I could almost remember hearing. And then my eyes moved down, landing on the bloody stump where his neck used to be.

There was no body. Just his head and those eyes that cut through me accusingly.

I jumped back, not even feeling the pain I knew was there in my scramble to get away from the decapitated head. I'd never seen a dead person before, other than on TV. It was gruesome, and I was sure I'd never forget it for the rest of my life… however long that might be.

My back met the wall, and I cracked my head against the crumbling sheetrock. From my new vantage point, I could see the room as a whole. I looked around in fear for my own life. Whoever had beheaded the man before me could still be there. He could be after me next.

The room came into focus—the bare, tobacco-stained walls, the lone couch in the center of the room, and the table in front of the couch covered with empty beer cans and ripped clothes—I couldn't remember any of it.

It was then I saw them—the body parts—mangled legs and arms. They were littered around the room like broken, bloodied doll parts. My eyes clashed with a set of long, blonde locks of hair drenched with blood. Her mouth was open and her dead eyes were staring accusingly at me.

Sarah.

My Sarah.

The girl I'd been dating for the last few months of my life.

I'd just told her I loved her, and we'd had sex for the first time a few months before. She was my first and I was hers. I knew once I had her that I was going to marry her. The way she opened up for me and trusted me with the most innocent parts of herself… I realized in that moment she was undeniably special. Yet there she was—dead—decapitated like the stranger beside her and screaming out into the morbid solitude around me.

I was in shock. I knew that because as badly as I wanted to go to her, I couldn't move. It was too gruesome of a sight. Blood splatter covered the space, painting the room a rusty red, as if some abstract artist had just finished painting a masterpiece.

It was a slaughter. There was so much death.

Who could've done such a thing? And where was that person now?

Why had I survived?

There were so many unanswered questions.

Looking down at my blood-soaked shirt, I lifted it to check for cuts. There was nothing. It was then that I took notice of my hands. The rusted color of dried blood was smeared all over them. It was caked in my cuticles, dried streaks running up my arms. Some had crusted in my arm hair, making it stick on end. It was all over me… and it wasn't mine. It was *theirs*.

There were only the dead people… and me. Their bodies were mutilated in ways that made my stomach instantly sour. I closed my eyes against the scene, and images filled my mind. There were pictures of screaming and running. They were begging to live — Sarah, begging *me* to live—staring at me with fear while crying. It was all so real.

I blinked away the images. I couldn't remember the events that led me to the moment I was in, but something told me I was responsible. A twinge of doubt and guilt tickled the back of my conscious. I wasn't sure why or how, but I'd killed Sarah and the stranger. I'd ripped them limb from limb and beheaded them like a madman.

Panic thickened in my gut and I turned to the side, puking all over the dirty, wooden floor. The sour smell of beer and things I couldn't remember eating teased my nostrils, making my stomach empty even more.

I was a monster. I was sick and demented, and I didn't even know it. My reality had somehow shifted, and I was in another universe—one where I wasn't the young, carefree boy I'd always been, but a dangerous, bloodthirsty freak.

I needed to get out of the room. Away from everything before me. I couldn't take it anymore. Couldn't look at the disaster I'd caused. I scrambled to my feet. The blood rushed from my head, making me feel dizzy.

I had two options: I could run... or I could go to the police station and confess to murders that I didn't remember committing.

Both options were taken away from me by the loud banging on the door.

"Christopher Jacobs!" a man with a deep voice called through the door. "FBI!"

After that proclamation, the door came crashing in, wood splintering and flying into the space around me. The room filled with the authorities, their accusing eyes filling with disgust as they took in the scene around us. They trained their guns at my head, but everything became muffled and began to blur.

A single beeping noise filled my ears, nagging my beating head and forcing me to swallow and blink. The room spun and the men moved in slow motion toward me as I held my hands up. I was tossed to the ground, a knee in my back and my face pressed into the bloody floor beneath me, as I was cuffed. Suddenly, the beeping sound disappeared and I could hear clearly.

"Christopher Jacobs, you're under arrest for murder."

My life was over. I was as good as dead.

CHAPTER 1

LYLA EVANS

"**FUCK, BABY, I** can smell that sweet pussy all the way over here."

My eyes flashed his way, and I was met with a hairy face and rotting teeth. Quickly, I looked away.

"I'd kill every motherfucker in this place to feel those pouty lips on my dick," another inmate called out.

I looked straight ahead instead of into the eyes of the men who shouted out to me.

The words of the warden and the commanding officer at my interview moved through my mind.

Don't show fear. If you show fear, they'll eat you alive.

"I bet that shit tastes like strawberry pie. I could eat strawberry pie all day, baby."

You have to be assertive. Show them you won't take their mental abuse.

"Hey, Strawberry Shortcake, can I have a taste? Fuck, just looking at you makes me hungry."

Their words echoed all around me. The ones who weren't calling out derogatory things were laughing. They were having a good time at my expense. I was nothing but a joke to them.

Be very private about who you are when you're with the inmates. Don't talk about your personal life with other staff in front of the inmates. Even simple things, said over time, will paint a very detailed picture. Inmates are always listening. Always.

"Come here and let me tongue fuck your slippery clam, pretty girl."

Never turn your back on an inmate; don't let them walk behind you on the way to the blood pressure machine; don't turn your back as you dispose of sharps, etc.

"Look over here, sweet thing. Look at all this cock I got for you."

Make sure at least one custody officer is with you at all times: in the infirmary, treatment area, escorting, etc.

If my daddy knew the kind of job I was working, he'd roll over in his grave three times and pop open a beer to soothe his nerves. Not the nurse part, he always knew I wanted to go into nursing, but where I was a nurse was the problem.

The thought of his little girl working in a maximum-security prison full of hardened criminals would kill him if he weren't already dead. But he was dead. Had been for three years, and I was left to fend for myself.

God rest his sweet soul and bless him.

It was my first day and my nerves were definitely getting the best of me. Of course, it didn't help that I was locked inside. Watching the bars close behind me every time I moved further into the prison to the infirmary was enough to send me straight into an anxiety attack. It was suffocating in a way. I couldn't imagine being an inmate and not being able to leave.

When another round of bars closed behind me with a loud bang, I took a deep breath.

I was fresh out of nursing school. I'd done my clinicals for a family practice close to home, taking the temps of children and the blood pressure of the elderly. I was so thrilled to graduate and become a registered nurse. Looking back, I remember how excited I was about the possibility of working the labor and delivery floor at St. Francis Hospital. Bringing new life into the world and holding a newborn life in my hands was my ideal dream.

I was clueless.

Jobs were few and far between. With bills that needed to be paid and student loans that were soon to be knocking on my checkbook, I couldn't afford to be picky. Instead, I was walking halls full of men who had taken lives — ones with no remorse for their crimes.

I'd accepted a job in the infirmary at Fulton Rhodes Penitentiary, one of the most dangerous prisons on the East Coast.

"Hey, Red, how's about taking a ride on this hard cock?"

It got worse the more we walked.

"Don't look them in the eye," Officer Douglas said from the side of his mouth. Louder, and in a much harsher tone, he snarled to an inmate as we passed by, "Knock it off, Reid. Put your pecker back in your pants or I'm taking your ass to solitary."

I walked next to him toward the infirmary. Cells lined the halls around me, and the men inside them continued to call out filthy words that made my stomach turn. I knew when I took the job how hard it was going to be, but being spoken to that way wasn't something I was accustomed to.

Closing my eyes, I swallowed hard before taking a deep breath and schooling my expression. I couldn't let these men eat me alive on the first day. My daddy didn't raise me to be a quitter. I'd always been tough as nails, but losing my dad had softened me a bit. I was raw and hurt — afraid of everything that moved — and it wasn't like me. I'd always been able to handle being roughed up a little, but I was still sickened by the foul things that flew from the mouths of murderers.

Finally, we left the block and the final set of bars closed behind us. When we stepped into the infirmary, I was able to breathe again. The space was empty except for the beds that lined the crisp, white walls. The sharp scent of antiseptic stung my nostrils, but after the pungent odor of the men on the block, the hospital smell was welcomed. I'd never been more thankful to be inside of a germfree environment.

"Here we are," Officer Douglas said. "Dr. Giles will be with you shortly."

He backed out of the room with an awkward smile. The bars opened with the loud clicking I knew I needed to get used to, and then closed behind him with a final bang.

I was alone. The room around me haunted me with its bare walls and grey and white shadows of sin. Alone—in a maximum-security prison with murders, rapist, and God only knew what else just outside the room.

Great.

I picked up a stethoscope from the counter, the cold steel burning my fingertips. When I set it down, the noise echoed throughout the room, sending chills down my spine. I didn't know if I'd ever get used to working in such a place.

There were many beds. Some were hidden behind the closed separator curtains, making me nervous that I wasn't alone. That there might be a sleeping inmate behind one of those curtains. Maybe he would wake up at any minute to rape and murder me.

It could happen.

I jumped when a buzzer sounded and a door I hadn't noticed in the room opened. A man, who I could only assume was Dr. Giles, entered the room. His jacket was as white as the walls around us, his eyes just as cold, but his smile was warm. I guessed that would have to be enough.

"You must be Lyla. I'm so glad you're here. We've been shorthanded for far too long."

Suddenly, the room felt warmer and his icy eyes melted into a friendly brown.

I nodded and smiled. "I'm glad to be here." It was a lie. I wasn't glad—I was scared. I felt dirty and cold, but still, a job was a job.

I spent the next hour following Dr. Giles around the infirmary and getting to know the space and where everything was located. He pointed out the machinery, explaining that a few of the machines were older and had certain tweaks. Apparently, when it came to hardened inmates, top-of-the-line equipment wasn't all that important.

"The good news is that you'll never get bored here." He smiled. "There's something new every day."

That sounded promising. I didn't bother to ask what some of the "new" things would be. My imagination was already going nuts with the possibilities.

"Your main responsibility until you get comfortable here will be intake screenings. You'll spend most of your time doing those. When a new inmate comes in, you'll do a full work up. You'll then fill out a four-page document on each inmate's physical and mental health status."

He flittered around the infirmary, speaking quickly, making it nearly impossible to remember everything.

"Those documents are important, so don't skim on them. If we're going to be safe here, we need to understand exactly who it is we're working with. When an inmate enters our facility, it's important to understand all their health issues—be it mental or physical. Trust me. It could save your life."

It was a lot to take in. My worry must have shown on my face because Dr. Giles reached out and laid a hand on my arm. "You'll get the hang of it."

He moved on and continued. I followed.

"In addition, you'll be expected to administer doses of medication. Many inmates in the system are on medicine, and we're responsible for making sure they receive it. Your other duties include coordinating outside services for inmates and overseeing care management for HIV-positive patients. You'll see a lot of that here. That and Hepatitis C. These men are locked together for most of their lives. You need to understand that certain relationships ensue."

I nodded my understanding.

"Let's see… what else?" He tapped his pen against his chin. "Oh yes. When it's time for an inmate to leave, we'll coordinate with the correctional department to facilitate the patient's discharge and arrange for continued care and medications outside. There may even be times when you'll also run a hospice unit."

He stopped and turned to take in my reaction. "Lyla, your job here is vital. I know working in a prison infirmary isn't ideal, but you might be surprised to find that this job is extremely rewarding. We can even play a role in decisions on early releases for ailing inmates. It depends on the inmate and their situation, but we occasionally put a great deal of effort into compassionate releases." He smiled.

He loved his job and was proud of it. That was reassuring.

Turning, he began to talk again. "Lab work is done on-site, and medications are provided by the state pharmacy. With several inmates sometimes crowded into the same cell, and especially with their sexual relationships, infection control is key. If we get a transmissible disease, we've got a crisis on our hands."

Picking up a folder, he began to thumb through the documents. "Any questions so far?" He peeked up at me over the rims of his reading glasses.

I shook my head. Truth be told, I had a ton of questions, but I was too nervous to ask. Removing his glasses, he set his folder to the side.

"Lyla, working in a penitentiary takes some acclimation. We work closely with the officers to ensure our safety in an environment much more regimented than the outside world. We're prohibited from even bringing a cell phone into the facility, as I'm sure you realized when you were brought in. It's not necessarily a warm, bright environment. In fact, it tends to be dark. The equipment isn't state-of-the-art and discussing anything personal inside these walls is considered inappropriate behavior and is not accepted. There are boundaries. If this job is something you don't think you can do, I'll understand. Don't be afraid to walk away. You wouldn't be the first."

I processed all the information I'd received in such a short period. It was a lot, but I knew I could do it. Honestly, I didn't have much of a choice. With a forced smile and my nerves close to snapping, I nodded. "I can do this," I said with false positivity.

He smiled and put his glasses back on. "That's good to hear."

THE FIRST WEEK at my new job consisted of intake screenings. I worked under three corrections officers as I looked over each naked inmate, administered a physical, and asked a multitude of questions to get a grasp on their mental state. I'd never seen so many penises in my life. *Big. Small. Short. Long.* I could see them when I closed my eyes.

On top of that, there was so much paperwork that my eyes would blur. By the time I was done, my wrist ached from writing so much and my eyes burned from reading. It was exhausting work.

When I wasn't doing intake screenings, I was giving the diabetics their insulin and dispensing hydrochlorothiazide to the inmates with high blood pressure. It was a busy job, and when I went home at night, I fell into my bed and slept like the dead.

On my second week, I spent most of my time in the infirmary with Dr. Giles. He gave me tour after tour of the prison, thankfully when the inmates were at rec time or eating lunch. When I wasn't doing that, I was making buy lists for the supply closet and disinfecting the clinical areas.

I was just returning to the infirmary from five intake screenings when a loud alarm began to ring out. Red lights flashed, illuminating the walls with quick bursts. Fear struck me deep. I'd seen prison movies. Alarms ringing and flashing lights were usually a bad thing.

Dr. Giles patted my arm. "You'll get used to it. This happens a lot."

I'd had yet to experience a lockdown, but there were two other nurses and a physician's assistant who worked at Fulton. We took shifts—four on and four off—which meant poor Dr. Giles spent most of his life at the prison.

He moved across the room and began setting up a few beds.

"It won't be long now until a few of these beds are filled. The alarms usually mean a fight. These boys fight dirty, so be prepared for blood."

Nodding, I swallowed. I'd already been there two weeks, but I wasn't ready for this part of the job.

The alarm silenced, and the bars began to click and clank. The room filled with raucous noise as the COs pulled in three inmates. Like Dr. Giles said they would be, their khaki uniforms were covered in blood. One of them was out cold.

The room became busy, and I assisted Dr. Giles as he stitched and patched up the inmates. Apparently, getting shanked in prison was a real possibility.

"It doesn't matter how many times the COs toss the cells; they always find ways to hide their weapons."

Uneasily, I kept to my task without responding. I didn't even want to think about where they hid their weapons. Diana, a friend of mine, swore they shoved things like that up their asses. Just thinking about it made me shiver.

The inmate Dr. Giles was currently working on pulled at his restraints and cursed in rage. I stood to the side as a needle was jabbed into his arm, making him relax and lie back.

Dr. Giles smiled up at me. "Scared you, huh?"

"A little."

"Don't worry. When they're rowdy like this, the officers keep watch."

My eyes moved around the room. When I saw three officers waiting by the door, I felt safer.

"Besides, this guy's not one you have to worry about," he said, pulling his suture tighter.

"Oh? And which inmates should I worry about?"

"Hmmm, good question. I guess the most dangerous inmate on the block is a guy named X. He's been here ten years for two counts of murder. Slaughtered his girlfriend and her friend, and I do mean *slaughtered*. I saw the crime-scene photos." He shook his head. "Anyway, he gets in a lot of trouble around here. He doesn't talk much, but you'll see him often. When you do, just patch him up and move him out as quickly as you can."

"X? What kind of a name is that?"

"It's a name given by other inmates. The lifers like to forget the life they used to have. You'll find a lot of them go by nicknames. The boys named him X because his cell is lined with X marks. No one knows why he does it. He's a strange one. Like I said, he's a scary guy. Just keep an eye out."

And as if he'd somehow summoned them, the alarms went off again. I covered my ears and clenched my eyes closed. This was really happening. It was like an extremely bad movie, and it was my life.

The room lit up with red. Soon, the noises stopped and the lights dimmed until they were out completely. The officers moved quickly, bringing in a fresh batch of inmates.

"Looks like it's going to be a busy day," an officer said with a smile. I didn't know his name, and it was the first time I had seen him.

When my eyes moved from the officer to the inmate he had cuffed at his side, everything and everyone in the room disappeared.

Breathless, chest heaving, I stared at the giant who enveloped the room around us. My heart slammed against my ribs as I took in his large frame. The sheer size of him was overwhelming. His sweat-drenched uniform clung to the tapered V of his torso, displaying every curve and cave of his muscles.

He stood rigid; his six-foot-four frame and wide shoulders filling the doorway behind him. His thick chest and shoulders demanded to be released from his khaki uniform, which was stretched tightly over his tanned skin. His head was down, and I stared at his shaved head while taking in the many jailhouse tattoos that moved up his neck and down his exposed forearms.

As he raised his head, he looked up and raked me with the ice-cold stare of a sinner. His eyes were royal blue, a strange contrast to his bronzed skin. They stood out as he peered at me beneath thick, ebony brows. His shadowy eyes moved across my face, and his expression darkened.

His nose was long and arrow-shaped, his nostrils flaring angrily with each breath. With a squared jaw and thick, moist lips, he was beautiful and treacherous. Evil radiated from him, even though he had a face that was obviously chiseled by angels.

His glare blazed into me, stopping my breath and paralyzing me where I stood. He was gorgeous, he was dangerous, and I'd never been so taken aback by my hormones as they went wild through my body in thanks to my rapidly beating heart.

"Well, speak of the devil," Dr. Giles said, taking my attention away from the dark angel who was staring me down. "What did you do this time, X?"

X.

This beautiful creature was the madman named X?

He was the slaughterer of men — the taker of life — the killer. A sinner with the body of a God and the face of a fallen angel, he was beautiful death — gorgeous hell. He was everything I was afraid of, and luckily for me, since I was new and Dr. Giles was busy, I was the one to provide him with care.

CHAPTER 2

CHRISTOPHER JACOBS
AKA-X

I SPENT TOO much time in medical. It wasn't by choice. It was either the infirmary or the hole. Neither offered any sort of reprieve, but seeing her standing there with her bright, innocent eyes and long, red hair, I could almost forget I was stuck in hell.

Before I murdered Sarah, and Michael Welch, the guy who I later found out during my trial was a friend of hers from high school, in a psychotic rage, I had never used my fists. I was a lover, not a fighter. A nineteen-year-old momma's boy—a rack of bones with unmarred skin and a bright, welcoming expression. Life was filled with tantalizing, exciting possibilities, and no one was more excited to embark on discovering those possibilities than me.

And then I snapped.

I went fucking crazy... mental. Apparently, I lost my mind, torturing and killing the girl I loved. I ripped their flesh apart with a kitchen knife and pulled their insides out.

My stomach rolled just thinking about it.

I could still smell them—the scent of their rotting guts on my fingers. Could still remember the look of absolute fear and death painted on their faces. All the blood that streaked the room. The memories weren't sweet. They were catastrophic. The images broke me down every day and haunted me with terrible nightmares every night.

There was no relief. Not ever.

I wasn't sure what caused my break. Hell, I didn't even remember it, but since then, I'd spent the last ten years of my life fighting to survive—for balance in a place that was completely unbalanced—unhinged from reality and decent people.

There was more crime inside the walls of a penitentiary than outside. More drugs. More murder. More rape. There was more of everything, yet there was so much less. More than just your freedom was taken away. Your values were snatched from you. The ability to distinguish right from wrong was obliterated. It was all tossed into the trash with your belongings and anything you had left of the life you used to live.

Life without the chance of parole. That was what they gave me. However, not a day went by that I actually felt alive. It was if I'd been given the death penalty. My heart had stopped beating, and my brains turned to mush. I was nothing but a number in a building full them, but the minute I laid eyes on the new nurse, life filled me—bright and breathless—salvation.

She was life. I wasn't.

The only reason I didn't get the death penalty was because I pled guilty to all counts. My public defender pushed me to do that even though I had no memory of the murders. He said there was too much evidence against me. If I didn't plead guilty, I'd be sentenced to death. Most days I wished I were. I wished someone would take me away from everything and everyone. I had nothing. I *was* nothing.

I lost everyone. My mother, the person who was supposed to love me no matter what, disowned me. She wouldn't even look at me in the courtroom. Finally, she stopped coming to my trial. Two years later, the warden came to my cell and informed me that she'd died from a massive heart attack. She'd died alone in our home. I wasn't there for her.

I missed her funeral because of bad behavior. After receiving the news, I'd flipped my shit. I barely remember bashing in the head of one of the COs. The last threads of myself were pulled away that day.

My home, the one I grew up in, was sold six months later, effectively killing any memories of the boy I used to be. Christopher Jacobs died in the room with Sarah and Michael — I'd murdered him, too — slaughtered him just as I slaughtered the others. All that was left was X — an enigma that even I didn't understand, a murderer, a dangerous, wild man without emotion or regard — a killer of all things.

That was all I was anymore, and the inmates around me thought it was a feat to conquer me. Lord knew they tried constantly, especially the newbies. They wanted to assert themselves — show dominance and earn a place in the high ranks of the prison. In their search for the top, they had to go through me. Not because I wanted them to fuck with me, but because those in the higher ranks forced it.

Their climb to the top in a place where rank was important was the reason for my visit to the infirmary. I was minding my business, locked away in my own thoughts as I collected the wash from the industrial dryer. It wasn't that I hated working in the laundry, but it was hot and strenuous. However, it was a good workout on the days when I didn't get yard time for a run.

I should've known it was too convenient that I was in the laundry alone. After being in the pen for ten years, I knew how things worked. Rarely were you ever alone, and when you were, it was because someone had paid off a CO.

Chills ran up my spine, warning me that I was no longer alone in the laundry. I sensed him behind me before I felt his fist on the back of my head.

What kind of pussy hit a man from behind?

I leaned forward from the exertion of his hit before turning around to face the coward. The room behind him filled with the familiar faces of the Mexican Mafia, one of the most dangerous gangs in the joint. They were mostly known for drug trafficking, extortion, and murder, but I'd seen it all from this particular gang. Nothing was beneath them, and they played dirty.

They were identifiable by the number thirteen that was tattooed on their cheeks—the number thirteen because it represented the thirteenth letter in the alphabet—the letter M.

Carlos Perez, their leader, stood in the middle with crossed arms and waited for me to retaliate, but I didn't hit the coward back yet. I always gave them at least one. A freebie so to speak. He could still walk away, and I wanted to convey that with my expression.

He wasn't familiar. He was a newbie, a dumbass trying to gain entrance into one of the most lethal gangs on the block. I fought a lot of newbies for this reason. Apparently, it took balls to find the biggest motherfucker behind bars and take him down. Luckily for me, I was that man. It gave me an excuse to rip fuckers apart whenever they were stupid enough to run up on me.

Gaining access into a gang in prison gave you a certain level of protection. For the smaller guys with no fighting skills, a gang was a smart move. You might get your ass kicked for entry, but with a band of brothers behind you, you weren't likely to get your ass kicked again. For them, it was worth it.

Most of the gangs stuck to their own. The Mexican Mafia and La Nuestra Familia preferred Latinos. La Nuestra Familia, which was Spanish for 'the family', wasn't as dangerous as the Mexican Mafia. Instead of dabbling in the hardcore stuff, they were more known for their work in sex trade. They communicated with their members on the outside, ordered hits, and organized one hell of a smuggling ring.

Not to mention that becoming a part of the Familia took years, versus a quick initiation fight into the Mafia. Ernesto Gonzalez, the leader of the Familia, required a complex initiation process where the recruit was responsible for demonstrating their potential and righteousness.

The Black Guerillas and the 803 were mostly black, although there would be the occasional white guy who thought he was a brother. They ran the right side of the yard. That crew mostly played dice and made Jump, or prison wine. They'd gather shit from the cafeteria and brew it in their cells. It was nasty as fuck, but it packed a punch.

The Black Guerilla Family, also known as the BGF, required a life pledge. Once you were in, the only way out was death. The prospective members were nominated by existing ones. They were identified by their tattoos as well, which was a dragon wound around a prison tower while holding an officer in its clutches.

The 803 consisted of the outcast black boys that were never nominated by a BGF member, and they were the least dangerous on the block. More than anything, they stuck together and watched each other's backs.

The whites stuck to their own as well, branching into multiple gangs from the Aryan Brotherhood to the Skulls.

The Aryan Brotherhood, or the AB, was a supremacist group. They walked their side of the yard with bald heads and racial tats, waiting for a fight. They were a ruthless gang who regularly murdered and grew out of control at times—so out of control, in fact, that even their own ranking members couldn't consider themselves safe.

And the skulls were the equivalent of the 803, just a group of white boys who needed someone to watch their backs. It was all political shit that led to death or the hole. Basically, Fulton Penn was one big cluster fuck of race wars, and I had no desire to be a part of any of their bullshit.

The newbies learned quickly that they were just sport for the high rankers. They would never gain an actual spot in the gangs. Instead, they were used for amusement. Like the poor punk who'd sucker punched me from behind. He didn't stand a chance. He was too weak. Still, that didn't stop the Mexicans from having a little fun watching me kick his ass.

Cracking my neck, I rubbed the raw spot on the back of my

shaved head where his knuckles had pressed and eyed him. I was giving him ample opportunity to turn tail and leave. I didn't know this new kid, but I knew he was at least a foot shorter than I was and had never lifted a weight in his life. I could tell by his puny arms.

Many of the inmates lifted weights in the prison, but they did it to bulk up... to better be able to protect themselves. Not me. Lifting was my only escape inside. I didn't lift weights to build muscle or to be the biggest motherfucker on the block. I did it to relieve tension. To press away all the bad memories.

His nostrils flared and he held his arms out at his sides, his hands opening and closing into tiny fists. He was scared, looking for acceptance. I didn't blame him. Prison was a scary place.

I looked him in the eye, taking notice of the fear that swam in his. His rapid heartbeat tapped against the side of his neck, and sweat glistened on the top of his brow. He was having second thoughts. Good. I didn't want to fight this kid, but if he wanted to go at it, I was going to protect myself.

I didn't speak often, so instead of talking to him, I lifted a brow, asking him if he seriously wanted to do this.

His expression shifted, and briefly, I thought he would be smart and walk away. But then he reached behind him, taking a paper blade from one of the gang members egging him on.

"Cut his heart out, bro. Earn your fucking spot," Carlos pushed.

Carlos was a real fucked-up piece of work—had been since the day he stepped foot on the block. He was the leader of the Mexican Mafia, but he didn't speak a drop of Spanish. Go figure. Somehow, though, he still managed to run shit. It never made any sense to me why a group of men would follow someone who couldn't even understand half of them.

Again, the newbie held up his paper blade, taking my attention away from Carlos and the guys behind him.

A fucking paper blade? *Seriously*? They were practically setting him up to fail.

I'd had a lot of weapons pulled on me over the years. From

toothbrush shanks to peeled paint balled up into hard paintballs to soda cans—inmates came up with all kinds of crazy shit to use. Being on the block meant becoming inventive. These boys pulled out some serious smarts when it came to making weapons.

It might sound crazy, but a whittled-down, sharpened toothbrush could do a lot of damage. Shit, I would know. I spent two days in the infirmary thanks to one of those bitches. The nasty scar it left behind was a constant reminder to never turn my back on another inmate.

And when it came to the fist-sized paintballs, those motherfuckers hurt like hell. Inmates put them in socks and slung them against your head. I'd felt a beating from one of those bitches. It was like getting socked by a cinderblock. I woke up a few hours later with a knot the size of my fist on the side of my head.

I had scars from some of the most ridiculous shit. Shivs. Shanks. Any weapon these assholes could manage, but paper blades were the dumbest. This small guy needed a big weapon, and I almost smiled at how ridiculous he looked holding the tiny, sharpened roll of papers. It was probably thirty pages from a National Geographic in the library.

Death by a research and science magazine. *Yeah, fucking right*.

Newbies favored the paper blade because they were easy to make, nothing more than rolling the paper up extremely tight, soaping it down, and salting it. It made the paper hard enough to punch through skin like metal. The main advantage to the paper blade was it could be unrolled and destroyed simply by flushing it down the john. That shit came in handy when the COs started to toss the cells.

Still, the blade was small, which meant for it to be effective, he needed to get close to me. Once I had my hands on him, it wouldn't matter what he was packing.

I stood there, unflinching, and waited for him to attack. And then he did. He moved quickly. His small stature gave him the advantage of speed, but he ran right into me, giving me the chance to yank him up before he could even swipe the blade my way.

The gang members covered their smiles behind their palms. They had obviously set him up to fail. These men were bored and watching some kid get his ass whipped was considered entertainment.

Fuck that.

I wasn't a dancing monkey.

Scooping the newbie up and pressing him against the wall with one hand, I yanked the paper blade from him and tossed him to the side like a sack of laundry. He scrambled back on his hands and knees, running into the group of watchers, all dying for some form of excitement.

Their smiles disappeared, and they peered angrily at me for not snapping on the dude and beating him within an inch of his life. That wasn't my thing.

I knew what was coming, but it didn't matter. As I held the paper blade in my hand, seven of the gang members surrounded me, pissed that I wasn't playing their game. Their tattoos were shiny from sweat, and their black hair was slicked back with oil. Dark brown eyes took in my stance, sizing me up for their attack.

My eyes skimmed over them as I tried to figure out which one would pounce first, but they surprised me when all seven jumped on me at once.

As I fought back, my fists flew and made contact several times. I didn't use the paper blade even if seven on one wasn't a fair fight. I was old school, so fuck it. If I was going to go down, I was going down swinging, but I held my own. It wasn't until one of them stuck me in the leg with a blade that I went down completely.

Officers filled the room at that moment, pulling the fight apart and ripping the paper blade from my fist without even noticing the other guy with his blade. As usual, they ignored everyone else who brandished a weapon. I was on their shit list and didn't have any of them in my pocket, which meant I was the one who always got the short straw.

No one ever said the COs were fair. Money and drugs were the only language they understood.

Before long, I was being cuffed and shuffled off to the infirmary. The smell of my blood filled my senses and sent my memories reeling. The gang members who jumped me laughed as I was hauled off, spitting onto the cold concrete at my feet.

My leg ached where the blade had entered, and my khakis were slowly turning rusty red. I walked to the infirmary without a limp and with my head held high. I wouldn't let those fuckers know how badly my leg hurt.

While three of us, Carlos included, went to the infirmary, the rest of them went back to their cells. A few of them, including the newbie, had run at the first sight of custody moving in. I smirked to myself, knowing that I'd at least gotten a piece of Carlos and some other asshole. I knew for sure that Carlos would need stitches. I'd felt his skin rip when I hit him.

Officer Reeves roughed me up on the way to the infirmary. He was a dirty bastard who thrived off excessive force. He had eyed me the first day I entered the block. I'd seen the way his eyes took me in, and I wondered if maybe he was thinking of trying to make me his bitch. Honestly, the way he'd looked me over was one of the main reasons I'd started lifting weights.

He kept his eyes on me for weeks until he finally approached me. Believe it or not, the COs posed more of a risk than the inmates did. When he made contact with me, I found out that the COs spent thousands gambling. There was somewhat of an officer-sanctioned "fight club" for entertainment. They'd put inmate against inmate and paid the winner a percentage. In his eyes, I was a prized fighter.

The winning inmate was given more than a percentage, though. They were given special privileges and rewards that were not usually found in the prison. Things were expunged from their records. Contraband was overlooked and sometimes even given to them. *Money. Drugs. Weapons. Protection. Women.* There was a lot to gain in the fighting ring, but nothing I wanted or needed.

I'd turned him down then, and I'd continued to do so for the last ten years. The bastard hated me for that and made my life hell. In his mind, if he kept it up, he'd break me. He wanted to use me as his own fighter dog. He wanted me to rip apart the competition and earn him thousands.

It wasn't going to happen.

Inmates were nothing to the COs. We were treated like dogs, fed and bred by the officers who had the money to invest in their animal. They rewarded and punished their asset just enough to make sure the big dogs stayed on top and the rest stayed exactly where they were meant to be.

It was lucrative, especially for a guy like me. Reeves wasn't the only one who had tried a time or two to get me to fight. Going against the COs was almost as dangerous as fighting in their club. It made you a target, something to be beaten down and destroyed for not obeying and jumping through their hoops, but none of it mattered to me. I fought to survive. *End of story.* The ones who had everything to gain and nothing to lose hated me for that.

"Move your ass, X," Officer Reeves said, pressing his baton into my back.

The bars clicked and clanked before banging into the open position. I followed Officer Reeves into the infirmary with my head down. The smell of the antiseptic in the room always made me feel nauseated.

I looked up, and there she was. The new nurse. She was wearing a pair of soft pink scrubs. There was nothing sexy about her clothes, but she looked so delicate and sweet. Honestly, she was the most beautiful creature I'd laid eyes on in my life.

I wasn't sure if it was her angelic beauty casting off her porcelain skin or the sheer mystery she appeared to be, but all I could do was stand there, stunned. She was simply breathtaking.

A tiny batch of freckles was scattered across her pert nose, and even from where I stood, I could see the swirls of caramel brown in her green eyes. Her lips were pink and pouty as if she were pondering life's greatest mysteries. Every now and again, she'd nibble the side of her lip as if she were unsure.

Most of her long, auburn hair was piled on top of her head, as if she'd run out of time when she was pulling it into a ponytail, and her baby pink scrubs hung from her tiny frame.

The muscle in my arm flexed beneath Officer Reeves' fingers as he ushered me to a nearby bed, and I had to tear my eyes away from her.

She was too pretty. Looked too sweet for such a sour place. She didn't belong there, and I was sure she knew that. If it was the last thing I did, I'd make sure she didn't stay long.

Officer Reeves pushed me back onto the bed, smirking down at me. He knew there was nothing I could do to him, so he could be as rough as he wanted. *Fucking power-hungry piece of shit.*

Stepping to the side, he took his spot next to the door. I watched as he eye-fucked the new nurse while she made her way across the room to collect supplies.

I turned away. I couldn't watch.

The bed he pushed me on was close to a window, which made me happy. I hadn't had yard time in days, and my body craved the sun. Birds chirped in the distance, and I could hear them through the thin pane of glass separating me from the outside world.

Closing my eyes, I pretended I wasn't stuck behind cinderblock walls and I was outside the barbed fencing. Ten years was a long time to be locked away. I was beginning to forget what it felt like to be free.

"It's a nice day out," a soft voice commented at my side.

Opening my eyes, I raked her face with my hard stare, connecting the fawn-colored freckles on her nose and cheeks. She swallowed hard. Looking away, she grabbed a pair of scissors to cut my khakis away from my wound.

I didn't respond. Instead, I turned away and let her do her job.

After she cut away the fabric, revealing the deep stab wound in my leg, she used cotton to soak up the blood that was still seeping from it. Her fingers trembled, showing her fear and insecurities.

Good.

She *should* be afraid of me. Hopefully, I'd scare her off and she'd leave her position as soon as possible. The truth was that I knew these people. The officers. The inmates. And I knew they would eat her alive.

The inmates would visualize her naked. They'd think about all the graphic things they wanted to do to her body—sick, twisted, perverted things. It made my stomach turn. The rapists who roamed the halls would debate over how and when they would attack her.

The guards would be helpful for a while, but those bastards were just as dirty, if not dirtier, than the inmates were. Most of them weren't married and had no life outside of the prison walls. They spent countless hours with the lowest form of scum this world had to offer—men with nothing to lose and more time to gain—men so disgusting you wondered if they were ever human.

The guards who had been there too long were, in a way, taught and trained by the inmates who would die there. They were deprived of a female's sweet touch, so they, too, would plot ways to get her alone, rub up against her, and talk dirty to her until not even the hottest of showers could wash away the stench of their breath.

Anger began to swim behind my eyes. Fury toward any person who thought hiring her was a good idea. But then she laid her glove-covered fingers across my hard skin, and I looked into her eyes.

"This might sting a little, Mr. X." She smiled sheepishly.

She was right. Her smile stung me somewhere deep. Some place I hadn't wanted to acknowledge for a long time. One I couldn't afford to retain. It was too soft—too sensitive for a place like prison.

I didn't like it. She needed to go.

CHAPTER 3

LYLA

HE WAS HARD. His body was like granite and just as carved and beautiful as a Greek statue. Later, when I was home, alone and safe, I'd be ashamed of every lustful thought I had over the inmate in front of me, but in that moment, I couldn't think logically. I tried to keep my hands from shaking, but it was like they had a mind of their own. All they could think about was the feel of his muscles beneath them.

Dr. Giles was across the room, patching up another inmate. He wasn't paying me any attention, and I was deathly afraid I was going to do something wrong.

Taking this job wasn't a great idea. The more X stared at me, obviously trying to rattle me, the more nervous and unsure I became. His emotionless eyes moved over my face without blinking. He could see my fear, or at least smell it. Predators could sense terror, and this man was the epitome of one.

I schooled my expression and silently begged my hands to settle. Shaky hands made my fear obvious, and we weren't supposed to show we were afraid. Already, I was failing.

After cleaning his wound, I examined it. It was deep. Even though I knew he had to be in an immeasurable amount of pain, he didn't flinch. Not even when I packed the wound tightly with gauze.

My eyes moved over his body, taking note of the many scrapes and scars that marred his skin. He was everything Dr. Giles said he was—an emotionless monster out for blood—out for death. His arms, chest, and sides were like a tribute to his violent tendencies. The tats running down his back and arms did little to hide the scars that graced his body.

It was obvious he was in a lot of fights, considering the marks on his body. Moving my eyes over his flesh, I counted over fifteen wounds, all healed over, and some more than once. My hands trembled again slightly. It wasn't from fear, but out of curiosity. I wanted to run my fingers over his skin and feel the ridges and bumps of his scars. I wanted to know if I touched them, could I feel the pain behind them? Would he allow me to feel his pain?

It made me wonder how many fights he'd been in to have so many scars, and those were just the visible ones. It made me wonder *why* he'd been in so many and how he'd managed to stay alive each time. I thought about a lot of things I probably shouldn't care about, but that didn't seem to stop the questions from producing one after another.

"How's that feel?" I asked, hoping to deter his attention.

His stare made me feel tiny and insignificant. As if I weren't good enough to clean the blood from his wounds. Maybe I wasn't. Perhaps I wasn't yet good enough at this job, but I had to get better. I had to work so that I could live. Because of that, I wouldn't give up. At least not yet.

He didn't respond to my question. Instead, he nodded his head and lowered his eyes, allowing me a brief reprieve from his heated stare. I took a deep breath while I could and continued to work.

He seethed from his seat, hate pouring off him in waves, as his eyes shifted around. They landed on another inmate across the room and they locked eyes, staring death and daggers at each other. If it weren't for the two COs standing between them, they'd be killing each other instead of sitting there promising death with their expressions.

I stitched him up, my needle piercing his skin and closing the gaping wound. He sat stoic as if he were in no pain, and I was in awe of him in that moment. I couldn't handle a paper cut, much less a stabbing. Yet, it was nothing for inmate X. He didn't flinch or make a single noise. He sat as still as stone, glaring at the other inmate, and obviously plotting his death.

When I was done, I cleaned his wound once more and bandaged his leg. I noticed his thighs were almost as big as I was as I wrapped one tightly, making sure to apply lots of pressure. Moving to get the tape, I accidently brushed against his knee and he stiffened, scaring me and making me drop my supplies.

I kept my eyes on his as I leaned over and snatched the tape from the floor. The side of his mouth twitched like he was seconds away from laughing at me. The asshole was getting off on my fear, and it kind of pissed me off.

My brows pulled down in anger as I stood and finished securing the bandage. I was angry. My hands were no longer shaking and my pulse was rapid, but not because I was afraid. I was pissed off. Who did he think he was?

As I straightened my back, my green eyes locked with his royal blues. I refused to blink even though he stared at me intently without wavering. He obviously wanted to see my fear, but I wasn't having it. Although I was freaking out on the inside, I had to prove to him I could handle this—that I could handle him.

A moment later, Dr. Giles appeared next to me and examined my work.

"Nice work, Ms. Evans." He nodded his approval. "How's it feel, big guy?" he asked X.

Apparently, he'd built a rapport with many of the inmates. X glanced at him and gave a brief head dip.

Still, no words. It made me wonder if he was even capable of speaking.

"Good. Then I think you can go back to your cell."

Dr. Giles was gone at that and once again, I was standing there with the beast. He stood slowly, his eyes burning into me, and he waited for the officers to assist him back.

He moved away from me, limping a little as the guards flanked him. The space felt small with him in it, but as soon as he stepped away, it grew and I was suddenly able to get large amounts of oxygen. My head spun from the deep breaths I pulled in.

They stood by the exit and prepared to put cuffs back on him. I looked away and shook myself. There was still work to be done and patients to be attended to.

I turned away from the bed where I'd patched up X and started toward Dr. Giles to help with another inmate, but just as I did, all hell broke loose. The room lit up with red, flashing lights, and an alarm sounded.

The entire room paused, everyone unsure of what to do next. We'd had lockdowns, but never with inmates in the infirmary at the time. My eyes flittered across the room, counting the amount of inmates in the room versus the amount of COs. Panic shot through my limbs. There I was in a room with dangerous criminals… and we were outnumbered. There were more inmates than staff.

The sharp alarm pierced my conscious and my eyes scanned the room again, watching as the remaining staff fell to the floor.

Men pray and women faint.

Dr. Giles' words moved through my mind.

In other words, when the shit hit the fan the way it was now, get down. *Get to the floor and cover your head.* If and when more officers came running in, they would take down anyone standing or wearing khakis. That was the biggest reason the medical staff wasn't allowed to wear anything khaki-colored. They would even go as far as sending you home at the gate if you did.

Know your surroundings. Exits. Quick escape routes. You never know when you'll need that information. This also includes fire extinguishers, fire alarms, etc.

My legs collapsed beneath me, and my face stung against the cold Formica flooring. As I lay on the floor, I lifted my head and took in the room and all the exits. If I needed to, I could run, but the stupid doors were all locked… hence the word *lockdown*.

The fear I felt before while looking into the eyes of a murderer was nothing compared the terror that swam in my veins now. I didn't know what was going on outside the infirmary, but I was worried that soon we'd have a problem on our hands as well.

Suddenly, we did.

Two inmates jumped up and slung a tray of medical supplies to the ground. The tools clinked against the tile in slow motion, and my eyes took in the many things that could be used as weapons.

Scalpels. Needles. You named it. Hell, even a harmless stethoscope could be wrapped around someone's neck and used to choke them to death. Everywhere I looked, the medical instruments were available on the floor, begging the inmates to pick them up and use them.

Of course, they went straight for the scalpels. They snatched them up and began waving them around the room, ready to cut someone. I closed my eyes and swallowed hard. This was it. This was the end of me—of Lyla Evans.

What in the world made me think I could do a job like this?

I was too soft. Too afraid of my own damn shadow. And now, I was seconds away from being slaughtered in a prison.

The officers nearby pulled batons and pepper spray, hoping to deter an attack, but as I watched the scene unfold, I somehow knew those things would be useless against the inmates.

I glanced over to where Dr. Giles had been. It was then I realized he had moved from the side of the room and locked himself in his office. His eyes locked with mine, and he motioned for me to join him. I could see his mouth moving through the thick glass as he told me to, *Come On. Run.*

My brain screamed that word on repeat.

Run. Run. Run, Lyla.

With arms and legs that felt like Jell-O, I stood in the midst of all the chaos, but my feet were planted to the floor. I was able to stand, but the fear was too thick and I couldn't move. Instead, I stood there like an idiot, hoping no one noticed me.

The two officers that were guarding X came to help take down the maniacs with scalpels. I watched as the guys were brought down, and I felt like I could breathe again.

Once I gained my composure and was able to move my legs, I started toward Dr. Giles' office, but I stopped when something out of the corner of my eye caught my attention. Turning, my eyes locked with X's. He stood there, shackled helplessly in the doorway, watching the scene before him. The inmates could've easily attacked him, and he wouldn't have been able to protect himself.

His expression shifted and his eyes softened, revealing something unexpected.

Fear.

X was afraid, and that didn't suit him at all. A big man like him didn't know fear. He didn't experience those types of feelings. And yet, there he stood, not ten feet away from me with terror in his eyes.

A strange feeling moved over me as I stood there staring at him. A feeling that I didn't understand. It was heated and protective. *Scary and dark.* A feeling I instantly tried to banish. I couldn't think of these inmates as anything more than chained animals. They were vicious and dangerous, regardless of the fear that swam in X's eyes.

I looked again and somehow, I knew. I just knew that the fear he was experiencing probably for the first time in his life wasn't for himself. It was for me. X, the slaughterer of people—the taker of lives—the sick, maniacal monster—was afraid *for* me. The realization made the darkness inside of me shift, and for the first time since he entered the infirmary, I wondered if maybe X wasn't as dangerous as everyone assumed he was.

CHAPTER 4

X

FUCK. **THE SHIT** *would* hit the fan the minute the COs shackled me. It was my luck. There I was, standing to the side of the room with a big, red target on my chest and my arms and legs tied, literally.

I knew it wouldn't be long before one of the inmates pulled some stupid shit and took advantage of the lockdown. Having a lockdown wasn't unusual. I was sure there was probably a fight somewhere in the prison, but this was the first time I'd been shackled during one.

Maybe things would run smoothly. Maybe the COs would keep things under control until the lockdown was over. But my hopes soon crashed. Carlos moved, and then he was standing there with a scalpel in his hand. I knew it wouldn't be long before that fucker stabbed me in the heart, and I wouldn't even be able to defend myself. Maybe that was the way it was supposed to end for me. Shit, honestly, it was better than rotting behind bars. I stood straighter, taunting him to make his move.

Looking across the room, my eyes met Carlos and I watched

as the side of his mouth lifted in a malicious smirk. He was coming for me, and all I could think was, *Bring it, motherfucker.*

I straightened my spine and waited for his attack, but then my view of Carlos was blocked when the new nurse stood. Ms. Evans, Dr. Giles had called her. She was standing in the middle of the room with two crazed inmates holding scalpels and four of the weakest officers on staff. And I could do nothing to protect her.

I pulled against my restraints as realization moved over me. Carlos would have much more fun slicing her to pieces than he would me. She was beautiful and unflawed. Just the thought of the scalpel touching her milky skin made me crazy.

Thankfully, my insanity lasted seconds. The officers were able to detain the inmates, and things went back to running as smoothly as possible. I was lucky for once. Instead of watching the new nurse get diced to pieces, I was being shuffled off to my cell.

Once the officers left me to my sanctuary, I reached under my bed and grabbed a loose screw from the frame. Standing, I looked over the wall in front of me and sighed.

There were so many X marks. So many regrets. Carlos had gotten away with a few stitches, but the other guy I'd beaten pretty badly.

Reluctantly, I etched another X into the concrete wall, scrapings of sand and my remorse falling to the floor at my feet. When I was done, I lay in my bed and reflected like usual. I was lucky the fight didn't send me to the hole. I was sure it was because of my injury, but I was still thankful nevertheless.

Reaching down, I ran my palm over my fresh cut. My leg throbbed with my heartbeat. Slinging my pillow to the foot of my bed, I propped my injured leg on it and thought of the new nurse. She was angelic. I couldn't stop thinking about her fiery hair and emerald eyes.

Why the hell would they let her work in a place like this?

Why would she even want to work in a place like this?

There had to be a way to get her to quit, if she hadn't already.

A maximum-security prison wasn't a place for a woman like her. She was too pretty — too soft — too womanly. The inmates would eat her alive, and I couldn't stand by and watch that happen.

Feeling helpless wasn't something I was used to, but for the first time since I was a nineteen-year-old punk, I experienced it. It was all because of her. It was terrifying. I couldn't afford to feel like that when more than half of the prison wanted to see me break. If they discovered my weakness, I would be helpless to resist them. I'd been careful, not connecting to too many and keeping to myself, but the new nurse was going to throw a wrench into my life of solitude.

I had no choice. I had to get her out of there if it was the last thing I did. She'd learn to fear me, hate me even. And when I'd pushed too hard, she'd run. At least, I hoped she would. Then she'd be safe and so would I.

I lay back on my bed and settled my arms behind my head. My leg still throbbed a bit, but I pushed the pain away as I ran ideas through my head. Starting the next day, I'd put my plan into action. I gave her a week, if that, before she was running like a scared little girl.

Bye, bye, little Red.

I WASN'T SURE how long I'd slept, but I woke up to the sound of someone saying my name.

"X, wake the fuck up, man."

I sat up cautiously, nervous that I was about to be taken off guard. It was dinnertime, and I could smell the food wafting in from the chow hall. My stomach rumbled and I turned, setting my feet to the cold floor. Looking up, I saw Scoop standing at my open cell door, ready for the chow line, and I relaxed a little.

Scoop was one of the few people in the prison I was okay with. I didn't talk to him much, but he talked enough for the both of us. Luckily for me, his cell was right beside mine, which meant some nights I'd fall asleep to his constant chatter.

He'd come in three years after me on a bullshit self-defense charge. Apparently, killing the motherfucker who was trying to kill you was enough to get you fifteen years.

"Fucking Carlos and his boys got you, huh?" he asked.

I nodded.

I didn't bother asking how he knew. Scoop always knew everything, hence his nickname. Scoop had the scoop. If you ever wanted to know what was going down on the block or in the yard, he was your man. His memory was on point, too. He knew everyone's records and the details of each of their crimes. I meant sick, twisted shit, too.

He was vigilant—always watching and relaying the information to those who asked for it, which made him a dangerous adversary and fucking awesome ally. He'd saved my ass a few times just by threatening to open his mouth and reveal some fucked-up secret. No one feared him, but they definitely feared the shit he had running around in his head.

The bad news was his knowledge also put a target on his back, which meant a few of the fights I got into were because I was protecting him. He couldn't defend himself without a gun. He was small and fragile, which meant if he got near his attacker, he was done for.

He'd earned more respect than haters though, which was a good thing, and he wore that respect around him like a suit of armor. It was kind of funny actually.

I stood, my leg still aching, and worked the kinks out of my shoulders and neck.

"You okay, man?" he asked.

Again, I nodded.

"A fucking paper blade to the leg... that sucks, bro. Does it hurt?" He stepped closer to my cell opening and leaned against a bar.

I could hardly believe I'd missed the loud call for chow time or the clinking of my cell opening. Apparently, I'd slept like death.

I shrugged, not wanting to admit how much my leg hurt. I trusted Scoop with my life, but if others found out how bad my leg was hurt, they'd use it as an opportunity to come at me again.

He smiled and winked at me, understanding my reluctance. There were ears everywhere.

"I said it's chow time," Officer Reeves said. He came up behind Scoop with his usual sarcastic smirk. "It's not time for making love, ladies. Either you want to eat or you want to fuck. So move your asses."

I hated that son of bitch.

Scoop chuckled to himself and started toward the chow line. "Come on, X. No ass for you today. I'm fucking starving."

He was being sarcastic, obviously, but Officer Reeves' lips curled in revulsion.

They left instead of waiting for me, and I was glad. I needed to feel my leg out and change. Flinching at my first step, I managed to walk without a limp after a few more, hiding the proof of my injury.

Custody had slipped a fresh uniform in my cell while I was sleeping, so I quickly changed before falling in at the end of the line and walking down the stairs to the cafeteria. I deposited my bloody uniform into the laundry chute before meeting up with Scoop.

We waited like children with our lunch trays in hand, and I took in my surroundings, reading the mood of the room.

Dinner was everyone's favorite part of the day, other than rec time, of course. The food was tasteless, but it was food. And sometimes during dinner, we'd get a dry piece of cake with something that resembled icing. It was a treat considering the alternative.

Everyone was tired from the day, so dinnertime was usually more laid back and friendly. There'd be jokes among the groups and banter between friends and gang affiliations.

Today, it was different. The mood was so tense you could cut through it with the cheap, plastic forks they made us use. I watched as at least two different gangs sized me up from afar. They eyed my hurt leg and grinned with conspiracy tight in their lips.

Scoop picked up on the mood too. Once we had our trays full, we retreated to the side of the cafeteria to eat in silence. Once we were done, we went back to our cells and waited for lights out. The day had been a bust, one that included a nasty leg injury, but at least I had a new purpose. I had something to occupy my time, and that thing was getting rid of the new nurse.

I'd given her my own kind of green light, and starting tomorrow, it would be her time to go.

CHAPTER 5

LYLA

I WASN'T GOING to go back. After leaving the prison for the day, I spent ten minutes in my car, staring off into the nothing and thinking about how afraid I was of going back in there. I drove to my crappy, one-bedroom apartment in a total daze. When I got home, I searched the refrigerator, starving, only to find there was nothing in my place to eat.

I wasn't even Ramen noodle rich. There wasn't a scrap of crusty bread or a piece of moldy cheese. I was broke — completely broke with no one to turn to. Even if there were someone, I was too proud to do so. Instead, I drank a big glass of water, showered, and went to bed knowing that no matter how badly I never wanted to go back to the prison, I didn't have any choice. It was either work or starve to death on the streets.

A benefit of working at the prison, however, was I was able to get a free breakfast and lunch when I was at work. Sure, it was food prepared by inmates. I didn't even want to think about what was done to it, but it was food. The meals tasted horrible, but anything was better than the pain of starving. I had to eat it until

I could afford to buy my own.

Falling asleep within minutes, I slept like I hadn't in days. I woke to my cell ringing on my bedside table. Looking at the alarm clock blinking back at me, I saw it was ten minutes away from going off.

Great. I could've used that ten minutes.

Snatching my cell from the table, I saw that it was my friend Diana calling. I'd met her the second day of nursing school. My bag broke under the strain of those ungodly large books, and she'd laughed and helped me carry them to my car.

Park close to your classes and use your trunk as a locker, she'd said.

Her words were a lifesaver over the next few semesters. It was impossible to carry around all those books.

Over the next few days after that, we'd been in all the same classes. We spent hour upon hour studying and working on assignments together.

"Hello?" I said into my cell.

"Seen any ass fucking yet?" she asked with a chuckle.

"Seriously?" My voice broke, heavy with sleep.

"Yes, seriously. You work in a prison full of men who haven't seen a naked woman in years. There's some serious ass fucking going on in there." She laughed.

Shaking my head, I rubbed at my eyes and sat up in bed. "How's the job hunting going?" I changed the subject.

"Eh, it's going. I have an interview today at University Hospital. What about you? What's it like working in a max clinic?"

I answered carefully. "It's definitely different. It's nothing like working in a hospital, I'm sure. There are so many rules you have to follow just to stay safe. I have to watch my back constantly, and I don't know who I can trust.

"We have lockdowns almost every day because there are fights all the time. We had one yesterday, and two inmates got their hands on a few scalpels. Luckily, the officers took them down pretty easily."

"Jesus, Lyla, that sounds terrible. Are you sure you want to go back?"

That was the million-dollar question.

Did I want to go back? *Hell no.*

Was I going to go back? *Hell yes.*

I sighed, thinking about my empty refrigerator and tiny apartment. I'd be lucky to have enough gas to get me to work over the next few days.

"I don't have a choice. Bills come every month and I have to feed myself," I said, just as my stomach rolled with hunger pain.

The line went quiet, and I heard her take a deep breath. "Just be careful, okay? Those inmates are ruthless. I watched a documentary about a prison once. It's some serious shit. You never know what they'll do. Just keep your ass covered and your head up."

I chuckled. "Got it."

"Good. Love you, miss you," she sang.

I smiled. "Love you, miss you, too."

Hanging up, I lay back against my pillows. I didn't have long before I had to get ready for my next shift. When I closed my eyes, X flashed through my memory. I thought about the fear that was etched on his face the last time I saw him.

My heart thudded.

I could only hope that my next few shifts would be monotonous. I didn't think I could handle it if every time I went to work something dangerous happened.

MY NEXT DAY at work was uneventful. I spent most of it cleaning the infirmary, counting sharps, and filling out reports. We had a few inmates come in for medication and blood work, but I drove to my apartment after my shift feeling much better about my decision to stay.

I'd even managed to snag a small bag of chips from the prison without anyone noticing or asking questions. I'd never been one to steal, but I was hungry and the bag was just sitting on Dr. Giles' desk. I had to do it. An apple from the cafeteria weighed in my pocket also. I was starving at breakfast, but after some eggs and a muffin, I decided to save the apple for dinner.

On day three, I sat in the parking lot, struggling with myself about whether to drive away like a bat out of hell or to get out of the car and go into work. A few days off to reflect might have been nice, but it was impossible because of my financial state. Dr. Giles had called the night before to check on me, which I thought was nice. I knew it was because he was worried I wouldn't come back, but he had no idea I had no other choice.

I assured him I was fine, but now, sitting in front of the looming cinderblock building, I was having second and third thoughts. My eyes followed the barbed wire along the top of the fencing, and I wondered if it was as sharp and cold as the men inside. I wondered if it sliced away at any soul who stepped through the fencing. Then again, most of those inside were deemed soulless, so I guess it didn't matter much to them.

Closing my eyes, I envisioned X's piercing blues. I remembered the fear I'd seen in them during the lockdown. It was the strangest thing. One second, he was vulnerable and afraid, and then next, the hardened killer was back and he was staring daggers at me. It was almost as if his mask had slipped—as if his armor had fallen out of place for the briefest of moments.

I secured my phone in my center console and stuffed my purse under the seat. With one last breath, I grabbed my badge from where it hung on the rearview mirror and tucked the hairs that had fallen from my ponytail behind my ear.

As I pushed my door open, it cracked and creaked. It wasn't a new car. I doubted I'd ever own anything new, but it was mine. Thanks to a little extra on my student loans, I was able to buy it with cash. Of course, now I was hoping I'd be able to pay those loans back.

I hadn't planned for things to be like this. My mom died when

I was five from a brain aneurism, and my dad never remarried. For years, it was just us against the world. He worked for CSI, which meant he was always bringing home stories about his job. He never considered the fact that I might have nightmares, but I guessed he knew me better than anyone else did because I loved his stories, no matter how twisted some of the criminals were.

But my daddy was gone now. Without him, the world felt like a bigger, scarier place. It wasn't like I knew my dad was going to die and leave me all alone in the world. I didn't blame him; I blamed the asshole that shot him while he was on a case. Because of that man, I woke up every day scared of the future. I hated not knowing what was next—not being able to make plans because I wasn't sure what the following day would hold. It was scary.

A few of the COs were walking in the parking lot toward the building. They were starting their next shift as well. I wondered if they ever had days when they wanted to run away from it all. Did they ever feel afraid of their job?

Swallowing my anxiety, I slammed my car door shut and turned to walk inside. After the usual metal detector and turning out my pockets, I grabbed my car keys and badge and headed to find an officer to escort me to the infirmary.

"Hey, Lyla, glad you came back." I glanced up to see Officer Douglas smiling down at me. "We had a bet going on how long you'd last here. You just won me a hundred bucks," he joked, his eyes crinkling with his smile.

He was the nicest CO in Fulton and my favorite escort. A tall, broad man in his mid-forties, he had bright blue eyes and a bald head. He looked stacked, like a man who lifted weights and played football in his younger days. His once strong and taut body was now replaced by a beer gut and a double chin from too many doughnuts and not enough exercise.

He wasn't attractive, but his friendliness made up for it. He'd been there through all the shifts I'd worked so far. From what I could tell, he was a jokester. He loved to make everyone laugh. But even though he was a comedian, he still did his job. When it came to the inmates, he was all business.

"Gee, thanks." I laughed. "I appreciate the vote of confidence, Officer Douglas."

He laughed. "Don't give me that Officer Douglas crap. Just call me Duggie." He playfully nudged me with his elbow. "You'll do fine here. Got it?"

I nodded as I followed him down the long hallway leading to the block.

I hated that we even had to go through the block to get to the infirmary. Whoever built the prison all those years ago wasn't thinking very clearly.

The place was set up in levels, each more stifling and suffocating than the last. The first level was for civilians, those coming to see an inmate for visitation or to simply pay for canteen. You'd see the occasional lawyer bustle up to the desk and demand to see an inmate or a mother crying because she couldn't see her son since she had missed visiting hours by five minutes.

Then there was the next level, where you were searched and processed before being allowed to go on to the next level. This required a badge, which I'd gotten on day one, and a few minutes in the control room to be checked in.

As they buzzed me through, I entered the last level, better known as the block. It was the place where the inmates lived and breathed. The walk through was hell, and I hated it. Officer Douglas was a good bodyguard, but I doubted his ability to protect me against a hundred sex-starved criminals.

As I plucked up my courage, I put in my imaginary earplugs and held my head high. The bars opened, clinking the whole way, and then we stepped in. The minute the bars closed behind us, the inmates began to taunt me.

"Here, kitty, kitty. Come here and let Daddy pet that sweet pussy."

Accidently, I looked his way. His wide eyes moved over my body, leaving chills in their wake. His greasy fingers grabbed the bars, and he shoved his face into them trying to get a better look at me. Instantly, I felt dirty and in need of a shower.

"Hey, Strawberry Shortcake, I see you're back for more. Just let me put a finger in, baby."

I ignored the onslaught of name-calling and kept my focus on the door that would ultimately be put between the demons and me. Douglas slammed his baton across the bars, making me jump, but also reminding them to shut up.

"Respect, boys!" he called out. "Remember your manners when a lady's present."

He smiled down at me awkwardly, and I nodded my appreciation.

It didn't matter, though. They kept talking. Their words were vile, each cutting into me and making me feel nauseated. I was their daily entertainment, a redheaded piece of ass for them to toy with. I'd dealt with catcalls in my life, but this was different. These men weren't dirty-minded frat boys or construction workers. These hardened criminals didn't give a damn about how it made them look or how I felt about it.

We moved deeper into the block toward the infirmary, and I cried inside knowing that I had no other options. I had to take their verbal abuse. It was my life now.

My eyes scanned the hall, bars as far as I could see, and then I turned my head and my eyes clashed with X. He was standing at the bars in only his khaki pants. His bare, tattooed chest glistened under the dim lighting. Against my will, my eyes dipped low, taking in his beautiful cuts and dips. Physically, he was amazing. Too bad I couldn't say the same about his mental state.

Catching myself, I moved my eyes away from his naked chest. Again, my eyes clashed with his, and he lifted a knowing brow. He shook his head at me, as if telling me I shouldn't be there. He was right. I wanted to be anywhere but there.

I peeled my eyes away from him and continued the walk down the mile. His eyes burned into my back, leaving a strange tingle down my spine.

As we finally reached the door, I gazed up at the camera and schooled my expression. I didn't want control to see how desperate I was to be on the other side and away from the inmates. The buzzer sounded, giving me a brief high, and I practically sprinted through into the infirmary.

Dr. Giles stood over an inmate, listening to his breathing with a steel face. As I removed my sweater and tossed it behind the chair at the nurses' desk, I glanced at Ginger, another nurse. I was there to relieve her of her shift. I'd only met Ginger once since she was usually gone before I got there, but she was a nice girl.

She'd been at the prison for two years, and I wasn't sure if it was working with the inmates or the way she was raised, but she was much stronger than I was. Nothing seemed to bother her, and I could only hope I'd be same soon.

Her name didn't suit her. She was short and stocky, her pixie cut sporting a box-blonde color on the tips. She was standing next to Giles, ready for any orders he spat out. She met my eyes and smiled, rolling her eyes as if to let me know it had already been a crappy day. I chuckled to myself, nodding at her and locking my car keys into the top drawer before going through my paces.

A few officers were posted around the inmate's bed, which meant he was dangerous. A fight must have happened already. Ginger was right; this shift was going to be crappy. I'd come in hoping to do nothing more than intake screenings. Those were easy and I didn't have to deal with the dangerous ones as much. Apparently, I wasn't that lucky.

As I approached Giles, he turned to me with a grimace.

"Morning, Ms. Evans. I need you to call transport here. This patient needs to be moved to the hospital."

Nodding, I grabbed the chart when he handed it over. I was relieved to see that the inmate wasn't injured, just sick. That meant no fights yet. Maybe the day would be a quiet one.

Dr. Giles turned on his heels and walked toward the officers, pulling the curtain and disappearing behind it. Going to the phone, I pressed the extension for transport and waited for an answer.

"Transport," a gruff voice rang out on the other line.

"This is Nurse Evans. Dr. Giles needs an inmate transported immediately to the hospital."

Scanning the chart, the word *flu* stuck out at me. The flu in a prison was never a good thing. It meant the infirmary was going to be packed, and the flu season had barely begun.

This particular inmate was having breathing issues. With respiratory issues and outdated equipment, sending him to the hospital was the only option.

As I relayed the patient information to transport, Dr. Giles reappeared and stood next to me, scribbling wildly onto a clipboard before returning it to its resting place.

"Are they coming?" he asked.

"Yes, sir, they're waiting for a few officers to return and they'll head this way."

"Good. Hopefully no one else will come down with this. Get ready, Ms. Evans, it looks like the rough season is starting early. We've never had a flu patient this soon in the year. I loathe flu season." The wrinkles across his forehead deepened as he focused back on his paperwork.

A few minutes later, the printer spat out a few sheets and Dr. Giles stuck them into a manila envelope. He scribbled the patient's name across the front and laid it on the top of the nurses' desk.

"I'm heading into my office to call the hospital and make sure they have a bed for him. That will save transport a few minutes," he said.

As he walked in and sat at his desk, I watched him carefully. He pulled his glasses from his face as he dialed the number and sat back. Rubbing his eyes and nose, he sighed deeply before rambling off to whoever was on the other end. His once-brown hair was now heavily grayed and his stress was obvious in the strain of his shoulders.

When he reentered the unit, he went back to the sick inmate.

"Good news for you, Patterson. You're going to the hospital. I've got you cleared for chest X-rays and a full workup. It looks like you'll be getting a small break from this place."

When I stepped around the curtain, the inmate was smiling as if he'd just won the lottery. I'd never seen someone so happy about a visit to the hospital.

"Thanks, Doc," Patterson replied.

He didn't look sick, except for the flushed cheeks and the glistening eyes of someone with a high fever.

I left Dr. Giles' side to go back to the computer and finish some paperwork. As I sat, the door buzzer went off and the bars clicked open to let in a CO and another inmate. He was a scrawny old man, his teeth rotting and his wispy, gray hair standing on edge. He grinned at me as he came in, his eyes moving over my breasts in a vulgar manner.

The CO escorted him to a bed before taking up his post next to the curtain. Dr. Giles disappeared again, and I continued to do paperwork. I updated the charts and went into the back room to do inventory. We had to account for everything in the infirmary. If something went missing, it was a massive deal and resulted in a prison-wide shakedown.

The day was turning out okay. I stayed busy and didn't have to deal with many inmates. The hours ticked by quickly, and I found myself smiling during my busy work. That all changed the minute the familiar lockdown alarms sounded. I groaned and rolled my eyes when the red lights flickered throughout the room.

There was no telling what was going on outside the infirmary. Why couldn't the inmates behave themselves for just one freaking day?

I stood, preparing myself for the onslaught of inmates that were sure to come. Twenty minutes later, the door buzzed and the bars clinked open.

Five COs walked in, tugging inmates inside with them. As the first two entered, I looked them over and assessed their injuries the best I could. One was clutching his shoulder and was hunched over as if he'd been struck in the chest. The other held his face, blood pouring from his nose and mouth. Someone had obviously taken something large and hard against his face.

Then the third inmate entered, and my lungs deflated as all the air rushed from my body.

It was X again.

What was it about him? And why did my body respond to him every time he was near me?

He gazed around the room as if he was searching for something, and then his eyes landed on me. My day had just taken a turn for the worse, and I wasn't so sure I was unhappy about it.

CHAPTER 6

LYLA

HE WALKED IN like he owned the place. Lord knew he was there enough to own it. I stood still, expecting his dark expression to soften the way it had before, but it didn't change. His royal blue eyes skimmed my face, his dark brows pulling down in aggravation.

Why did he always look so annoyed with me? What had I done to him?

His gaze was sharp, and it cut right through me. He moved across the room, his eyes never leaving me, and sat down and did as the officers asked.

Grabbing the clipboard, I went to the first two, hoping Dr. Giles could take care of X this time, but I wasn't that lucky. Coming to my side, Giles took the clipboard from me and motioned me to X.

Grabbing another clipboard from the counter, I went to X's side, avoiding his accusing glare. Nervously, I scribbled a few notes on the paper about the time and date. My face flushed, and I knew it was because he was watching my every move. I schooled my face since showing any kind of emotion was forbidden, and then I looked at him.

"Hi again, X," I began.

I didn't expect a response since he never talked. He stared back at me, unblinking, with hate thick in his expression.

"Look, I know you're not one for small talk, but this could go a lot faster if you'd just answer a few questions for me," I pressed.

His thick lips shifted, and his voice broke through. It was rough and unused, but so deep I was sure it vibrated his muscled chest.

"Has anyone ever told you you're fucking annoying?" he asked, his voice cold and sinister.

I was shocked by his words, but instead of showing him, I looked down at the paper on my clipboard and took a breath.

My pen lingered over the place where I'd enter the inmate's name, but entering the name X didn't seem appropriate. Dr. Giles had told me his real name once before, but I couldn't remember it.

Ignoring his rude question, I began asking my own. "What's your name?"

I tapped the pen against the clipboard, prepared to write. My face ached with a smile I didn't feel as I waited for some kind of response.

"Leave," he simply stated.

I blinked. "Excuse me?"

"I said… leave. You don't belong here, and you know it."

His voice was becoming menacing, as if he was issuing a warning. I swallowed hard, my next words becoming lodged in my throat.

"I'm sorry." I attempted to smile. "I can't do that. This is my job."

"You're going to be eaten alive here. You know it, too. I can tell by the fear in your eyes and the way your hands tremble."

His scowl deepened, his knowing eyes digging into me and learning all my secrets.

"Stop it," I hissed.

SLAMMER

"Stop what? Stop telling the truth?"

I stepped away from him, the fear of the truth consuming me. If he knew how weak I was, that meant the rest of the inmates knew it, too.

"What's your name?" I tried to gain the upper hand and move past his scary words.

The side of his mouth lifted in a knowing smirk. He'd rattled me and he knew it.

"Fine, ignore my warning, but if you want to make me feel better, Miss Nurse, all you have to do is give my cock a nice, long kiss."

His crude words rolled around in my stomach, but instead of letting them bother me, I pressed on.

"Name?" I said forcefully, my teeth locked together, making my jaw ache.

He chuckled. "You're fucking delicious when you're angry. You know what they say—red on the head equals fire in the hole. I love a hard, angry fuck." He reached up with cuffed hands and ran a finger over his mouth seductively. "I suppose you should know what to call out when I'm making you come. My name's X."

Again, I swallowed my nerves, my eyes scanning the room for the nearest officer. He was being so crude and disgusting, yet somehow, it was completely different from when the men on the block did it. I couldn't explain how it was different. It just was.

"No. What's your real name?" I asked.

"I said… my name is X," he answered through gritted teeth.

My eyes followed his features from his dark eyes to his throbbing jaw. He was obviously not enjoying my question.

"Okay, let's try this again." I shifted from one foot to the other and blew a stray piece of hair from my face. "What's the name your mother gave you at birth?"

His jaw tightened even more. It was so tight I was sure he was grinding his teeth down. His expression darkened even more, and his dark skin reddened in anger. I'd hit a nerve, and I suddenly had the feeling I was about to get attacked. No one pushed X,

53

obviously, and yet there I was, pushing him like an idiot.

He sucked his bottom lip in, closing his eyes as if to breathe away his anger. His nostrils flared and his shoulders tensed.

My flight-or-fight response kicked in. Running away from the big, scary inmate was probably the best idea I'd had all day. But before I could move away from him, his eyes opened and his mask slipped once more, revealing softer eyes—eyes full of pain—full of hurt. I could practically see the sad memories I'd invoked swimming through his mind.

"Christopher Jacobs," he whispered.

He looked down at the shackles on his feet and his cuffed hands in his lap. I took the moment to breathe. Something had shifted in our little space, and it was as if I were examining two different men.

"Thank you, Christopher," I said with a smile.

Again, he looked up at me, his eyes taking in my expression before he nodded.

My eyes shifted across the room to Dr. Giles. His face was one full of shock. His brows were dipped in confusion. Obviously, no one had ever spoken to X. Or at least, he'd never spoken to anyone.

"Why are you here today?" I asked, scribbling his name across the top of the form.

"Fighting." He held out his hands, palms down and flexed his fingers so I could see his knuckles.

The cuffs around his wrists rattled, and he tugged at them a bit. His right hand was covered in blood and his knuckles busted open, revealing the tissue within.

How was it possible to hit someone so hard and do that kind of damage to yourself? I couldn't imagine being that strong.

After I jotted down a few notes, I placed the clipboard on the table beside the bed. "I need to check you out and make sure you didn't suffer any other injuries. Is that okay?"

"No problem. You check me out all you want, baby."

His eyes devoured my face once more, checking for my

reaction to his words. I'd never had anyone look at me the way he did. It was unnerving. It was, in a way, flattering, yet it made me uncomfortable at the same time.

I shook my head with disgust and stepped away. Leaving him, I went to the desk and retrieved my stethoscope and blood pressure cuff. When I got back to his side, I realized there was no way the cuff I had was going to fit around his gigantic arm. Instead, I wrapped the cuff around his forearm and placed the stethoscope against his large wrist.

His heartbeat was hard and steady, thumping in my ears as he eyed me suspiciously. The wild strands of hair that escaped my ponytail fell against my cheek, and I felt him shift. As he leaned over me, his breath brushed my ear and cheek, sending goose bumps down my back. He was close, and instead of smelling rotten like the other inmates, his scent was fresh—like the outside air and clean laundry.

I breathed him in, enjoying his manly scent before recalling myself.

What the hell was wrong with me? My actions were unprofessional and completely unacceptable. Not to mention, he was just as rude and perverted as the rest of the men on the block.

Pulling the stethoscope from my ears, I undid the cuff around his forearm. I jerked when his whispered breath skimmed my cheek.

"So how's the blood pressure?" he asked.

I jolted nervously and stepped away. Again, he grinned as if knowing my thoughts.

I busied myself, grabbing the clipboard and recording my findings. "Good," I stated in my most professional nurse voice. "Sit tight; I'll be right back."

After I left his side, I took a deep breath. I needed to get my shit together, and I needed to do it sooner rather than later. Looking over my shoulder at him, I caught him staring at my ass. His eyes flickered back up to me. If I wasn't mistaken, he blushed. It was a confusing action. One that I was sure I'd seen incorrectly.

I collected some supplies—gauze, antiseptic, and gloves—and then I walked back over to him. He didn't look me in the face this time. Instead, he eyed my supplies and held out his hands once I put on my gloves.

I cleaned his large hands, removing blood from them before stitching up the gaping wounds.

"Why do you do this to yourself?" I asked, the words coming before I had a chance to think them through.

I felt him stiffen.

"I have to," he responded.

"You don't have to fight. You could walk away."

He chuckled, a sound that was as dark and menacing as his knowing stare.

"Why is that funny? You think it's funny to walk away from a fight?"

"You're clueless, Red. I don't think it's funny; I think it's impossible."

"How so?"

I flipped his hands over, cleaning some minor cuts on his palms. They were smooth and dotted with calluses, but they were probably the only spot on his body without scars. Apparently, when you kept a closed fist, it protected your palms. I admired how large and strong his hands were as I ran my gloved fingers over them.

The muscles in his arm flexed, making the hard muscle in his forearm pop. Clearing my throat, I tried not to notice how totally beautiful his physical form was. I hadn't been turned on by a man in a long time. Not since before my dad died. Back then, I was young and able to take time away from the worries of life. But I found myself thinking crazy things when I looked at X's lean figure and tatted skin.

It was irrational. I knew that, but I couldn't help myself.

"If I don't fight, I die."

I paused and looked up at his face. My eyes moved over his tight features and lingered on the ink that crawled up the side of his neck.

I hadn't thought about the fact that he could be protecting himself. Who in their right mind would even try to fight such a large and scary creature? I'd always thought X was the instigator. It didn't make any sense for anyone to go against him without good reason, but evidently, I'd been wrong.

I wasn't saying he was a saint. Obviously, he wasn't since he was in prison for multiple counts of murder, but maybe, just *maybe*, he *was* protecting himself from the people within the walls of the most dangerous place I'd ever spent time.

I nodded my understanding since I didn't trust my voice.

As I dried his hands with clean gauze, I slipped back into professional mode and tried to forget the last few minutes of conversation. I couldn't afford to think of the inmates as anything but chained animals. Softening to these men couldn't be safe, and I wasn't about to put myself in any more danger than I already was.

Closing my eyes, I ran Dr. Giles' warnings and rules through my head again.

Inmates are pros at lying and faking symptoms. It's difficult, but if you examine the patient thoroughly, you should be able to determine whether they are actually hurt or just trying to earn a reprieve. You've already learned how to be a nurse. Now you have to learn how to take care of manipulative and dishonest patients.

I couldn't let myself be fooled. I had to remember who the man in front of me was. He was a criminal, one I was sure was trying to manipulate me.

Internally giving myself a shake, I cleared my throat once more. "Well, Mr. Jacobs," I said to him, trying to get our professional relationship back. "You're all stitched up. Do try to contain yourself from here on out. I'm not sure you have any more room on your body for more scars."

Again, he grinned. "Have you been looking at my body, Ms. Evans?"

I blushed. I felt it. It was hot and tingly as it rushed over my cheeks and down the back of my neck. I'd basically told him that I'd been staring at his body. I'd all but said I liked looking at his naked chest and strong, supple muscles.

Quickly, I changed the subject. "I'll get some triple antibiotic ointment, and then you can go back to your unit."

I turned and fled to the supply closet. Once inside, I pressed my back against the wall and covered my racing heart. This couldn't go on. I couldn't continue to treat this man.

I didn't look him in the face when I returned to his side. I'd patched him up, done my job, and now it was time for him to leave. Putting on fresh gloves, I rubbed the ointment onto his cuts, feeling his eyes cut through me the entire time.

I didn't breathe again until the COs had taken him from the room and returned him to his cell or to solitary. I wasn't sure where he was going and truthfully, it was none of my business. Christopher Jacobs, or X, was not my business. I was done even thinking about him, and I'd make sure Dr. Giles knew I wasn't comfortable treating him anymore.

CHAPTER 7

X

SOMETHING WAS HAPPENING to me. I couldn't put my finger on it, but something was changing. I didn't like change. It wasn't safe to change in prison. You had to stay vigilant, stay strong, and make sure the inmates knew not to fuck with you.

My mind was beginning to wander. It was filling with visions of red hair and emerald eyes—of a slim waist and wide hips—hips that could handle a large man like me. Daydreaming was forbidden in my world. I couldn't afford to lose focus on daily life. Losing myself in a dream world about a pretty nurse and her perky tits was a sure way to get myself killed.

At night, once it was lights out, I'd pump my cock hard and imagine how sweet she'd sound as she came all over me. I'd blow my load to the imaginary sounds of her in pleasure, and then I'd wake up the next morning hating myself for it. I couldn't keep this shit up, yet I couldn't help myself. She needed to go, but I wanted her to stay. It was fucking selfish.

The fighting escalated. I found myself in the infirmary almost every other day versus the usual two times a week. I'd watch her flitter around the room, sweetly taking care of the dirty inmates who stared at her ass and fucked her with their eyes.

It was wrong, but even I allowed myself the privilege of watching her lithe body move around the space. Every time I saw her, she grew more confident in her job. She smiled more at the nicer inmates, and the ones who were just there for their meds or to have their blood sugar checked.

The lucky bastards.

Being bathed in her sweet smile was a privilege they didn't understand. I understood it all too well. It got to the point where I craved her smile, but somehow, no matter how many times I went to the infirmary, she never tended to me. Probably because I was such a sick fuck the last time I spoke to her. I was doing what I had to do to push her away. I hadn't meant to get so fucking turned on by the dirty talk.

Instead of Red, I'd get stuck with Dr. Giles or on the days when Ms. Evans wasn't there, I'd get one of the less attractive nurses. Finally, I learned her schedule — four days on and four off. It was twisted, and honestly, it was a form of stalking, but it didn't matter to me. She became the thing I looked forward to.

She leaned over her desk, her perfect, heart-shaped ass sticking up, and I felt my mouth water. I imagined pulling her scrubs down and fucking her until I unloaded deep inside her. My dick twitched, ready to stand at attention, but once I saw two other inmates eyeing her ass, the anger seeped back in and my dick deflated like a fucking balloon.

One inmate cracked a smile at the other and licked his lips provocatively while the other one rubbed his hands together and pretended to spank the air like he was spanking her ass.

I cringed just thinking about their filthy hands on her perfect skin. The thought of their dirty mouths anywhere near her made my skin crawl with rage — raw and extreme — so hot it made me want to claw at my skin and rip it away from my body.

When she turned back around, her eyes flashed to me and I felt it in my chest. She straightened her posture and continued to care for the two sick fucks who openly stared at her ass and tits. She was clueless to what she was doing to them. Hell, what she was doing to me. Maybe that was why she was so fucking appealing. She didn't know she was gorgeous.

I wasn't paying any attention as Dr. Giles, who was cleaning a new cut on my cheek. My eyes lingered on her. I watched as her almond-shaped eyes shifted as she read the paper she was holding. She pressed the tip of the pen against her mouth, giving me a physical reaction.

It was such an innocent act, but just the sight of something touching her plump, pink lips was enough to send my cock standing high.

It was then I learned her name.

"Lyla?" Dr. Giles called out to her.

Her name was Lyla. It was such a beautiful name, and it matched her perfectly.

"Yes, sir?"

"Could you come stitch Mr. X up when you get a second?"

She blanched and her face whitened. Her plump lips tightened, showing her unhappiness with his request. She didn't want to be near me, and while that should've made me happy, it sent a twinge of sadness through me. I'd acted like a douche for a reason, and I'd obviously done a good job, but still, it sucked.

"Sure." She forced a smile.

She came my way, her eyes never reaching mine, and then she replaced her gloves with a fresh pair.

I sat still, letting my eyes roam over her face as she stitched up my cheek. She didn't talk to me this time, and as much as I hated talking, I wanted her to. I didn't miss the way her fingers trembled or how she kept swallowing her nerves. I hated myself in that moment because I knew how uncomfortable she was around me. Me—a murderer—someone not worthy of her smile.

It was bullshit that I was even daydreaming about a woman like her. I gave up the rights to anyone when I decided to lose my fucking mind and decapitate two people.

Looking away from her, I kept my eyes locked on the wall over her shoulder. I was too dirty to even look at her. Too evil to touch her or to even think about it.

Her gloves snapped when she pulled them from her fingers.

"All done," she said with a false smile.

She had yet to look me in the eye, and I decided I was okay with that. It didn't matter, and it wouldn't pay to become too attached to someone.

I was taken back to my cell and left there until chow time. I couldn't keep this shit up, fighting every day just for the chance to see Lyla. If I did, it wouldn't be long until I was sent to the hole, but then again, it was worth it. Seeing her was like being in the sun, and that was worth being in the dark for a day or two as far as I was concerned.

I'd hear the things the COs would say about her. They'd talk about her ass and her tits. The perverted things they said made my blood boil—made me want to rip them to shreds the way I knew I could.

I hated the fucking COs, most of them anyway. Officer Douglas was an okay dude, but the rest deserved to be ripped apart for even thinking the foul things they did. Especially since the ones talking the most shit had wives and kids at home.

Lying in my bed, I listened as two COs walked up and down the block talking shit.

"She's got a sweet little ass on her. I bet she could take a mean fucking," Officer Stone said while swinging his baton.

I'd never liked Officer Stone, mainly because he looked like a pedophile. This fucker wore glasses that looked like they were made in the seventies and had enough grease in his hair to fry a whole chicken. I swear if I found out he drove a friendly van, I'd snap. I could just picture him luring children in with promises of candy and bikes.

I'd heard from Scoop that he was a shady motherfucker. There had even been hearsay about him raping a few of the smaller guys on the block. One supposedly went on to hang himself in his cell with his bed sheets. But that was before I was on the block, so there was no telling if it was even true.

"Yeah, but I hate escorting her. She makes the inmates crazy. It makes me wonder if the warden knew what he was doing," Officer Parks replied.

"I bet he wants to fuck her, too. That's probably why the bastard hired her."

They laughed. The fuckers *laughed*, and I wanted to rip their faces off. *No*. I wanted to rip their heads off. I wanted to see their dead eyes glaze over with the shroud of nothingness.

Their limp dicks would never touch her, at least not while I was there. I'd get my ass kicked every day and end up in the hole for the rest of my life before I let it happen.

The COs were dirty, hiding behind their badges to get away with everything. The fight club, the mistreatment of the inmates who didn't deserve it, I'd seen it all over the last ten years, but I wouldn't think twice about beating one of those fuckers to death if it came to the mistreatment of Lyla.

On the days she worked, she'd pass my cell. I'd stand at the bars and watch her openly. Most of the inmates did. I hated the tenseness in her shoulders and the way she'd hug herself as she walked down the block.

I'd hear the vile things the inmates would say to her and I'd grip the bars with white knuckles, wishing I could shut them up with my fists.

I knew in the back of my mind that it wouldn't be long before I snapped again. Before I went mentally crazy and ripped one of the COs or inmates to shreds. It was all because of her. I wanted her to stay, but she needed to go. I couldn't take the chance that I would kill someone. Fighting them and breaking a nose here or there was okay, but murdering was deeper. I wasn't sure I could do it again. I didn't think I could handle taking another life.

THE SUDDEN STING of alcohol brushing against the scrape on my elbow brought me out of my thoughts. Luckily for me, Dr. Giles was busy when I was brought into the infirmary and even though I knew she didn't want to, Lyla had to tend to me.

It caught me off guard, and I hissed at the sting. It wasn't often I showed my pain, and that was obvious in her expression when she looked up at me.

"Really? After everything you've been in here for, you're going to show pain for a little scrape like this?" she asked.

The side of her mouth lifted in a semblance of a smile, and it made me feel lighter.

I didn't respond. Instead, I focused on keeping my hands to myself as she continued to clean me up. It was hard work not to reach out and finger her hair or cheek, to fill my hands with her tits and ass. It took a lot to not run my knuckle over her fair skin and touch her soft lips.

I was a dead man for sure. I wasn't sure how much longer I could keep it up while living inside my head with the new nurse.

She looked up into my face, looking for more signs of pain, but I didn't flinch again. The last time was a fluke. You didn't feel pain when you were already dead inside, and I'd been dead for the last ten years.

Most of the fights I'd gotten into were nothing. It was just me trying to show everyone that I could protect myself. I hated the fighting. Hated everything about it. The men fought me hard, punching me when I gave them a chance, but these days, I didn't even feel their hits anymore. I didn't feel anything except for when I was with Lyla. Maybe that was why I was becoming addicted to her.

She was a drug. She made me high, and I waited every day for another hit of her. Closing my eyes, I breathed her in as I listened to Prichard, the inmate I'd fought, bitching on the other side of the infirmary.

"The motherfucker broke my nose, Doc!" he yelled.

I grinned to myself when Lyla turned away to take a blood-soaked gauze to the red Hazmat bag. The mouthy fucker deserved it. He should've known better than to come at me. It wasn't my fault he'd found out his wife was fucking another dude on the outside, and he should've known I wasn't going to back down when he decided to take his anger out on the person in front of him in the chow line.

When she came back into my curtained space with the doctor, he looked over my cuts and then told the COs to return me to my cell.

Thank fuck. One more time I'd gotten away with it without being put in the hole. I knew my chances were running slim.

The COs nudged me to my feet and then escorted me out. The loud doors shut behind me, and we began walking down the block toward my cell.

"Damn, man, she was looking hot today. Her ass is begging for my dick. I'd like to bend her sweet ass over and show her what a real man can do," Officer Parks said as if I were deaf and couldn't hear him.

He reached down and adjusted his balls, making anger and disgust roll through my gut.

"No shit," Officer Stone agreed. "I want to shove my dick down her throat and make the bitch face fuck me. I swear, if I ever get her alone in a dark place somewhere around here…" He chuckled. "Some place where they'll never hear her screams."

And just like that, I was done.

My face fell, and the anger that was simmering in my stomach exploded. It filled me, rushing through my veins like hot lava and heating them to a dangerous point.

There was once a nurse who accused Officer Stone of rape, but nothing ever came from it. Instead, she'd lost her job and I'd never seen her again.

When I thought of them doing those things to Lyla, I could feel myself losing control. My body began to shake, and, without realizing it, I began to pull at the restraints holding my hands together.

"I say we tag team that ass. No one would believe her with

both of us saying she's a liar."

They laughed, and I snapped.

The room around me faded away, and all I saw was red. I turned on them, pulling away from them with a growl and making them step back in surprise. They grabbed for their batons. They knew pepper spray wouldn't work on me. It'd been used on me too many times already.

I reached for Officer Stone, my cuffed hands going around his slim neck, and I didn't even feel it when Officer Parks began to beat me in the back unmercifully with his baton.

Stone's face turned red as I choked the life out of him. When I couldn't take the aggravation of Parks hitting me anymore, I turned on him. I yanked the baton from his hands and beat him, each hit releasing some of the anger within.

In the distance, I heard the alarms ringing and the other inmates in their cells egging me on, but I pushed it all out of my mind. Instead, I continued to beat the two officers until they were on the ground at my feet.

Their faces morphed into one bloody mass, but I didn't stop… I couldn't stop. The monster had been freed, and he was hungry for revenge and chaos.

I felt arms on me, pulling at me, trying to stop me, but I turned and pushed them away. It wasn't until one of the COs struck me in the nuts that I was brought to my knees.

I gazed up, seeing several COs standing around me before they all moved to attack. It didn't matter that I'd stopped beating Stone and Parks. I'd attacked two of their own… and that meant I was in for the worse ass beating of my life.

They all beat me at the same time, their fists and batons hitting me everywhere until I was flat on the concrete floor. I felt my skin splitting, old wounds opening, and I could smell the blood all around me.

Flashes of the past rumbled through my mind. The murders — the dead eyes that stared back at me after I'd mutilated their bodies. *Sarah.*

"Come on, boy!" one of the COs yelled. "Let's see you fight back now."

Soon, I didn't feel their hits anymore. I just felt the pressure of their blows against my head and back. Until, finally, I began to get dizzy. The roar of the inmates filled my ears as the bars that held them back shifted and blurred.

I knew it wouldn't be long before I was out cold. The last thing I saw before everything went black was the butt of a baton coming straight for my face.

CHAPTER 8

LYLA

TEN MINUTES AFTER the alarms went off, the room filled with chaos. Two COs were brought in, beaten half to death, and Dr. Giles was on the phones calling for an emergency transport.

Officer Parks was unrecognizable, and Officer Stone's pulse was weak. I rushed to their sides, administering everything I could to keep them alive. The door opened again, and then they were bringing in the inmate who'd beat them.

I couldn't see his face through all the blood, but I knew by his physique that it was X.

He really *was* the monster everyone claimed. I'd softened to him over the few weeks that I'd been working there. I'd even considered the fact that everyone was wrong about him, but apparently, I was the one who was wrong. So freaking wrong.

He'd beaten two COs almost to death with his bare hands and their own batons while he was shackled and cuffed. I wouldn't have thought it possible if I hadn't seen the two officers with my own two eyes.

"What the hell happened?" Officer Douglas asked when a

group of COs came in with blood spatter all over their uniforms.

"He fell down the stairs. Lots and lots of stairs," an officer panted, clearly out of breath from bringing the beast better known as X down.

Obviously, they'd beaten X, but rather than say that and deal with reports and all the craziness, they were all going to agree he'd fallen down the stairs. It was like watching a messed-up prison movie.

"We came in, and he was beating Parks and Stone. I've never seen anything like it. Then he just ran. We pursued, but he got caught up on a set of stairs," another officer agreed with the first. "Poor bastard. It's not like he had anywhere he could run to."

Officer Douglas looked at them suspiciously since obviously, they were lying, but then he shook his head and placed his hands on his hips.

"Go put in a report," he said.

He looked my way and shrugged. We were both shocked. I could tell by the look on his face. X fought, we knew that considering he was in the infirmary all the time, but it was still unlike him to snap on the COs. He was escalating… fast.

The other COs cleared the room, leaving me in the infirmary with two dying officers and the monster who'd tried to kill them. We ran IVs for the officers and prepared them for transport, and once the ambulance came, Dr. Giles called the hospital to warn them ahead of time.

During all this, X was out cold in a bed, waiting to be checked. One minute, everything was moving fast and the next, it was slow. After the COs were done, I found myself standing over X, watching his deep breaths move his hard chest up and down.

Slowly, I peeled his bloody uniform away from his body, reminding myself every few seconds that no matter how beautiful he was, he was evil. It wasn't hard because every time I closed my eyes, I saw the officers' faces in my mind.

I cleaned him up, putting more stitches in his body and checking for any signs of internal bleeding. He was badly beaten, bruised from head to toe, but honestly, what had he expected? He needed to learn that he couldn't go around beating on people. As bad as it sounded, I was starting to think that he had gotten exactly what he deserved.

Once Dr. Giles and I finished checking him over and taking his vitals, I sat beside his bed and kept watch as I filled out some paperwork. All the while, I tried to process what had just happened. The images of the beaten officers were flashing throughout my mind.

My head spun with the onslaught of grotesque pictures. My mind flipped from X, to Officer Stone, back to X, and then to Officer Parks. Constant back and forth, like my body was swaying in a rowboat. Not long after, my raging headache began. Thankfully, the infirmary remained quiet for the rest of the day. I went home that night and collapsed on my bed, falling in a deep, coma-like sleep.

X WAS AWAKE when I returned the following day for my next shift. Staying away from him as much as I could, I even avoided eye contact. I couldn't look at him, but this time, it wasn't because of the severe attraction I felt for him. I was angry for being deceived. I was beginning to think he was a somewhat decent guy, and then he went and did something so monstrous that I couldn't look at him the same.

We received word that the two officers were expected to make a full recovery, which was good news, but when Dr. Giles told X that information, he didn't flinch.

How could a person be so cold about another person's life? Was it really that easy for him to discard their lives like trash? The very thought disgusted me, and it repulsed me more that I was naive enough to think he was simply misunderstood. It wasn't something I even wanted to comprehend.

I'd just returned from my lunch break when Dr. Giles asked me to please change X's bandages. I didn't want to, but I didn't have much choice. I had to uncuff him and remove his restraints before I could remove his old bandages and clean his wounds, but as I did so, I felt his heated stare all over my face.

"You're ignoring me." He stated the obvious. "You're angry with me."

He never initiated conversation. I considered not responding, but I was so mad I couldn't help myself.

"Ya think?" I spat sarcastically.

At that, he did something that angered me even more. He grinned. The sick bastard had the audacity to smile at me.

"You think this is funny, Christopher? You think you can just go around and beat people within an inch of their lives, and nothing's supposed to happen to you?" I asked rhetorical questions. I didn't want or expect his answers. "Well, you can't." I cut him off before he could even think about answering. "You got exactly what you deserved."

I knew the minute his entire body tensed that I'd pushed too far. It wasn't my job to punish the inmates. It was my job to nurse them back to health and send them on their way.

His eyes darkened, his brows pulling down into an angry expression. It was then that I realized I was there, standing over a dangerous murder, and he wasn't cuffed or shackled. There I was chastising a man who could reach up and choke the life out of me for being a bitch to him.

Quickly, I scanned the room for the COs in case I needed to scream for them. And when X lifted his arm to scratch the back of his neck, I flinched as if he were about to hit me.

His expression shifted from anger to rage, and his lips tightened. He moved closer, tugging me into his space with soft hands. My breath stopped as my imagination went wild with all the vile and terrible things he could do to me, but instead, his eyes softened and dipped to my lips when I licked them nervously.

"Lyla, I would never put my hands on you. Never. Do you

believe that?" he asked.

My breath hitched when his unique scent swarmed all around me. It was strange to hear him say my name in such a personal manner, and the way he said it knocked me off my game. He was begging me with his eyes to trust him, but I couldn't do that.

I didn't believe him. He was a dangerous criminal—a liar—a manipulator. Dr. Giles had warned me about the inmates, and I couldn't forget that. They lied. They cheated. They killed. I worked in a penitentiary—not in a jail full of men with minor offenses. A maximum-security penitentiary full of murders and rapist—the lowest of the low—the most evil people on earth—and Christopher Jacobs was among them.

"No," I whispered, earning myself a scowl from the giant. "I don't trust you. You're a murderer and a liar."

He released me and I pulled away quickly, gathering as much space as possible between the two of us.

Something that resembled hurt moved over his expression before his mask slipped back into place. Cold and calculated—sinister. "Good," he said sternly. "You might survive this place after all." Lying back, he turned away from me.

Stepping away, I backed into the curtain behind me, and then I left his space and went straight for the supply closet to get away. I needed to breathe, and I couldn't do that whenever X was anywhere near me.

CHAPTER 9

LYLA

I ENJOYED MY four days off, spending time cleaning my apartment and catching up on laundry at the local laundry mat. Diana conned me into going to her place for dinner and movies, and I opened up to her about some of the things affecting me at work.

She had a thing about men in uniforms, so I told her about the officers. I told her about Officer Douglas, aka Duggie, and explained how he was the nicest CO in the place. Even though I trusted him, I had a hard time trusting the others.

We talked about a few of the inmates. I told her about X and how he was constantly in the infirmary. When she asked what he looked like, I explained without actually revealing how gorgeous he was.

"Sweetie, can I say something without you thinking I'm totally fucked up in the head?" she asked before hiding her face behind her massive wineglass.

I laughed. "Sure, but I already know you're fucked up in the head."

"That's the truth. Okay, so this X character you're going on about sounds fuckable." She grinned.

"Oh my God, you didn't just say that." I shook my head and took another sip of my red wine.

"Yes, honey, I did. Look, I know you're not really into the hardcore stuff, but he sounds like he could put a serious fucking on a bitch." She sat her glass down on the table in front of her with a clink. "All I'm saying is I'd like to be that bitch."

Obviously, she'd had too much wine, but I couldn't help but shake my head. I didn't bother mentioning the fact I'd been thinking some of the same things before he went all crazy and tried to kill two of our COs.

"Just think, Lyla, he's been locked up without pussy for ten years. Could you imagine what he'd do in the sack? Just thinking about what he'd do to my lovely lady makes her drool."

Covering my face, I laughed. "Your lovely lady? Seriously, Di?"

"Yes. She's lovely, and she likes it rough."

Spending the night out with Diana was just what I needed. She was completely unhinged, but she knew how to let her hair down and have a good time. That was exactly what I needed after an extremely stressful four days in the infirmary.

WHEN I WENT back to work, X was still in the infirmary. It was the longest he'd had to stay since I started working at Fulton.

Tossing my jacket over the back of the chair, I went straight to work on the paperwork and kept my eyes away from the part of the room I knew he was. I didn't want to look at him for two reasons. One was because of what he'd done to the two officers, and the other was because I knew every time I looked at him, I'd think about what Diana said. I knew I'd picture him on top of me, pumping like madman and growling like beast.

Feeling my nipples harden inside my bra, and I closed my eyes to shake my thoughts away. I was in the middle of my second deep breath when Dr. Giles came up to me and touched me on my shoulder. Gasping, I jumped since I wasn't expecting him.

He laughed. "Sorry. I didn't mean to scare you."

"It's okay. I'm just jumpy today."

"Ginger took care of most of the paperwork before she left for the day, but if you want, you can go check on X. He seems to be doing well, but some of his bruising is starting to worry me."

My shoulders dropped in defeat, but I nodded and smiled. "Okay, will do."

I went into his curtained space, sliding on a pair of latex gloves and readying myself for the conversation I'd have to smile through.

"Oh, God, not you again," he growled.

He was obviously in a foul mood.

"Yep, I'm back. How are you feeling today, Mr. Jacobs?"

He chuckled, the sound vibrating with its usual rich tenor. "Oh, so it's Mr. Jacobs now? What happened to Christopher?"

"Calling you Christopher was unprofessional of me. From now on, you're Mr. Jacobs."

"I'm not sure how that's going to sound when you're screaming my name, but whatever floats your boat, bad girl."

I ignored his words and took his blood pressure. Once I was done with that, I shined my light in his eyes to check the dilation. The bruises on his face were turning color, but they still looked terrible.

"So what changed?"

Sighing, I asked, "What do you mean?"

"I mean, what changed? Why am I suddenly Mr. Jacobs? You might as well call me X like the rest of them."

"Maybe I should," I snapped in a hiss. "Especially since it's obvious you're the guy they say you are."

I knew my words made no sense to him. He had no way of knowing what my thoughts had been like over the weeks. He had no idea that I was slowly coming around to him—slowly thinking that maybe he wasn't a terrible monster, but he'd proved me so wrong.

"I've never been more wrong," I said.

His blue eyes moved over my face as he tried to figure me out. I could practically hear the wheels turning in his head.

"Wrong about what?" he asked.

I didn't hesitate. "Wrong about you. I was starting to think that maybe…" I stopped. "Never mind what I was thinking. I was obviously wrong."

I gasped when he reached out and pulled me close. His heated breath skimmed the side of my cheek, and I breathed him in instead of calling for help. He moved his face, his lips inches from mine, and I silently hoped that he would kiss me. It was wrong, so wrong, but I wanted to feel his lips on mine.

"Don't ever *think* anything. You should always know, especially when dealing with inmates."

I pulled my arm from his grasp and tried to move away, but he held me strong. When I shifted, my chest rubbed against his and he closed his eyes in pleasure. Finally, I tugged my arm free and backed away, taking large pulls of oxygen to slow my beating heart.

His eyes raked across my face, trying to determine what I was thinking.

"You're upset with me."

I was. I wasn't about to deny it.

Shaking my head in annoyance, I blew out a breath and looked at the ceiling. "You know what? I am. I'm upset. Why'd you do it, Christopher? Why'd you beat those officers? I was starting to think you weren't the monster everyone said you were, but then you had to go and… Never mind, just forget it."

I was heated and when his lips tilted in a sexy grin, I felt my anger spike.

"You're smiling? You think what you did is funny? Because I assure you, it isn't. You could've killed them."

I knew I was raising my voice too much, and I was starting to worry the people outside his curtained space could hear me. But I was so hot, bothered, and angry with myself for it that I wanted to take it all out on him.

"Yes, I'm smiling, but not because of that."

"Then why are you smiling?"

"You called me Christopher again."

Rolling my eyes, I pressed into his chest in exasperation. When I realized I'd touched him so personally, I pulled my hands away quickly with wide eyes. I didn't need to poke the bear. Plus, getting comfortable with the inmates was strictly forbidden.

Before I could pull away, he reached out, grabbed my hands, and pressed them back into his chest. His eyes devoured my face, waiting to see what kind of reaction I'd have.

I gasped and pulled against his hold, but the strangest thing was that I didn't feel like I was in danger in any way. The look in his eyes wasn't scary; it was as if he was testing his limits with me. He was curious, and I couldn't deny the fact that I was, too.

He was hard and hot beneath my palms, his muscles twitching against my fingertips as if begging me for more.

"What are you doing?" I whispered. My eyes flittered around the space, seeing that the curtain was covering us completely.

He closed his eyes and breathed deep, as if he was getting some sort of relief from my touch.

"I've been in this place for ten years. For all those years, the only touch I've felt has been either out of hate or for medical purposes. This is…" He paused, his hands pressing my palms deeper into his chest. "Your touch… it makes me feel alive again."

His eyes opened, and his gaze was soft as he looked me in the eye. I was so confused. He was two different men —one with the authorities and other inmates, and one with me. Still, I couldn't help but feel like maybe I was being played for a fool.

I pulled my hands away like he was on fire when the curtain keeping us blocked from the rest of the infirmary was whipped back.

Officer Douglas poked his head in with a worried smile. "You okay, Ms. Evans? It was quiet in here."

Smiling through my beating heart, I nodded. "Yeah, I was just finishing up."

I stayed away from X for the rest of my shift, busying myself with paperwork and intake.

The following day, when I checked on him, I kept my eyes away from his face and stayed strictly professional. I'd gotten comfortable with working in the infirmary and with the way things worked. I went about caring for the inmates with a smile, and I was actually starting to feel good about taking the job.

My bills were all caught up, and there was food in my refrigerator and gas in my car. Slowly but surely, things were coming around.

I'd just given Mr. Davis his insulin and was headed to Dr. Giles' office to let him know I was going to grab some lunch, when a hand reached out from behind one of the curtains and grabbed me. Pulling me into the curtained room, he covered my mouth to keep my scream locked in.

His hot hand moved across my lips, making my stomach roll with disgust, and his foul breath cascaded across my cheek as be begun to whisper.

"Shhh. Don't make a sound or I'll tear you apart."

My mind went a million miles a second as I tried to remember which COs were in the room and where they were posted. But before I could make a noise, something sharp was jabbed into my back.

My eyes widened as all the things he could do to me went swirling through my mind. Suddenly, the alarm starting ringing and the lights began to flash as all of Fulton went on lockdown.

"Right on time," he said, his lips sliding against the side of my face.

Nausea thickened in my throat and my heart sped up when I realized he'd planned this. At that moment, the COs were running around like crazy trying to get the prison back in order. No one was even thinking about me or where I was. I was sure of it.

The inmate took his hand away from my mouth, sure that I wouldn't scream, and whatever he was jabbing me in the back with was moved to my throat. Cold, sharp metal pressed against me and dug into my skin when I swallowed hard.

Quickly, I ran the names of the inmates in the infirmary through my head, but I couldn't for the life of me figure out who it was behind me. All I knew was that he was tall and smelled like vomit.

With large hands, he caressed my breasts, making my breath catch in my chest. I wanted to scream, but I knew if I made any noise, he'd slit my throat. His hand moved down the front of me, skimming my stomach before he grabbed me between my legs.

"Fuck, baby, your pussy's warm. I can feel it through your pants."

I was going to be sick. I was going to throw up and end up getting my throat cut. I wasn't sure how much longer I could hold it down. The bile was already burning the back of my throat.

Suddenly, I was being turned and my eyes collided with Carlos Perez. I'd learned a lot about Carlos. Like the fact that he was the leader of one of the most dangerous gangs in Fulton.

His eyes glazed over, and a demonic happiness filled his expression. He moved closer, his chest pressing to mine, and his heated breath filled my nostrils. The smell was so terrible that I gagged.

His eyes darted around the space, searching through a small slit in the curtain, before he refocused on me. The alarm continued to blare through my brain, and I began to pray that maybe it was still going off because they were searching for me.

His eyes glistened, and I knew he was high on something. I inhaled sharply, wishing I could run, but with something sharp still pressed tightly against my throat, I knew I had to remain still.

Again, he moved his free hand down over my breasts and grinned. Dizziness swept over me, and I began to worry that I was going to faint. As if knowing I was getting weak, he moved even closer, resting his thigh between my legs.

Something tickled the side of my neck, and I knew from the tiny sting on my throat that it was my own blood trickling down. I was bleeding. I had no doubt in my mind that this man was going to rape and murder me right under the CO's noses.

His hand left my breasts and began to move down until his fingers were brushing the top of my pants. Roughly, he pulled at the elastic waistband and shoved his hand down them. I gasped, a tiny squeak pushing past my lips.

"Make a noise and you die."

He forced me against the bed, the rails digging into my back. Fear coursed through me, sharp and alarming. I didn't want to get on the bed, but I also didn't want to die. In the back of my mind, I continued to pray that someone would come and help me. But then again, someone coming could also push him to slit my throat even faster.

"Get on the bed."

Doing as he asked, I sat on the bed and pulled my legs up. I could feel my blood running down my chest and between my breasts.

Reaching between us, he untied my scrubs with one quick pull of the string. Closing my eyes, I prayed harder than I had in my entire life. I prayed that when I opened my eyes, he'd be gone, but when I finally did, he was still there, looming over me with something sharp in one hand and palming his hard penis through his uniform with the other.

"Spread your legs. Let me see your pussy."

I was being violated in so many ways, and I was mortified. There wasn't anything I could do, even though a scream was slowly working its way up my throat. I was beginning to think that maybe death was better than being raped.

The flashing lights stopped, and I knew it wouldn't be long before the alarm shut off as well. As soon as it was quiet, I'd make a noise. Even if it meant dying, I'd make some kind of sound to let the COs know I wasn't okay.

He pushed at my shoulders, and I lay back with a stiff spine. I began to open my thighs, cool air rushing past my knees and across my cotton panties.

"Lose the panties," he growled.

His fingers shifted, and the blade stung my neck once more. Finally, he pulled the blade away long enough to reach down and unzip his khakis. He backed up a little to tug them down over his hips, revealing his hard cock.

I took the chance while I had it. Kicking him back, I screamed as loud as I could. The bed rolled from beneath me as I jumped off and made a run for the curtain blocking us in. My screams weren't loud enough to be heard over the alarm, but I kept screaming anyway.

Carlos grabbed me by my ponytail and yanked me back. Again, I screamed. Something stung my arm, but I didn't care. I continued to pull against his hold, knowing that if someone didn't come soon, he was going to kill me.

I pulled until I finally got free again. But as I ran, my foot caught a power cord and I fell into the curtain. As I floundered in the fabric, I searched for an opening. Before I could find one, I was being pulled by the hair again. He pushed me down onto my knees. Dropping to all fours, I tried to crawl away. My knees ached against the cold, hard floor.

At that, he was on me, trying to flip me over so he could climb on top of me. I fought back, sure that any second he'd get tired of me and cut me open. Finally, he got me onto my back, his heavy body pinning me to the floor.

Reaching up, he pushed my hair from my face and shook his head at me. "Stupid little bitch. Didn't I tell you? I told you I'd kill you." He raised the makeshift knife and pressed it against my throat, stinging the skin in a new spot.

He looked down at me with a flushed face, spit flying from his mouth with every hard breath he took. He was going to kill me. I screamed again, trying to save myself once more.

All of a sudden, the weight of him was gone, and I no longer felt the sharp knife against my throat. My eyes flew open, and air rushed into my lungs. It was then that I heard the shuffling beside me. Looking over, I couldn't believe what I was seeing.

My attacker was pinned to the wall by his throat, a menacing figure with long, muscular arms and broad shoulders breathing over him with fire in his eyes.

X.

He stood there, growling into Carlos' face, wearing nothing by the hospital gown he'd been in during his stay in the infirmary. The back was open, revealing a long, muscled back, slim hips, a perfectly round ass, and thick thighs. His skin was tight and tan, and it was rippling with each move he made.

I stared in shock, still trying to come to terms with everything going on around me. I'd almost died. I'd almost been raped and killed, which had been my biggest fear since the first time I'd stepped foot into Fulton Rhodes Penitentiary.

"I'm going to kill you," X hissed in Carlos' face.

The alarm had stopped, but I could still hear remnants of it ringing.

Carlos was turning white, his lips a strange shade of blue, and it was then I realized that X was literally choking the life out of him.

Jumping to my feet, I stood on shaking legs before I moved across the room to where X was slowly killing my attacker. My arm burned when I reached out and placed my hand on his shoulder.

His head snapped my way with wide eyes.

"Don't," I started. I was out of breath and couldn't finish my sentence. Sucking in oxygen, I tried again. "Don't kill him," I whispered.

I definitely wanted him dead. After all, he'd almost raped and murdered me, but at the same time, I knew it was wrong. I didn't want X to get into any more trouble than he was already in.

His eyes softened even though his hands stayed tight around Carlo's throat. "But he was going to…"

I stopped him. "I know, but don't do this. Please," I begged.

The muscle in his arm shifted as he released the hold he had on Carlos. With X's hand gone, Carlos slumped to the ground, gasping for breath.

X turned toward me, his eyes moving over my face with concern. He clenched his teeth and the muscle along his jaw popped. Reaching up, I placed my palm against his cheek, feeling the warmth of his skin and thanking God that he came when he did.

There was a strange emotion in his eyes before he closed them, pressing his face into my palm, enjoying my touch. When he opened them again, they moved down my neck and to my arm. "You're bleeding."

My arm was burning where I'd been cut, and my throat was still stinging as if the knife was still there. "I'm okay," I whispered. Physically I was just fine, but I wasn't sure I'd be okay mentally ever again.

"I'm sorry," he said remorsefully.

I couldn't believe my ears. He'd just saved my life, and he was apologizing to me. "For what? You saved my life, Christopher."

"No. I'm sorry I didn't get to you sooner. That stupid fucking alarm." He stopped. "I didn't hear you. I'm so sorry I didn't hear you."

He looked as if he was about to lose it again. His eyes were wild, his lips tight. Using my thumb, I swiped under his eyes and let my fingers slide down the side of his face.

"Don't ever apologize to me again. Thank you so much. I can't express to you how much…"

Suddenly, the curtain flew back. Officer Douglas and Officer Reeves were staring back at us. Thankfully, I'd already pulled my hand away; otherwise, there was no telling what it might have looked like.

There I was, standing in front of X in nothing but my panties and shirt, with my hair down and blood on my neck and arm.

Before I could say anything, the COs moved in, snatching X

away from me and slinging him to the floor.

"No," I shouted. "Stop!"

But either they didn't hear me, or they weren't listening, because they were digging their knees into his back and putting him in cuffs.

His eyes met mine from the floor, his face contorting in some unrecognizable expression.

"Duggie, please stop. Just listen to me," I yelled as I reached down and began pulling on Officer Douglas' arm.

Getting the CO's attention, I quickly explained what happened. When I told them that X had saved me, their eyes went wide in shock.

Surely, someone who'd murdered two people wouldn't give two shits about me, but he did. He came in and saved me, and something in his eyes told me he'd do it again and again if I needed him to.

He stood against the wall, still cuffed, and I watched as his carefully placed mask slipped back over his expression. Gone was my savior. In his stead was the monster. That was it. Christopher Jacobs was only wearing a monster mask. I was sure of it. *Especially* now.

Leaning against the bedrail, I watched as the COs put Carlos in restraints and hauled him off to solitary confinement. Everything began moving in slow motion as Officer Douglas handed me my scrubs. Pulling them over my hips, I covered myself. I couldn't even believe I'd stood there as long as I had without any pants on.

I was in shock.

At that moment, Dr. Giles arrived. He leaned over me, calling out to the COs for supplies even though they had no idea where to look for it. I hadn't even noticed the large amount of blood that was running down the front of my shirt.

"Lyla, put pressure on your neck until I get back," he said, rushing from the space toward the supply closet.

I reached up and covered the cut on my neck. Everything

around me began to move quickly as Dr. Giles tended to my cuts. I heard nothing as I sat and replayed X rescuing me through my mind like a rerun of my favorite show.

I couldn't make sense out of it. Nothing I'd learned about him over the last few weeks was fitting. It was like I had different pieces to several puzzles. I freaking hated puzzles, but something in my gut told me that things were off when it came to X. Things just weren't right.

"Lyla? Can you hear me?" Dr. Giles asked, trying to get my attention.

"Yes," I mumbled. I was slowly coming out of my shock, and the room around me was starting to come into focus. Relief filled his wrinkled face.

"Your neck wound isn't too bad, but the one on your arm required several stitches. I'm sending you home for the rest of the day."

Stitches? He'd given me stitches, and I'd had no idea. Suddenly, I remembered giving X stitches and him not even flinching.

Was this how he felt? Cold and emotionless? Full of shock and fear?

I nodded instead of talking.

After filling out an incident report, I left the prison and walked to my car. Starting my engine, I sat in the driver's seat and stared at myself in the rearview mirror. I couldn't wrap my head around the things that had happened. But the same question kept surfacing.

If X was such a cold-blooded murderer, why did he save me?

CHAPTER 10

X

I TORE MY eyes away from her as the door shut, cutting off the connection between us. She was going home for the day, which made perfect sense, and while I knew I'd miss her sunny smile, I couldn't help but hope she'd never come back.

She'd seen firsthand the demons that occupied every corner and shadow of this purgatory. I wouldn't always be there to save her, and even thinking of something happening to her when I wasn't there made my blood boil.

Closing my eyes, I could still see her piercing green gaze and the haunted look that moved over it. I could still see the way her face contorted in agony as the scum of the fucking earth violated her. It was a memory that was sure to be etched in my brain for the rest of my life. It would stick the way the lifeless eyes of those I murdered did. Except I felt more fear seeing Lyla hurt than I ever did when I realized I'd murdered people.

It was sad to say, but I couldn't abide by her getting hurt. *Ever*.

The cuffs were tighter than usual on my wrists as the COs escorted me back to my bed. I hated being in restraints all the time. They were symbols of my enslavement, taunting me and reminding me that I was forever locked behind the bare walls of this dark and lifeless place. A place where innocent women could be raped and murdered not five feet away from those who were meant to protect them.

Hope didn't reside in Fulton. There was no such thing as a better day. There was only despair and fear. It thrived throughout the walls and into the ground to the point where Satan himself wouldn't dare enter.

We were all sinners. We all had secrets. When they finally released me from the infirmary and I was being escorted to the hole for what I had done to the COs, I passed the cells of hundreds of inmates. I cast a look into each one, seeing things the COs pretended not to see. Seeing what we really were.

Evil.

A few inmates looked at me and smiled, showing their appreciation for what I'd done to the COs, while other practically hissed through the bars holding them in.

"X on the block!" an inmate called out from somewhere above me.

Things came flying at me from different directions. Most of it was harmless—paper balls, wads of trash, and wrappers from the canteen. The COs pushed through the chaos, dragging me along with them.

Finally, we left the block and entered the darker part of Fulton. The hole was black, dark with shadows and grime. To be placed in solitary confinement was the equivalent of being shut in an inescapable cinderblock box. The walls closed in on you inch by excruciating inch while your mind started to do the same thing. As the space got smaller, your mind started to drift off to unknown, strange places. And if left there long enough, you walked out not sure if it was all a bad fucking nightmare or reality.

The air was musty and damp. The smell of a decaying basement flooded my nostrils. The crumbling tiles echoed in the guts of the withering dungeon as my feet shuffled along the floor.

When we came to my door, the sound of rusted hinges whined when they opened it. With an unsettling stride, I walked in. As one CO watched my every move, a hand poised on his baton, the other bent over to unlatch me from my restraints.

I rubbed my hands over my leathery wrists, burned by how tight they'd made the cuffs. As they shut the door to my solitary confinement, I relaxed for a moment and prepared my mind for the mental disconnect I would surely feel once I'd spent some time in the fucking place. I closed my eyes and imagined I was in my own cell. Only in my own cell did I feel somewhat at home, and I hadn't been in there since before my attack on the COs.

I sat in the darkness and rested my head in my hands. By then, I was sure the entire prison would know I'd saved the pretty redhead in medical. They would think I was getting soft, which meant there would be hell to pay when I got out of the hole.

I didn't regret saving her, but I did regret forming any kind of attachment to anyone or anything, and I'd definitely done that with Lyla. Prison wasn't a place for that. Forming attachments was dangerous because it gave the other inmates leverage. It didn't pay to have any weaknesses in prison, and Lyla had become one for me… whether she knew it or not.

A WEEK.

That was how long I was stuck in the darkness of the hole. It was a disgusting place. One filled with vermin and feces. There was no such thing as being comfortable. There was no such thing as clean. The hole was meant to be torture, and it was.

And worse than the hole was the fact that I spent most of my time there thinking about Lyla. I craved her sunny disposition and the life she brought into the room. I longed to hear her tiny giggle or see her sweet smile. Simply put, I wanted her to quit. I hoped that when I got out and put back into my cell, I'd find out from

Scoop that she'd ran and never looked back. At the same time, I knew her leaving meant I would have nothing to look forward to anymore.

Time in prison was different than time outside. Days felt like weeks and weeks felt like years, but my week in the hole felt more like ten years. When they finally opened the door to let me out, the light stung my eyes and my legs ached from disuse when I walked back to my cell.

Once I was back in my cell, I stood in the middle of my space and stared at the wall adorned with my signatures. I counted the Xs to myself almost every day, mourning the sight of them.

Stepping closer to the wall, I ran my fingers over their roughness and lowered my head in sadness. I'd never wanted any of this. I never wanted to hurt anyone, but they were always pushing me—always attacking.

Why couldn't they just let me serve my time in peace?

Going back to my bed, I pulled out my trusty screw and began etching three new Xs into the wall—two for the COs and one for Carlos. My jaw ached as I clenched my teeth together. Etching the Xs felt like I was etching into my soul, digging myself a hole deeper and deeper to hell.

Once I was done, I sat on my bed and put my screw back into its place.

Three hundred and forty-six.

That was how many fights I'd been in since I got to Fulton. How many times I'd lost myself and hurt another human being. That included the two murders I'd committed.

My eyes moved over the Xs. I'd have to look at them for the rest of my life. I'd add them every day I needed to until someone was finally able to take me out. X became my name mostly because everyone thought the Xs were marks of victory. But in reality, they were headstones. Tiny graves for each of my victims, whether they were dead or not. It was a place where I could go every day and mourn the things I'd done. I could grieve the loss of the boy I used to be.

The Xs were a place where I could be sad over all I'd lost, my sanity included. They screamed at me from the wall, keeping me accountable for all that I'd done in my life—reminding me every day that I was a monster.

I was just a shell of the person I used to be—hard on the outside and empty on the inside. Those marks were my own personal tombstone, reminding me every day that I was just as dead as the ones I'd murdered.

As night crept over Fulton, the familiar sound of snoring filled the block. Things settled down quickly at night. Closing my eyes, I reserved my energy for what the following day would bring.

Which motherfucker would try and take me on tomorrow?

They knew I was weak, mentally and physically. If anyone were going to try and take me out, it would be then.

I glanced over at my wall once more, the Xs standing out like shadowed souls in the night, Sarah's being the biggest on top, and then Lyla filled my head. I'd shown her a side of myself that I never should've. Flashes of her face moved through my memory—terrified and bloodied. Again, I could feel anger churning in my stomach.

It didn't pay to care for another person in this world, and I knew as I closed my eyes and began to fall asleep that caring for Lyla the way I did was surely going to be the death of me.

THE FOLLOWING DAY I found Carlos dead inside one of the industrial dryers. I pulled open the handle, ready to put in a load, and was met with the smell of burnt flesh and blood. His melting flesh hung from his bones, and he was bent into an unnatural position from his tumble in the heated barrel of death.

The other inmates in the laundry with me went nuts, and it wasn't long before COs came spilling into the room. The inmates were lined against the wall, forced to watch as his body was removed from the dryer piece by melted piece. It was graphic, and I found myself closing my eyes and seeing flashes of the scene that landed me in Fulton.

Talk about who'd murdered Carlos spread through the prison like fire, lighting the minds of murderers and gang members. Some thought the COs had done it as payback for his attack on a prison employee, but most of his brothers in the Mexican Mafia placed the blame at my cell door. It was common knowledge that Carlos and I had bad blood. Hell, just a week before, I'd almost killed him with my bare hands for his attack on Lyla, but it wasn't me.

I knew from that point on I'd have to sleep with my eyes open. Jose Alvarez, Carlos' right-hand man, stepped up as the leader of the Mafia, and his eyes were glued to me, blaming me for the loss of his brother and former leader. Shit was about to get real in Fulton.

CHAPTER II

LYLA

I TOOK A week off from work, missing my four-day shift. I worried about my bills being paid, but I couldn't go back yet. Thankfully, I found out on my second day off that I was paid for my leave because of what happened. That made it easier to relax and take advantage of my time away from Fulton. It gave me time to reflect on the incident.

That was what I'd taken to calling my attack—the incident. I couldn't bring myself to say the word rape. I couldn't think about the fact that I'd almost been murdered. I had the cuts and bruises to prove it, but I made sure to keep my eyes away from them when I looked at myself in the mirror.

I didn't tell Diana about what happened. I didn't need anyone trying to talk me into quitting, as I was already doing that to myself enough. Using my week off to my advantage, I put in applications at local medical offices and a few hospitals, but I had no bites. When it was time for me to go back to work, I drove to the prison with what felt like a ball lodged in my throat.

The sense of dread that loomed over me was suffocating, and

I felt as though an elephant had taken up residence on my chest. I'd had patients describe a heart attack to me before, and if I was going by their explanations, then I was definitely having a massive one.

I sat in the parking lot, building up my courage, and when I had less than five minutes to clock in, I pushed my car door open and climbed out. Breathing deeply, I put one foot in front of the other until I was stepping into the warm air of the prison.

When I walked the block to the infirmary, I shut out all the shouts and usual vile language. You'd think that after a month of working in the infirmary, the men would've gotten used to me by now, but still, they acted as if I were fresh meat and they were starving.

I submerged myself in work, filling my day with intake screenings so that I wouldn't have to go face to face with X, but there were only so many new inmates. After stressing over seeing him, I realized my worry was for nothing. Right after I went home, X left the infirmary.

He was sent straight to solitary for his attack on the COs. It was well deserved, but still, it bothered me knowing he was locked in such a terrible place after he'd rescued me. Not that my life was any more important than the COs, but you'd think one would cancel the other out.

As bad as it sounded, I wasn't sad when I found out that Carlos had been murdered. I didn't even want to think about who'd killed him. I probably should've felt guilty knowing that his attack on me had something to do with his untimely death, but I had none.

Rumors moved around the prison about who had ultimately taken his life, and X seemed to be the number-one pick. I wanted to believe differently, but I couldn't forget about the fire that was in his eyes the day he saved me. He wanted to kill him then, but instead, he had waited.

Of course, I couldn't forget the fact that Carlos was the leader of a lethal gang. Gang violence was an everyday occurrence in

Fulton. The simple fact was, no one would ever know what really happened to him, but there was one less killer in the world.

It was wrong, but every day that I worked, I waited with bated breath for X to enter the infirmary. Wanting him there meant another lockdown for the prison. It meant some guy on the block was going to get his ass kicked by X, and it meant X getting hurt as well, but I was selfish. I wanted the opportunity to thank him properly and if I were being honest with myself, I wanted to see him.

My eyes kept flickering to the door. Every time it opened, I'd hold my breath, but it was never X.

"Who you waiting for?" a voice asked from my side.

When I looked over, I saw an inmate sitting up in bed. It was a little guy the inmates liked to call Scoop. His real name was Evan Moore. He was serving fifteen years for self-defense and had already been at Fulton for seven. I'd only seen him a handful of times, but he wasn't a very scary guy.

He was short and skinny. Something about him reminded me of a little mouse. I thought it was his tiny, button nose or his pointy ears, but either way, I found myself smiling at him.

"No one."

"So how you liking Fulton so far? To be honest, I'm surprised you're still here considering."

He lifted a shoulder and grimaced. I knew without him saying that he was talking about the attack.

And then I remembered some things I'd heard about Scoop. Things like he was X's friend and that he knew everything there was to know about every inmate on the block. It was wrong, but my curious nature was getting the best of me. I wanted to know more about X.

Ignoring his earlier question, I went straight for the kill. "So you're friends with X?"

The side of his mouth tilted in a knowing grin. "That I am."

I was hoping he'd just automatically tell me things about X, but he was obviously going to make me work for it. Swallowing my pride, I nodded and continued my line of questioning.

"How is he doing? He was pretty banged up the last time I was here."

"Don't know. He was in the hole for a week, and now all this shit with Carlos. I haven't been able to talk to him much." He scratched the side of his neck and opened his mouth like he wanted to say more. Grinning, he did. "Being in the hole is hell, but looking at you now, I'd say you were worth it."

Maybe Scoop didn't know everything he thought he did. He had his facts all messed up. X didn't go to solitary because of me; he went there because he'd beaten two COs so badly they had to be rushed to the hospital.

"I had nothing to do with his attack on the COs," I insisted.

He lifted a blond brow and looked at me as if I were insane. "You really have no idea, do you?"

"No, I don't. Why don't you fill me in?"

Again, he smirked, shaking his head in disbelief. "X was defending your honor. Stone and Parks were talking so much shit about you. They were even joking about getting you alone and raping you. I guess he couldn't take it, and he snapped." He shrugged like it was no big deal. "You should know X is crazy protective when it comes to the people he cares about."

I could hardly believe my ears.

Swallowing hard, I let his words run though my brain, trying to make sense of everything. "Wait. What makes you think X cares about me? I'm just a nurse. I could lose my job if it were anything more."

When he stood from his bed, he seemed no worse for the wear, which made me wonder why he was even there to begin with.

"You're not very smart are you, Ms. Lyla?" He started toward the door as if he were just going to leave. There were no COs around him, and I knew without asking that he wasn't supposed to be in the infirmary. "Trust me. X cares. He cares, and it's eating him up inside."

I laughed and shook my head. "You're wrong. X doesn't care

about anything. Everyone knows he's a monster." The words burned the back of my tongue.

He'd saved me, and I knew in the back of my mind that he was far from being a monster, but he was in prison for murder. There was more bad than good inside him.

"You're not very observant. Do you have any idea why X is in prison, Ms. Lyla?"

"Yes. He slaughtered two people. He's a murderer."

"Yep. He *allegedly* slaughtered two people with a kitchen knife. But there's one common factor about everyday kitchen knives—they're dull as shit. You'd have to be one strong son of bitch to cut through bone with one of those. I've seen pictures of X before he was put in prison. He might be a big motherfucker now, but back then, he wasn't much bigger than minute. I find it hard to believe that he was able to cut off one body part, much less multiple off two people, with a dull kitchen knife. Look it up."

I'd had my own experiences with dull knives in my kitchen. I could barely cut a piece of chicken, much less a body part. But then again, I wasn't X. However, if what Scoop was saying was true, then maybe it was something to look into.

My dad worked for the police department for many years. Set-ups happened all the time. People were arrested for crimes they didn't commit on a weekly basis. Who was to say that didn't happen to Christopher as well? I'd had my own doubts about the man he was. I sat on the fence when it came to X, but I couldn't deny the desire that swam in my stomach for him. Finding out he wasn't the monster everyone thought he was would make me feel a lot better about that desire.

Scoop smiled at me from across the room and nodded. "You're getting it. X isn't the monster. He does what he has to do to survive."

And then he was gone, leaving the room silent. For the first time since I started working there, I noticed I was completely alone inside the infirmary. How had that happened? How was Scoop able to get me alone without an officer present? Obviously, the little guy had more pull in the prison than I realized.

I spent the rest of the time at work trying to figure out how to get Christopher's file. I needed to read over it. If Scoop was right, and I had a feeling he was, something was definitely wrong.

Had Christopher Jacobs been put in prison for a crime he didn't commit?

I administered meds and went about work in a zombie-like state, my mind running over the details of everything I'd heard about X's crimes.

Suddenly, the bars clinked open and the buzzer sounded as four COs came in carrying X's limp body. They moved him through the room, struggling to carry his heavy weight, and then they laid him on the closest bed they could get to.

Running to his bedside, I began to examine him. "What happened?"

There had been no lockdown—no alarms or flashing lights.

"Don't know. Reeves found him this way in his cell."

Opening his eyes, I flashed a light in and his pupils didn't change. Something was definitely wrong. Rushing to the phone, I plucked the receiver from the base and began dialing.

"Transport," the usual gruff voice answered.

"I need an emergency transport STAT."

Dr. Giles came in then, his white lab coat flying behind him as he moved with a quick stride. "What's going on?"

I explained as he did his own examination.

Finally, transport showed up and began to load his large frame onto a stretcher. Going to his side, my fingers ached to touch his face.

Before they began to move him, his eyes popped open. I gasped as he took in my face, his eyes scanning me with worry etched deep into his brow.

"Lyla." My name crept from his lips in a whispered struggle.

He tried to sit up before collapsing back onto the bed. I pressed my palms into his hot chest and forced him to stay down.

"Shhh. Just relax. You're going to the hospital. Something's wrong. Promise me you'll behave and I'll be there as soon as I can," I whispered in a rush.

His eyes cleared before he nodded his understanding.

At that, he was gone, transport rushing him from the infirmary. I had the strangest feeling that they'd taken a tiny piece of me with them, leaving me feeling incomplete and awkward.

CHAPTER 12

X

THE MORNING WAS uneventful. Apparently, I'd been wrong about the inmates coming at me during my weakest point. I grabbed breakfast and ate in silence as Scoop ran his cocksucker about some shit going down on the block. I wasn't all in the conversation—instead, my head kept swimming in the shit that happened over the last few weeks—drowning in Lyla. I was sure those thoughts had a lot to do with the headaches that kept me up at night.

"So your girl's back in the clinic," Scoop said, finally catching my attention.

I looked up from my eggs, and he chuckled. "I thought that would get your attention."

"Shut the fuck up," I muttered, digging back into my breakfast.

He laughed and shook his head. His eyes moved around the cafeteria, and his face cleared. Leaning forward, he cleared his throat. "Listen, maybe you should take a break from the infirmary for a bit. I know you want to protect her, but let the COs do their job."

I snorted. "Those fucks can't protect their own asses, much less Lyla's."

"That's true sometimes, but the boys are talking, and I think maybe you should lay off on your visits."

Dropping my fork, I gritted my teeth. "What are they saying?"

"Not much, but everyone knows you saved her from Carlos. They're saying you killed him because he attacked her. You don't want them connecting the two of you. That could be more dangerous for her."

He was right. I had to lay off going to the infirmary. Getting close to Lyla was dangerous for her. Instead of responding, I nodded my understanding and pushed my tray away.

After breakfast, I always went to laundry to get my day started. The smell of death still lingered around the laundry room. I was sure they'd never get all of Carlos out of the dryer he'd died in, and when I loaded it every morning, I could still see his bent, melted body inside. It was a fucked-up way to die, but I couldn't shake the feeling that he deserved it. I'd seen him do worse to other inmates.

Today was different. Usually, I made plans to get into a fight so I could see Lyla, but I knew I couldn't do that anymore. It wasn't safe for her. I watched my back while I worked, knowing the inmates would pull some shit. The Mexican Mafia lived by the credo: *An eye for an eye*. I was sure they were going to try to kill me the same way Carlos had died. I wasn't interested in taking a ride in the dryer.

The rumors were still flying. Death threats had been carved in the cinderblock outside my cell. Word was getting around that I was weak just like I knew it would. I figured it wouldn't be long before someone pulled some shit.

I walked into the laundry, and my stomach dropped. Inside were three members of the Black Guerillas, and they were busy holding down one of the boys from the 803. He was young and new to the block, and he cried as they fucked him roughly in the ass.

They had him bent over one of the folding tables while they took turns raping him. Blood seeped down the back of his dark thighs, glistening in the muddy light of the laundry room. He was beaten pretty badly. His lip was split and one of his eyes was swollen shut, but still, he begged them to stop.

"Take it like a man, bitch boy," the one of top of him whispered into his ear.

I closed my eyes against the scene, the sounds of their bodies slapping against his echoing throughout the room alongside the sounds of the washers and dryers. Disgust rolled around my gut, sending spicy bile up the back of my throat.

When I opened my eyes, his eyes were bugged while the one behind him choked the life out of him and continued to drill his hard cock into his bloody ass.

I should've walked away. I should've minded my own business for once, but I couldn't. He was so young and defenseless. It was wrong to let this continue. I went at them with full force, ripping them away from him. They pulled up their pants with a curse. I shuffled the young boy out of the laundry, him dropping to the floor on weak knees, and then I stood there and waited for the three of them to attack me.

"That was a bad idea, motherfucker," Jerome said.

We'd never really talked to each other before, but he was a big motherfucker... almost as big as I was. He moved toward me, his two boys flanking him, and I stiffened my spine. The room smelled of laundry soap, burnt flesh, sweat, and blood, which was smeared in a rusty mark of the beast on Jerome's khaki pants.

"You should've just minded your own damn business, white boy."

They cornered me; the one on Jerome's right, I thought his name was Marcus, ran his palm over his thick, black cornrows and smirked. I tried to figure out which one would come at me first, but it didn't matter. I was weak and tired, and I wasn't sure I could take on all three.

Jerome moved, almost putting a hole through my stomach he

punched me so hard. I folded over and gasped, but before I could go at him, they jumped me. I blocked my head, knowing the headaches I kept getting meant I wasn't fully healed from the beating I got from the COs.

My fist connected with two of them, knocking them back and earning myself a second or two without hits. They moved in again, but before they could attack, a loud banging noise stopped them.

We turned, finding Officer Douglas standing beside the metal folding table. Again, he slammed his baton against it.

"That's enough," he growled.

Great. Officer Douglas being there meant I was probably going to go back to the hole. That was the last thing I wanted, but I couldn't just stand there and watch while some poor fucker got ass raped.

But he surprised me. Instead of calling for other COs and throwing the four of us in restraints, he came into the laundry and nodded toward Jerome.

"Get your boys out of here and don't let me catch you in the laundry again."

Jerome promised me revenge with his eyes before the three of them left the room. *Fucking awesome.* Another lethal gang to worry about. My death was imminent at this point. The guy they'd raped had left without comment. He wasn't stupid. He knew ratting on the Guerillas was like signing his own death certificate.

I stood there, taking in Officer Douglas and trying to figure him out, but instead of staying for a talk, he nodded and turned to walk out of the room.

"Try to stay of trouble, X."

With those words, he was gone, leaving me to do the laundry in peace until the rest of the laundry crew came in. I spent three hours washing, drying, and folding, all while sweating in the heat of the room. The humidity made everything sticky and wet. When I got back to my cell, my muscles were sore and my uniform was soaked.

THE HEADACHES HAD gotten worse. Soon, they were accompanied by dizziness. I knew I should've gone to the infirmary, but I also knew going around Lyla was dangerous for us both. One minute I was standing in my cell, waiting for the Cos to run the line for chow time, and the next, I was waking up in the infirmary with Lyla standing above me. It had been so long since I saw her face that my heart rate instantly sped up.

She was there. Scoop told me she'd came back, but I almost didn't believe him. Now, I could see with my own two eyes that it was true. That was bad and fucking great at the same time. Seeing her there and knowing she was okay was like a rush. I wanted to reach out and touch her skin—feel that she was real—but I didn't want to jeopardize her job or get my ass kicked by a CO for touching a prison employee.

The ride to the hospital was spent replaying her worried face over and over in my mind. She acted like she cared about me. It was much more than the usual worry a nurse showed for her patient. She looked like a woman worried about her man, and something about that made a strange ache burn in my chest.

I wanted her. God, help me, I wanted her. But it wasn't because I hadn't touched a woman since I was nineteen; it was because my body craved her—no other woman—just her.

There were so many tests and scans. I was put in one machine after the other while armed officers waited. Being tested and scanned meant all restraints had to be removed and without restraints, I was considered a flight risk. They had no idea that leaving was the last thing I wanted. Sure, I wanted to be free, but I wanted to see Lyla again more.

Once the doctors were finished with me, they put me in a room and cuffed me to the bed. The armed officers were posted outside my room, but I was left alone in a place of comfort with a

TV. No wonder inmates liked a trip to the hospital. It was like a tiny vacation from our reality.

After watching TV for an hour, I began to doze off. My body was more relaxed than it had been in years. For the first time in a long time, nothing hurt. Even the tiny headaches I'd been getting had decided to give me a reprieve.

My eyes fluttered closed and sleep was moving over me when suddenly my door opened and Lyla stepped in.

She was still in her scrubs, letting me know she'd come straight to the hospital after her shift. She slowly moved across the room toward my bed, her green eyes scanning my face with insecurity.

"You're here," I said, sitting up.

She nodded.

She was so beautiful. So fucking beautiful, and it was wrong but it felt amazing knowing she'd came there for me. No other inmate—just me.

"I knew you couldn't resist me," I joked, trying to lighten the mood.

A tiny smile pulled at her lips, and then disappeared as worry lowered her brows.

"I'm glad you came." The words rushed from my lips, and I meant them. It wasn't a hit to my pride to admit it. I was happy she was there, and I wanted her to know that.

"Come here," I said, reaching out my free hand. I didn't want her to be afraid of me. She was the last person in the world I'd hurt. But I needed her close to me.

She moved stiffly toward the side of my bed and swallowed hard, her throat bobbing up and down.

"I'd never hurt you, Lyla. Not ever." Truer words had never been spoken.

Her eyes scanned my face once more, and then she moved closer, her thigh rubbing the rail of my bed. Slowly, I lifted my free hand toward her as if I were about to pet a wounded puppy, and when my fingertips met her cheek, she closed her eyes and sighed as if she felt as much pleasure from my touch as I felt from touching her.

This was really happening. I'd dreamed about it for weeks, but she was really there and I was touching her. Letting my fingers linger on the side of her cheek and then down her neck, I watched as her eyes dilated and her cheeks flushed. I wanted to follow the flush with my fingers when it moved down her neck and into her top.

Shaking herself, she reached down and plucked a clipboard from the side of my bed. I watched as her jade eyes scanned the document, and a tiny smile twitched her plump lips.

"You're going to be okay," she said.

She had no idea how right she was. I was definitely going to be okay. As long she was there and I had her full attention, nothing could hurt me.

"I am now."

And I was. I was more okay in that moment than I had been in my entire life.

CHAPTER 13
LYLA

I COULDN'T BELIEVE what I was doing. I was being as manipulative as the inmates. I was lying to get what I wanted, and I wanted to get to X.

Seeing him cuffed to the hospital bed was unnerving. He didn't look like himself. He wasn't the X from the block. His usual dark nature had been wiped clean and all that was left was a pale version of him—weak and unsure of what was going on inside his body.

But when he touched me and gazed up at me with warmth in his eyes, I wasn't sure I wanted to acknowledge the emotions that moved over my heart. His promise to never hurt me had touched me all the way to the very depths of my soul in a place I'd never been touched. And even though everyone else was afraid of X, I knew he was telling me the truth. He'd never hurt me no matter what.

He'd had opportunities to over the last few weeks, and yet, he was the one person in the prison who'd gone out of his way to save me. Why would he do that if he had any plans at all to hurt me himself?

His thumb shifted beneath my eye, the calloused pad rough against my cheek, and I melted into his palm. All my inhibitions lifted in that moment, and something unseen passed between us. He had somehow managed to make me his, and I wasn't even sure he knew it.

"How'd you get in here?" he asked, his big, warm hand engulfing both of my frozen ones.

"I walked in." I shrugged.

I didn't want to divulge all the manipulative things I'd done to sneak in to see him. It wasn't something I was proud of, and trust me, the little angel conscience on my shoulder was bitching me out for it.

I took a seat in the chair next to his bed and removed my hands from his. When he was touching me, I couldn't think straight. All my focus went to the point where his heat met my cold skin, and that was all I could think about. The COs outside his door laughed out loud, making me startle. It wouldn't be long before they were coming in to check on me.

"Before I left work, Dr. Giles got a phone call from the hospital. I watched as he wrote your room number down in his files."

He listened, not saying a word as his royal eyes moved over my face, landing on my lips. They were so deep, pools of emotion that I wanted to dive into.

"How'd you get past Ramirez and Reeves?" he asked, nodding to the door where the two COs were posted.

Pulling papers from my purse, I held them out for him to see—papers I'd taken from the infirmary—with Dr. Giles' signature, which I'd forged.

"I showed them these and told them they couldn't come in with me because of confidentiality. They're outside waiting for my call. I'm supposed to scream if you try to attack me. Although…" My eyes flickered to the hand that was handcuffed to the bed. "I'm not sure there's much you could do even if you wanted to."

"You lied for me," he stated.

I nodded.

"Why?"

"I need to talk to you."

There was no need to beat around the bush. I needed to know if he was innocent. I needed to know that I wasn't sick for being so attracted to a man who was capable of slaughter. I'd gone to bed so many nights hating myself for the way I felt just thinking of his dark skin and blue eyes. It was lust—raw and unadulterated—and it was so wrong considering our circumstances.

"Then talk." He lifted a confused brow, his eyes becoming suspicious.

"Did you kill Carlos?"

He didn't even think about it. "No," he said right away.

I stood, moving closer to the side of his bed. Reaching out, I took his free hand in mine, his much warmer than my own. He didn't try to stop me as I inspected his hands. They were rough. Scars and scrapes covered his knuckles, bearing witness to the many fights he'd been in.

When I flipped them over, my eyes moved over his palms. They were smooth, except on his fingertips, which were calloused and spoke of hard work. With the flick of his middle finger, he skimmed it across my own palm, sending goose bumps up my arm into my shoulder.

He watched me intently for my reaction to his touch, and I knew he could see the red blush that was spreading across my cheeks. Closing my eyes, I swallowed hard and continued my inspection.

I traced every inch of his palms, the natural lines dug into his skin from left to right, but there were no signs of scarring. I tried to picture how young and innocent he could've been, but all I could see were his bulging muscles and deadly expression. Had Scoop been right? Was Christopher set up?

The weight of all the accusation came crashing down on me, weakening my knees.

"Are you okay?" he asked, reaching out with his free hand to hold me steady.

"I'm okay." Stepping away, I looked him over from his shaved head, which was slowly growing back in, to his thick lips. "Christopher, I need to ask you some things. I need you to let me in, and I need you to be honest with me. Okay?"

His eyebrows furrowed, but he nodded. "Okay."

"Do you remember the night you killed those people?"

I was normally one to beat around the bush, but I knew it wouldn't be long before the COs were tapping at the door and coming in.

His shoulders stiffened and his eyes slid away from me. He didn't want to answer.

Reaching out, I placed my hand against his cheek and turned his head my way. Instead of opening his eyes, he pressed his cheek further into my palm and sighed.

"It's important," I whispered, afraid to break the strange spell that had begun to shift between us. "Please tell me what happened."

Finally, his eyes met mine, but it wasn't the X I was used to seeing. His mask had slipped once again and instead of the usual hard stare, fear moved in. Suddenly, I could see the nineteen-year-old boy he used to be. I could imagine how afraid he was in that moment.

"I can't," he said, his voice cracking in aggravation.

"Please, Christopher, I need to know," I begged.

He looked at the ceiling as if trying to find the answers, blowing out a hard breath. "You don't understand; I can't remember doing it." His eyes searched mine beseechingly. After a minute, he closed his eyes and shook his head.

"Try," I rasped. "Just try."

"You don't think I've *tried*?" He exploded, making me jump back.

I looked at the door, sure the COs would come bursting in, but nothing happened.

"I'm sorry, Lyla. I didn't mean to yell at you." He reached up, running his fingers down my arm softly. "It's all a blur. I went to my girlfriend's house for dinner. That's all I remember. She's all I remember—her long blonde hair and red lips."

"So you don't remember anything about the murders, yet you confessed?"

He looked at me, sadness overtaking his face, turning it dark. "I killed them. Their blood was all over my hands. I can still smell it. I feel the guilt of their murders every day, and I will for the rest of my life."

He gawked at his hands, as if he still couldn't believe he'd actually done such a thing. Taking his face between my palms, I gazed deep into his eyes. He looked so helpless, lying there with so many questions and confusion in his eyes. He was almost childlike.

"You didn't do this, Christopher," I said, trying to convince myself as well. "You're too good. You couldn't have done those things."

He clenched his eyes closed tightly and shook his head. "No. I did. I know I did."

"Look at your hands," I said, taking his hands in mine and turning them palms up. "The person who murdered those people cut them apart with a dull kitchen knife. It would be almost impossible for you to do that *now*, much less when you were younger and weaker." I wanted to hear him admit that he was innocent. I needed it. "Think about the boy you used to be, Christopher. Is that something you think you're capable of?"

He wasn't looking at his palms, his eyes darting all around the room.

"Look at them!" I yelled.

His eyes clashed with mine before they dipped down and scanned his palms.

"I did those things, Lyla. I remember the blood. I remember all of it. I was scared and I was angry, but I don't remember why. I don't care what you think because I know what I did. I earned every X I ever marked on my walls. I hurt people. It's the only thing I'm good at."

"The Xs on your walls? That's why you mark them? For the people you hurt?"

He looked me in the eye, taking me in and making me feel exposed.

"The Xs are my graveyard. They remind me of the monster I've become. Every time I hurt someone, I mark it on the wall. I mourn each and every one of them every day. I mourn them, and I mourn the boy I used to be. He's gone, Lyla, and he's never coming back."

My heart broke for him. Every day, he stared at that wall, counting his sins and reliving some of his worst nightmares over and over again. He wasn't an evil monster. He wasn't counting his Xs as victories. Instead, it was his way of owning up to what he'd done.

Picturing him in his cold, dark cell alone, mourning the loss of his life outside Fulton, being reminded every day of the terrible things he'd supposedly done, made me want to cry for him.

How could he have lived like that for ten long years?

Tears pricked at my eyes, and I stood and turned away. My time was coming up soon anyway. It wouldn't be long before the COs came in.

"I'll see you when you get back to Fulton." I grabbed my purse and the paperwork I'd pulled out.

As I turned to leave, he reached out and grabbed my hand. Warmth crawled up to my elbow, sending tingles up my shoulder. His fingers intertwined with mine, and I closed my eyes at the sensation.

He tugged, pulling me onto his chest and making me gasp out loud. His free hand moved into the hair at my cheek, softly twisting into the strands I'd left free.

"Lyla." My name rushed from his lips like a prayer.

His eyes were glued to mine with a passion I couldn't continue to ignore. My stomach twisted and my brain filled with fog. Warmth rushed through me and I leaned closer, wanting so badly so feel the stubble of his cheeks against my face. He pushed his rough cheek against mine and a manly sound rushed past my ear, making my breathing accelerate.

Sliding his lips along my cheek, he kissed the side of my jaw, warm and soft. When he pulled back, his eyes went to mine, searching for any indication that I was okay with what was about to happen. Whatever he saw gave him permission because he moved quickly, pressing his hot lips against mine and sending my brain spiraling.

His lips were thick and soft, unmarred in their wickedness. I leaned into him, going onto the tips of my toes as I pressed for more. There was no denying it anymore—I wanted him. It was different from the way I'd wanted my high school boyfriend or the guy I dated for a few weeks while I was in nursing school. This want blazed inside of me, sending heated rushes down my spine and into my thighs.

No one had ever made me feel this way, and I knew that the tiny taste of him would never be enough. There was no going back. Time had stopped on our little moment, and I silently wished it to stay paused—to sneak a lifetime into these few minutes with him.

When he ran his tongue along the seam of my lips, I let him in, tasting him as he sweetly sucked my tongue into him mouth. There was nothing else. There were no COs posted outside the door. No lifetime sentences stuck between us. There was only him and me, and his succulent lips taking me away to a place I hoped to visit often.

His fingers sifted through my hair before running along the base of my neck. I pulled away to release a tiny moan, and his grip on the back of my head tightened, pulling me deeper into his kiss. He growled against my mouth, letting me know he wanted me, and desire pooled between my legs in a wet slide of want.

A sound alerted me outside the door and I pulled away quickly, my hand flying to my swollen lips. Stepping away from his side, I adjusted myself and looked away from him. He was too tempting—too sexy—too ready to give me something I'd never experienced. Something primal and filled with sin. Something that made me clench my thighs tightly and lick at my lips to taste him.

I didn't trust myself to look him in the eyes again. As it was, I wanted to fall back into his arms. Knowing the expression on his face that awaited me, I couldn't take the chance of looking at him. Grabbing my purse, I turned toward the door. I had to get out of there before things went any further.

Before I could get there, Ramirez poked his head in.

"All good?" he asked, his eyes moving over my body as if he could sense my arousal.

Tucking my hair behind my ear, I looked up at him and gave him an innocent smile. "All good." With that, I left the room without looking back.

When I left the hospital, I took a deep breath and leaned against my car. My insides were screaming to be released, my breasts so sensitive I bit into my lip at the slightest touch of my bra.

X had knocked me off my feet with one hand cuffed to the bed. I could only imagine what he could do with them both.

OVER THE NEXT few days, I couldn't shake my thoughts of X. I could still feel his hands on my skin and every night I went to bed with my fingers in my panties and his soft growls on replay in my mind.

When I was at work, all I could think about was the words he'd said in the hospital. He couldn't remember murdering two people. He couldn't remember much of anything about the moments before the murders. His amnesia nagged me. Something was definitely off about his entire situation. I needed answers.

Dr. Giles had once told me he'd seen X's files. I wasn't sure how he'd gotten a peek at them. I was under the assumption they could only be viewed by those ranked captain or higher.

Officer Douglas was a captain, and we'd become friends since I started working at Fulton. He was a great guy, and we often worked the same shifts. I spent a lot of my time in conversation with him. He was a funny guy and always knew how to make my day better.

Maybe I could get him to show me X's file?

After a few days of hesitation, I finally had the opportunity to ask. Dr. Giles was at lunch and it was just Douglas and me in the infirmary. We were watching over an inmate who was being treated for vertigo. Luckily for me, the inmate was passed out and I had plenty of time to work up the nerve to ask Douglas for what I wanted.

I read over some paperwork, every now and again looking up and watching Douglas. He was leaning back in his chair, one leg cocked up on the desk with a cup of coffee in his hand. He turned up his radio, trying to listen to the codes with a furrowed brow.

"Can I ask you something?" I went for it. "Something just between us?"

His eyes darted my way, and a smile crossed his face. "What's up, buttercup?"

I chuckled at his friendly banter. "Dr. Giles told me he saw X's file. Was that bad? I mean, I know he seems like a scary guy, but every time I think about how he saved me from Carlos, I can't help but wonder, you know?"

Douglas' eyes lowered briefly before he removed his leg from the desk and turned toward me. His spine stiffened, and I thought for a second that maybe I should've kept my mouth shut.

"Lyla, don't doubt for a second what these boys are capable of doing. I know you want to think the best of everyone, but you saw yourself what he's capable of. Poor Stone and Parks." He shook his head. "He almost killed them with his hands cuffed, and we're still not sure who put Carlos Perez in that dryer."

I nodded my understanding. I wanted to confess his

innocence in Carlo's death, but I couldn't spill the beans about my hospital visit. Still, I couldn't see it. I'd seen what he was capable of, but I also was starting to understand the reasons behind everything he did.

Turning away, he began to type some things into the computer in front of him. When he was done, he twisted the monitor my way and nodded at the screen.

"See for yourself. Let's see if these pictures change your mind." He stood. "I'm going to check on our dizzy friend."

After he left me with the computer, I pulled up a chair and began flipping through the pictures. My stomach flipped, and my head swam with disgust as I took in each image.

Body parts lay strewn everywhere, arms and legs detached, and there was so much blood. It looked as if the entire room had been doused in it. Broken pieces of furniture were tossed around the room as if a tornado had touched down in the center. It was an unnatural disaster—a cluster of evil.

There was so much death—so much hate.

With a weak stomach, I looked over each picture carefully, searching for a clue. Each image painted the scene perfectly, letting the viewer know that a psychopath had indeed committed the crimes.

The final picture wasn't of the crime scene, but instead, it was a full body picture of X after he'd been arrested. I stared at it, memories of our kiss moving through my mind. His eyes were hot and full of lust then, but in the picture, he looked dazed and afraid.

His young body was unscarred and smaller, *much* smaller. His was still tall, but his muscles weren't as defined. No ink graced his skin, and he looked pale and confused. Prison had changed him. The cinderblock walls that held him in had transformed that boy in the picture to a hardened man. He wasn't the monster he claimed to be before Fulton. Fulton had bred that monster, and the inmates and COs had fed it.

My eyes moved over the picture, taking in the blood that covered his body. It was on his face, chest, and arms. He stood there, naked to the world with his arms out and his palms visible. And that was when I knew. He was too small to have committed the gruesome crime. He couldn't have been strong enough to cut through muscle and bone. X hadn't cut those people into pieces. He was innocent.

I sat back in my chair as the realization came crashing over me. Losing myself in that moment, I let snippets of crime scene information move through my mind. I was so lost in thought that when Douglas came up behind me and touched my shoulder, I jumped.

"So what's the verdict? Monster or not?" He studied my face, as if he were trying to figure me out.

"I don't know yet," I lied. "But I tend to find out."

CHAPTER 14

LYLA

MY FOUR DAYS off were exactly what I needed to recharge. The week had been hectic and with all the new information I had swirling around my brain, I was mentally exhausted. I needed help, and I knew exactly where I needed to go to get it.

When I got out of the shower, I wrapped myself in my robe and towel dried my hair. My day wasn't going to be pleasant, but if it meant possibly clearing Christopher's name, then I would do it. I'd do whatever it took. Maybe I was drugged by the mere thought of him. Perhaps his kiss had sent me on a downward spiral, but I meant to find out.

Slipping on my favorite jeans, I pulled on a T-shirt and a pair of socks. As I finished running my fingers through my curly hair, I added a touch of color to my face, which I hadn't done since I started at the prison, and sprayed on my favorite perfume.

Grabbing my purse and keys on the way out the door, I headed to the place I'd known all of my life. It was like a second home to me, and when I opened the doors of the station and stepped in, I immediately went back in time.

The scent of coffee was welcoming and the banter between the officers made me smile. Phones rang every few seconds and I took it all in, enjoying the wave of nostalgia it brought me.

I stood in the center of the police station, my eyes touching every wall and piece of furniture until I landed on the photo of my dad. There was a plaque next to his picture, a dedication from his fellow officers. Swallowing against the emotion that threatened to choke me, I closed my eyes and wished that I could hear his voice once more.

"Lyla?" a voice called from behind me.

When I turned around, Charlie, my dad's old boss, was standing there smiling back at me. "I must be seeing things." He chuckled.

"Hi, Mr. Charlie." I opened my arms, and he embraced me like he used to when I was younger. He had always doted on me.

"What are you doing here, carrot top?" He pulled away, taking in how much I'd changed since I'd last seen him at my dad's funeral. "You're not in any trouble, are you, sweetheart?"

I shook my head. "No, sir, but I could use some help. Do you have a few seconds?"

He motioned for me to follow him to his office, and when I walked in, I took a seat in the worn leather chair he offered. Looking around his office, my eyes moved over the pictures of his history as the police chief. He even had a picture of him and my dad together, both smiling at the camera after catching a murderer.

"It's been, what, two years since I've seen you? Not since your daddy's funeral."

"Three years." I swallowed hard, trying not to think about the pain being in his office brought. Trying not to think of the pain of missing my dad.

"My, how the time flies," he said sadly. "I'm sorry, darlin', I know your dad's a sore subject. I miss him, too. More and more every day. He was a great man and one hell of an officer."

I nodded as an image of my dad standing in his police uniform crossed my mind. He'd worked for Charlie for almost thirty years before he was shot three months shy of retiring. After thirty years of being shot at, sleep deprived, and kicked around, he'd died from a fatal shot to the head right before he was finished.

"He was," I muttered.

"So what can I do for you, sweet cheeks?" He leaned back in his chair and placed his clasped hands over his belly.

I had his full attention and suddenly, my nerves were getting the best of me. "I recently got a nursing job in the infirmary at Fulton Rhodes."

His eyes widened. "Lord, your daddy is probably rolling over in his grave, girl." He sat up, leaning over his desk. "He'd hate you working there. Hell, I'm not sure I like it very much. There are some nasty pieces of work in that place."

My mind went over the roster, knowing I could name half of the bad seeds he was talking about. I smiled and agreed. "There's an inmate there. His name's Christopher Jacobs. Ever heard of him?"

He closed his eyes and mumbled Christopher's name repeatedly, as if he were mulling through his memory bank.

"Let's see." He flipped on his computer and began searching. After a moment, his eyes widened and I could see the moment his memory was jogged.

"Christopher Jacobs. Oh yeah, I remember that one. He was a sick one. I couldn't get the images of that crime scene out of my head for weeks. What do you want to know?" His face turned serious.

"Can this be between you and me for now?" I asked, hoping I could confide in him.

"Yes, of course." His curiosity was getting the best of him.

"I think he's innocent." The words leapt from my mouth in a rush.

Charlie's face cleared, his eyes raking over my face, before he burst into laughter. "Please tell me you don't believe this monster when he says he's innocent. Didn't you know that every inmate in

Fulton is innocent? At least, that's what they tell everyone.

I shook my head, cutting him off. "No. He thinks he really did it, but some things aren't adding up."

His laughter stopped, and he swiped at the moisture under his eye. "Things like what?"

He watched me carefully, reading my every move like a book he'd read too many times. It was his job to interpret body movements, and Mr. Charlie was excellent at his job.

Filling him in on the details, I told him about Christopher's amnesia and my own experiences with the human body. I told him about how difficult it would've been to cut through muscle and bone, especially with a dull knife. He listened with concern in his eyes. Maybe he thought I was going crazy. Maybe I was, but something in my gut told me I was right, and my daddy always told me to follow my gut.

When I was done telling him my story, he stood from his desk and went to the door. Shutting us off from the rest of the precinct, he leaned against his desk in front of me instead of going back to his seat.

"Lyla, I love you like one of my own, and because of that, I'm going to tell you something." He pinched the bridge of his nose and took a breath. "Be careful which stones you turn over when it comes to criminals. You never know which one has a snake hiding under it. Jacobs is a snake if I ever saw one, and he's working you. Stay away from him. He's dangerous. You're not a police officer, and you're no detective. Do your job, and let me do mine."

Any hope I had of getting his help fell through the cracks. I didn't bother responding. Instead, I nodded and stood to leave. "Thanks for your help," I said as I turned for the door.

"Lyla, look at me."

I did as I was told, even though I wanted to bolt from the building. "Sir?"

"I'm sorry if I was hard on you, but I hear criminals claim to be innocent every day. I'll look into the case, because it's obvious it's something you're passionate about, but I can't make any promises." He lowered his eyes and sighed. "Come by tomorrow. I'll see what I can dig up."

I left the building unsure if I'd done the right thing. A weight had been lifted off my shoulders, but I wasn't sure if Charlie believed me or not. I hated to think I was just being tossed around because of who my dad was, but I had to hope that he'd at least take a look at it like he'd promised. As I climbed into my car, I knew it was going to be a restless night. I wasn't sure if I could wait until the next day to find out anything.

I SHOWED UP bright and early the next day with two cups of coffee in my hands. When I entered the police station, I was greeted by several familiar faces, and when I got to Charlie's office, he welcomed me with a wide smile, motioning me to come in.

"So let's talk. I spent most of the night digging, and you won't believe what I found."

He stood and motioned for me to follow. I was eagerly hoping he'd found something good. He led me to the records room. The room was large with boxes lining the walls—case numbers and names written on each one. It was an old school way to file, but it worked for them.

I sat at the table in the center of the room, placing my purse in the chair next to me. He set a box down on the table in front of me, and dust flew all around us. Pulling out a thick folder, he opened it and began laying crime scene pictures onto the table in front of me.

I'd seen them before, but still my stomach turned at the jagged flesh and blood before me. I schooled my expression, sure that he'd turn the pictures over if he knew how badly they affected me. The familiar mugshot of Christopher when he was just a boy was laid before me, and beside that was his confession.

"I looked over the pictures and after making some phone calls, I think you might be on to something, kid. His entire body is covered in blood, but his palms are clean. No cuts. No blood. Nothing." He sat down, his eyes filling with excitement. "At first, I thought maybe he'd just washed his hands, but he was taken straight in and this picture was snapped before he was even fingerprinted in the intake area."

Hope moved through my chest. I was right. I'd known it.

"That's all well and good, but here's where it really gets interesting." He leaned forward and lowered his voice. "During the investigation, they uncovered DNA under his nails. None of that DNA matched any of the victims."

I couldn't believe it. This was the big break I'd been hoping for. Someone else had been there, and Christopher had taken a piece of them without even realizing it.

"Tell me about the victims." I wanted to know everything I could about the case. I wasn't a police officer, but I'd lived my entire life with one of the best.

"Sarah Rizzuto was his girlfriend's name. This is the thing; her father was Anthony Rizzuto, one of the biggest mafia bosses on the East Coast. There are two families—the Lanza family and the Rizzuto family. The Rizzuto's were being watched by the FBI and had been for the last two years. They were suspected of drug dealing and human trafficking."

My stomach turned, and I felt the air around us get thick. This was more serious than I'd originally thought.

"And the other victim?" I asked.

"Michael Welch, a high school friend of Sarah's. About a month before the murders, the FBI noticed a young boy hanging around the Rizzuto's oldest daughter, Sarah. They suspected he was a recruit and took a bunch of surveillance photos of him."

He laid the photos on the table in front of me, and I realized they were pictures of Christopher, young and carefree. One of the pictures was of him with his arm around a pretty blonde. He was smiling in all the pictures. He looked so happy, and my heart ached for him.

"And then a week before the murders, Michael came into the picture. Again, they assumed he was a new recruit." He laid more surveillance pictures on the table of another young guy. He was walking along the sidewalk, looking down at his phone.

"I put in a call to a buddy of mine over at the FBI and he says when they busted the door in, Jacobs seemed disoriented and confused. He said someone had called in a tip about the murders, but they never figured out who it was. Before they even got the investigation under way, Jacobs had already signed a full confession. Case closed."

My heart was slamming against my chest. "He was framed," I whispered, my eyes scanning over the pictures once more.

"It looks that way."

I stood, ready to run from the room and tell the world, but Charlie reached out and grabbed my arm, stopping me.

"Lyla, listen to me. This is serious shit. We're talking drug cartels and human trafficking. If we open this case back up, it's going to get nasty. Blowing the whistle on this could have repercussions. Are you sure this is what you want to do?"

I didn't care about the repercussions. X was an innocent man serving a life sentence for crimes he didn't commit, and I was hell-bent on letting the world know. I wanted him to be freed. He deserved a second chance at life, and if I was being honest with myself, I wanted to be a part of that.

I FOUND MYSELF outside Fulton on my day off. I probably should've waited, but the excitement of the things I'd just learned was too much. Walking into the warden's office, I smiled at his secretary.

Curiosity moved across her aging face, streaks of grey

working themselves into her loose bun.

"Can I help you?"

"Yes, ma'am, I need to speak to the warden."

"Can I tell him who's here to see him?"

"My name's Lyla Evans. I'm a nurse in the infirmary for Fulton."

Finally, she smiled back at me. "Sure. Have a seat and I'll let him know you're here."

I sat in an uncomfortable chair and twiddled my thumbs. Finally, his door flew open and he stood there, looking over at me. He was short and stocky, older than I thought he'd be. His brows were bushy, his face stern, but he still managed to smile at me.

"Ms. Evans, please..." He held a hand out toward his open door. "Come on in."

He ushered me inside of his very luxurious office. Compared to the bleak, white-walled halls I walked every day, this was like a five-star resort. His rich leather furnishings shone in the sun that came through his large wall of windows, and his walls were a dark burgundy trimmed in gold.

A decanter on the far side of the room was filled with an amber liquid that I assumed was an expensive scotch. Pictures of senators and even the president lined his walls.

"So, Ms. Evans, how are you adapting here at Fulton?"

I sat in the chair in front of his desk and nodded. "Very well, thank you."

"Good. I'm glad to hear that. I was sorry to hear about your attack. Mr. Perez was a real piece of work. He'd been a problem here at Fulton since we received him." He leaned back in his chair, the leather squeaking. "I'm just glad the officers got to you in time."

He was obviously misinformed and didn't seem to have any grief over Carlos' death.

"The officers didn't save me. Mr. Christopher Jacobs did."

Surprise flickered in his eyes briefly before he was able to contain it.

"Is that so? Well, regardless, I'm glad." He looked away and adjusted a pile of papers on his desk. "So what can I do for you?"

Touching his forefingers together, he pressed them to his lips as he examined me with a steely look. It unnerved me, and I felt myself growing nervous.

"I have a friend in the sheriff's department, and after hearing about Mr. Jacobs and his past, some things didn't add up."

His brows lifted. "Some things?"

"Yes, sir."

I went on to explain, filling him in on my knowledge of the human body and the difficulty one would have cutting through muscle and bone with a dull kitchen knife. I went on to mention a few other tidbits of information. His eyes grew darker the more I talked, and a coldness settled over his expression. It was unnerving and the more I talked, the more uncomfortable I became. Something wasn't settling right with me.

A momentary look of fear passed over his expression, stopping me and allowing me to catch my breath. As soon as it did, it passed, his features smoothing and all emotion leaving his eyes.

The hairs on the back of my neck stood on end, and I suddenly realized that maybe coming to the warden wasn't my brightest idea. I wasn't a fool to the ways of law enforcement; I knew there were bad guys mingled in with the good, but the warden? Something about him gave me a bad feeling.

The temperature in the room grew colder, and something told me I needed to keep my mouth shut about everything else I'd found out. Still, I continued, explaining Sarah's connection to one of the largest mob bosses on the East Coast.

"Having the last name Rizzuto had put a massive target on Sarah's back and after looking over the files, the fact that her father was a part of the mob wasn't even mentioned. Plus, DNA was found under Christopher's nails that didn't match the victims." I swallowed against the knot in my throat.

"So they are thinking about reopening the case?" he asked, his lips thinning in what looked like anger. "What do they hope to get out of this?" He studied my face too sharply, making me feel as if he could hear my unsure thoughts.

"I'm not sure. Some of the information regarding the case seemed off. That's all I know." I stood, ready to flee his office. He was making me uneasy. Perhaps I was just being paranoid, but he seemed to be pissed off by the information I'd brought him.

He smiled, but it never reached his eyes. There was no kindness or even a twinkle in them, only ice. "Thank you for bringing this to my attention, Ms. Evans. I'll call the sheriff and have him fill me in on the details. I'm sure it will all get resolved soon enough."

His eyes shifted toward the phone on his desk before he reached out to shake my hand. It was cold and impersonal, faked. Once he let go of my hand, I turned and went for the door. He sat at his desk, unmoving.

When I closed the door behind me, I leaned against it to catch the breath I'd been holding. I hadn't stayed behind to eavesdrop, but suddenly, I could hear him talking on the other side of the door. My blood ran cold when his words reached my ears.

"Hey, it's me. We have a problem. Ms. Evans, the new nurse in the infirmary, paid me a little visit."

The room went quiet as he listened to the person on the other line speak. And then my worst fears came to light.

"It doesn't matter. She knows too much. Take care of it."

CHAPTER 15

X

MY VACATION FROM Fulton was too short. I was just starting to get comfortable with not having to look over my shoulder. Starting to enjoy the fact that I didn't have to worry about who was coming through my door and which gang was going to try to take me out.

As I sat back on my bed, staring at the grimy, white walls around me, I realized just how terrible being in prison was. It was the place where souls went to rot, and the smell, which I'd obvious gotten accustomed to over the years, was a product of those souls rotting… decaying and mixing with the smell of unwashed ass.

The nice, quiet hospital room was heaven compared to the moans and yelling that now blasted through my head. I closed my eyes tightly as they shut my cell door, wishing I could be back in the hospital again. I prayed that some asshole would jump me and kick my ass so badly I'd have to be returned.

After a moment of adjustment to the chaos, I realized Scoop had been calling my name from the cell next to mine.

"X!" he shouted in a whispered rush.

"I'm here," I replied, not moving from the bed. My head still hurt slightly, and I really didn't want to get up.

"I've heard some news. There's been a breakthrough in your case. Some evidence came out that you might be innocent."

"What?" I sat up, ignoring the pain that shot through my head. Walking to the bars, I leaned against the wall as I listened.

"Apparently, your little girlfriend did some digging and came up with some stuff. Did she come see you in the hospital?"

"Yeah." I stopped asking him a long time ago how he knew things. He was a Houdini. He was everywhere and nowhere at the same time.

"And?" He was prying. I knew I could trust Scoop with my feelings for her, but giving him that kind of power over me wasn't what I wanted.

"And nothing. She told me I didn't do it, and you know what?"

"What?" His voice grew soft and curious.

"I think I'm beginning to believe her."

He grew silent. After a few minutes, I realized he had gone back to his bed. I retreated to mine and sat staring at the wall, the Xs burning into my retinas. The first two ran along the top of the wall and weren't as deep as the newer, fresher ones, but they hurt the worst. I was just a scrawny, scared kid when I first etched them in, tears streaming down my face. I sat for weeks staring at them, repeating their names over and over again.

I pictured Moira and Anthony, Mr. and Mrs. Rizzuto, Sarah's parents, as they shook my hand and welcomed me into their lavish home the first time I'd met them. They were such pleasant people. It was a shame they'd lost their daughter so tragically.

They loved each other so deeply, and I envied that. I could see it in their eyes every time they looked at each other, and I remember hoping that one day Sarah and I would be the same.

Soon after, Mr. Rizzuto hired me to be his errand boy and to do some yard work. I was hard up for money. With me trying to help my mom out and maybe save for college, I needed to save every penny I made. He treated me like a son, even though I'd only been dating Sarah for a few months. He even offered to help with my college tuition.

They were good people. At least, I'd thought they were. It wasn't until later that I found out what kind of people they really were. The drugs. The lies. They had a rap sheet a mile long, and Sarah had known the entire time. Still, the guilt of taking her away from them was thick and deadly.

Lying back, I closed my eyes and pushed away the memories. It was getting close to lights out, and I knew if I kept up that way of thinking, I'd wake up drenched and gasping from nightmares. Instead, I thought of Lyla and smiled. Drifting off, I dreamt of her sweet kisses and soft sighs. I couldn't wait to see her again.

"It's my first time," Sarah said, her lips open in pleasure.

"Mine, too."

I moved my body into hers, the feeling so extreme I could barely hold back the raw, lustful noises that spilled from my lips.

"I love you so much, Christopher," she panted.

"I love you, too."

And then the room around me shifted, and I wasn't having sex with Sarah anymore. Instead, I was sitting in a chair across from her father, Mr. Rizzuto. He was sitting on the plush white couching and looking back at me with a smile. He held out an envelope and pushed it into my chest. I took it.

"Look inside," he said, taking a drag from his cigar.

I opened the envelope, and my jaw hit the floor. It was full of money. I pulled it out and counted a thousand dollars.

"This is too much," I said, confused.

He stood and came to me, patting me on the back like a proud father. "You deserve it. You've been doing an amazing job around here. Christmas is right around the corner. Go buy your mother something nice."

I looked down at the money in my hand, and when I looked up again, the room was different. I stood, my eyes taking in the blood-covered scene around me. My heartbeat quickened and panic filled my gut.

My eyes shifted around the room, landing on a dark figure. He carried

Sarah's lifeless body in his arms. Rage consumed me and I tackled him to the ground, my stomach spinning when one of Sarah's arms fell to the floor before the rest of her.

I clawed at his dark face, kicking and punching with everything I had. Suddenly, the room began to spin and blur, and my arms felt too heavy to move. I felt drunk, but I never drank.

The faceless man fought back, and then he spun me, his heavy frame pushing me into the hardwood floor. I reached desperately for his face once more, but I only reached his neck. I dug my claws in, ripping at his skin and making him yell out.

I'd gotten a piece of that son of bitch.

The blur thickened, and the sounds around me became muffled. Darkness moved over me, but before I passed out, the last thing I saw was Sarah's decapitated head and her lifeless eyes staring back at me.

I sat up with a jolt, shaking, my body covered with beads of sweat. Cold seeped into my veins, and I glanced around, terrified. The dark prison walls stared back at me, bringing me back to reality. I grabbed my chest, expecting my heart to pound a hole right through it. As I breathed, I could hear Scoop from my cell door.

"X? You okay?" he asked, leaning against the bars.

"Yeah, I'm okay. Why didn't you wake me up?"

Once again, I'd missed the call for chow line up and the sounds of my cell opening. It was breakfast time, and I never slept past it. Officer Reeves was going to have my ass if I didn't quit fucking up.

"I've been calling your name since they started to run the line, man. Are you sure you're okay?"

I wasn't okay. I'd had nightmares about that night for the past ten years, but never had there been another person, never had there been a faceless man that I had to fight. I was almost positive it was more than a nightmare. It was a memory.

After ten years, things were coming to light. I hadn't done it. Someone else was there. He'd killed them, my girlfriend and her friend.

The shocking reality hit me like an anvil and I sat back, straining to remember more, but nothing else came to me. One thing was for sure, I'd been drugged. It was the reason I couldn't' remember much about the night of the murders. I was framed.

The pieces were slowly falling into place. Things I'd never thought about before moved into my brain. Things like the fact I would've never been able to cut someone into pieces with a dull knife. Lyla was right. I used to be so weak. Why hadn't I realized that before?

Excitement rushed through me. For the first time in ten long years, I wasn't being choked by guilt. It was sad that Sarah and her friend were dead. It was a sadness I was sure to carry around for the rest of my life, but I hadn't done it. Lyla was right. I was innocent.

CHAPTER 16

X

THE NEXT DAY, I went looking for a fight every chance I had. Shouldering past the men on the block, I hoped to piss them off enough for them to swing at me. I practically seethed at the inmates during chow time, wishing a motherfucker would come at me. I was a like a rabid racehorse, foaming at the mouth and chomping at the bit.

I knew Lyla was back at work, and I wanted to see her. If things had changed since our kiss, I wanted to know before I let myself get too involved. Hell, I was already fucking involved. Maybe she would come in and act completely different toward me. If she were a smart girl, that was exactly what she'd do. I knew having anything to do with me was a bad idea; she should know it, too. Even if I was innocent.

The dynamics of being in prison had changed for me, though. No matter how much I pushed, no one would fight me. Also, I wasn't being watching constantly, and it seemed as though people were going out of their way to avoid me. I meant to the point where they were walking on the other side of the hall in avoidance. It was just my luck. The moment I needed the inmates out for my blood, they wanted nothing to do with me. Maybe my beating the hell out of the COs was enough to deter them.

After a few days, however, I realized it had been a rare, short-lived fluke. Rumors about me murdering Carlos moved around the block like hot lava, pouring from the mouths of those who had no fucking clue. Because of that, it became obvious Jose was out for revenge. He sat staring at me every chance he got, his thought processes above him like grey clouds of contempt. I was sure he was mulling it over, trying to figure out how and when he wanted to go about killing me. After all, I'd supposedly killed his brother.

His gang knew the situation and they were his constant surveillance, waiting for the perfect moment to catch me off guard. For three days, they watched and waited, expecting at any moment to be able to take me down. Finally, they got their chance.

I was working laundry when I felt the similar chill pass down my spine. Ten years of paranoia had honed my sixth sense. I knew when someone was behind me. Turning quickly, I found six of his guys surrounding me, all brandishing a weapon. Two of them had socks full of paint balls. They slung them around like David about to take on Goliath. The others had paper blades lodged in their fists.

As I waited impatiently for them to attack, the hairs on the back of my neck stood on edge. A paintball sock was swung at my head, while the two with blades moved in. I deflected the blades instinctively and tried to duck at the same time, but the paintballs caught me in the side of the head, sending an ache so extreme through my brain that I thought I'd pass out on the first hit.

My teeth rattled and then the familiar ache worked its way through my cerebrum and the headache started again. It was the same old twinge that sent me to the hospital. There was no healing from a head injury in prison when you had a big target on your back.

I ripped the sock out of his grasp and used it against him, catching him across the jaw. He fell to the ground in agony, spitting out blood and a tooth. Five moved in at once, and one sliced my arm with the blade. I wrestled another one away, but then their fists began to fly at me and I could only block so much.

I took down four of them, leaving the last two standing and ready to strike. Their blades caught the light coming into a barred window, and it reflected in my eyes. They were dangerous and tenacious, like bulldogs waiting to take down a bull.

The alarms began to ring out, alerting the staff of the fight. Within a few seconds, COs moved in to diffuse the situation. They hauled off the ones who weren't bleeding and took them straight to the hole. The others, and myself, were taken to medical, which was a good thing considering I was already starting to feel dizzy.

The moment I entered the infirmary, I looked around for Lyla. I knew she would be angry with me for another fight, but I didn't care. I'd learned to love the heat she displayed in a moment of anger. It was sexy, a raw reaction that made the blood pump straight to my cock and my brain swim with need.

My head throbbed in the bright lights, and I closed my eyes for a moment. Head pain was no fucking joke.

Opening them, I looked around for Lyla, but she was nowhere to be seen. I sat on the bed, waiting for Ginger or Giles to come in and see me. When the curtain came back, Giles stepped in. A familiar redhead followed him, and her eyes lit up with raw anger and excitement when they landed on me.

She was there. I'd never been happier to see her face.

Her cheeks were flushed as she gazed at me from behind him. Her features were soft, begging me to touch them, as she helped Giles get some vitals and check my pupils.

"Damn it, X, you just got out of the hospital with a head injury. Why do you keep doing this to yourself?" he asked.

But I didn't answer him. I wasn't paying him any attention. All I could hear was the soft slide of her scrubs as she moved around the room. I tensed when she pressed a finger to my wrist to check my pulse. I could see her counting in her head, trying not to look me in the eye for fear of losing her place.

"Douglas, I need some room. Could you back up to the curtain for a moment?" Dr. Giles asked.

Officer Douglas nodded before leaving. I saw him through the slit in the curtain as he walked around checking on other inmates before he returned to the desk. From that moment, his eyes never left my face as he stared me down through the tiny slit.

"What happened this time?" Lyla whispered when Giles left the curtained space for his suture kit.

Thankfully, he closed the curtain all the way, making it impossible for Douglas to see us.

"I needed to see you. "I didn't bother blaming Jose and his boys. They did me a favor as far as I was concerned. My eyes penetrated hers, making her blush and look away.

"Are you okay?" Worry tugged at the corner of her sweet lips. "They could've killed you."

Reaching out, I ran a single finger over her cheek and down the side of her mouth. "I'm fine now." I dropped my hand to my side when Giles pulled the curtain back and reentered.

"If I had a dollar for every stitch I've put in your body, I'm be a rich man," he joked, his gravel-filled laugh filling the space around me.

I'd always pictured Giles as a father figure. Sure, I was a hardened inmate and he was a doctor, but if I'd had a different life, he would've been an amazing dad. It made me wonder if he had children of his own. The staff in medical was smart, they knew better than to talk about their personal lives. I knew a ton about the COs, but next to nothing about the nurses and Giles. I supposed that was the point.

The side of my mouth lifted at him with his words and the sound of his happy laughter, and if I wasn't mistaken, a gleam reached his eyes that portrayed a level of comfort that wasn't allowed in our respective positions. It made me long for a family and a life I no longer had.

Quickly, I looked away and kept my eyes on Lyla as Giles worked to stitch up my arm. As if she couldn't handle the heat between us, she left the space and went to the desk to work on paperwork.

Tossing his bloody needle onto the metal tray, Dr. Giles pulled off his latex gloves and smiled at me. "Your arm's all done, but because of that noggin of yours, I'm going to have to keep you here for a few days. I can't send you back to your cell with a busted-up brain, now can I?"

I shook my head.

He didn't know it, but he was actually doing me a huge favor. I wanted to be around Lyla and if I had to use my head injury to do it, so be it.

When Giles left my side and went to her to tell her I was staying for a while, her eyes flittered my way and a tiny smile spread across her lips. She wanted me there just as bad as I wanted to be there, and it was time I took full advantage of our situation.

FOR TWO DAYS, I watched Lyla flitter around the room like a little dragonfly. She took care of patients and blushed every time she felt my eyes on her. My cock grew hard every time I imagined her without her oversized scrubs. And every time she let her hair down before pulling it back up, I imagined what those strands would feel like against my chest as she rode me.

I was a sick man, but I was a sick man who was about to explode from wanting Lyla so much. Everything about her was turning me on, and it had nothing to do with the fact that it had been ten years since I'd had sex. It was her smile, her smell, and the curves of her body, which I could see through her clothes when she leaned certain ways or reached for supplies.

On the second day, I'd reached my limit. When she came in to check on me, I took advantage of the closed curtain. The infirmary was quiet, no new inmates in the room. Actually, I was the only patient that day. Douglas had taken the silence of the room as an invitation to nap, and Dr. Giles was going over patient files in his office.

She checked my blood pressure, her latex-covered fingers grazing my arms and sending chills down into my stomach and deep into my balls. They grew heavy as my cock grew hard, and the urge to reach down and relieve myself was almost more than I could stand.

The skin of her fingertips was blocked by a barrier of latex, and I longed to feel her skin against mine. Reaching out, I took her hand in mine and slowly peeled the gloves from her fingers. She swallowed, her eyes meeting mine, but she didn't stop me.

"Christopher." My name rushed from her lips in a whisper.

Lifting her hand to my chest, I sighed when her fingers grazed my chest hairs. "Say it again."

She closed her eyes and ran her fingers over my hot skin, leaving me panting for more breath. Leaning in, her eyes a swirl of hypnotized greens, she whispered my name again.

I lost it.

Standing, I pulled her to me and her small frame molded against mine. Without regard for the sleeping officer outside the curtain or Dr. Giles, who could walk in at any moment, I crushed my lips to her and took everything I'd been dreaming of from the moment she joined the block.

I tasted her, fed on the sweetness of her mouth like the greedy criminal I was. She moaned into me, swiping the air from my lungs and making my cock strain against the zipper of my khakis painfully. My balls ached between my thighs, heavy and ready to be unloaded.

Fuck the rules. Fuck solitary, which I was sure to get when we were caught. Fuck it all. I wanted to crawl inside of her. Explode into her depths. And it was more than obvious by the way she began to climb me, lifting her leg on my thigh and rubbing herself against my hard dick, that she wanted it, too.

I was a murderer, at least allegedly. A filthy criminal who had no right to touch her sweetness or taste her thick desire, but fuck it. People took things they didn't deserve all the time. Why should I deny myself when no one else ever did?

Plus, from her flushed face and the glittering gaze full of lust and need, she needed me just as badly as I needed her, and I was all about giving her exactly what she desired.

CHAPTER 17

LYLA

HE WAS THERE. I was angry that he'd gotten himself hurt, but at the same time, I was so ecstatic to see his face. I'd spent some time digging into his case, and it was looking good. It wouldn't be long before his case reopened and people saw what I instinctively knew. Christopher Jacobs was innocent, at least innocent of his crimes.

When it came to everything else, he oozed sin. He was dark and dirty minded. I could practically see his unclean thoughts when he looked at me, and my body responded in a way that was unfamiliar. My thighs clenched on their own accord, and the tiny pearl nestled where no man dared go throbbed with just the thought of his touch. It was pure, raw, amazing torture.

He looked good, tall and lean, and everywhere I went, I could feel his eyes on me. Penetrating me, filling me with something unnamed. I found myself biting into my bottom lip to keep from growling with need. I wasn't sure how much longer I go without feeling his touch.

I wanted him more than my next breath. More than anything

I'd ever wanted before. So when he pulled me into a heated kiss, I threw myself into him and let him take over. I knew in the back of my mind that what I was doing was so wrong. Getting caught with my hands all over an inmate was a sure way to get terminated, but in that moment, I didn't care. All I cared about was alleviating the ache that was clawing at my pelvis like a rabid beast.

"This is wrong," he said, arching his neck so I could taste the saltiness of his skin. "I'm a monster, and you're…"

I took his words away from him when I sucked his bottom lip into my mouth. I didn't want to hear about how wrong it was… I just wanted him to take control. Wanted him to throw me onto the bed he was laying in seconds before, rip my scrubs off, and slam his hard cock into me. I wanted him to be the monster he claimed to be.

"Yes. You're so bad," I hissed against his mouth. "Show me how rotten you are. Be the bad guy, X. Be the monster."

We were whispering, taking in each moment before someone came in and stopped us.

Ripping his mouth from mine, he turned us and lifted me onto the bed. Cool air touched my hips as he tugged my scrubs down. Plucking my shoe off, he ripped one leg off, opening me to the room around us. My panties clung to my center, soaked with the desire he was pulling from me.

His eyes raked over me, and his teeth dug into his bottom lip. "Fuck, you smell amazing," he said, leaning down and running his nose along my inner thigh.

I gasped. The sensation of his face being so close to my opening and the tiny bundle of nerves that throbbed for his touch was enough to drive me mad.

"I'm going to eat you like you're my last meal," he growled against my thigh before he nipped at my soft skin and made me hiss in pleasured pain.

Before I could respond, he slipped a finger into the side of my panties and pulled them to the side. With a flat tongue, he licked from hole to nub, gathering my desire on his tongue and swallowing it like I was a special dessert. I leaned back against the bed and covered my mouth to keep the moan from escaping and alerting Dr. Giles or Douglas to our precarious situation.

He closed his eyes and groaned like I was the best thing he'd ever tasted, and then he moved up, sucking my sweet pearl between his lips and massaging it with his tongue. Breath rushed past my teeth in a quiet hiss, and I found myself fingering the back of his head to keep him place.

"So sweet. So fucking sweet," he mumbled, sucking at the sides of my pussy and releasing my flesh with a smack.

He sucked, fed on me like the starved man he was, and his sea blue eyes took in my expression as he devoured me. Rimming my clit with his tongue, he dug a single finger into my passage, sending pleasure down to my knees. A whispered noise I'd never made crept past my hand, sounding animalistic as he pulled out my inner sinner.

Right when I felt myself began to climb to orgasm, he pulled away with a sloppy smack. He wiped his glistening mouth with the back of his hand and grinned. At that, he was pulling my thighs to the edge of the bed and stepping between them.

"Consider this your warning," he said, tugging his khakis over his slim hips. "It's been ten years since I've tasted a woman. If you think I'm a monster now, just wait 'til I'm inside you."

My underwear strained and popped as he pulled them to the side even more. The threads around my hips begged to be snapped. Taking himself in his hand, he pumped twice with his fist before he pushed the rounded head of his penis into my moisture. I clawed at his back, pulling him into me, and begged with my eyes for more.

"Please, Christopher," I pleaded.

He shattered me, filling me to the hilt and pulling a sound I'd never made from me. It was the sound of my soul crumbling for him. It was the sound of my innocence dying. I wasn't completely inexperienced, but never had I been taken so roughly by someone so wicked.

"Shhh." He ran a calloused thumb over my lips, but I could tell by the feral look in his eyes that he was close to crumbling, too. "Fuck," he hissed.

He pumped his hips, first slow and steady, feeling my depths and relishing in the feeling of the two of us coming together. His strong fingers dug into my hips, making my flesh ache and only adding to the sensations rushing through my body.

With a groan, he moved quicker and his strokes became wild and untamed. The bed pressed against the wall, chipping into the old cinderblock and spreading broken pieces of white paint onto the sheet at my side. He took full control, his body owning mine, ripping away the flesh of my face, and staring into my emotions. He was a force as he took what was his since the minute I'd first laid eyes on him.

"Fuck, Lyla, I can't..." His words were broken and full of breath. It made me feel good to give him so much pleasure.

I wrapped my legs around his hips, pulling him deeper and harder with my ankles. He plunged into me, the sounds of our bodies getting louder and louder the faster he moved.

Throwing my head back, I let my mouth fall open in pleasure. I'd never felt anything so raw. It was unadulterated. Forbidden. Dark. Uncontrolled lust exploded into the space around me, splitting me into two and sending me to a place I'd never visited.

Leaning in, he rested his forehead against my shoulder and the sounds of his heated breaths were loud in my ear. Occasionally, he'd moan softly and something about such a large, dangerous man being brought to moans sent a spiral of sensation down in my core.

My orgasm clawed at my pelvic muscles, burning with want and need and teetering on the edge of greatness. "Yes," I cried, the sound coming out way louder than I wanted.

Reaching up, his large hand settled over my mouth, quieting me as he sped up and dug into me harder and deeper. The noises of our bodies echoed throughout the room, and the whiz of my hard breaths exploding from my nostrils was almost as loud.

"I'm going to come," he whispered in my ear. "Fuck, Lyla, feel me. Ah yeah, feel my cock. I'm going to come so deep in your sweet pussy, baby."

I was so close, and his filthy words sent me right over the edge. My body tightened around him, the nerves in my opening reaching out to their edges and giving me so much pleasure that my eyes rolled back in my head. My toes curled so hard I felt cramps developing in my feet and calves.

His movements became jerky as my body milked him hard, his hips drilling like a machine. Leaning over again, he bit into my shoulder, exploding inside of me. His teeth stung my flesh through my scrubs, and I hissed at the sensation of pain and pleasure. His heat filled me, warmth spilling out and onto the sheets beneath me. I'd never felt something so amazing.

His body relaxed into mine, his weight intensifying against me. Heated lips skimmed my cheek and neck before he placed a single kiss beneath my ear.

"I'll never be the same again," he said.

I wanted to tell him that he'd changed me, too, but no words formed against my tongue. It lay dead, like the rest of my muscles, in the bottom of my mouth, thick and useless. But it was the truth. I'd never be the same either. He'd taken my body and pushed it to the edge of every sensation possible.

Reaching out, I ran my fingers over his head, the spiked hairs of his new growth tickling my fingertips.

"I want to stay a part of you forever." His words whizzed past my ear as he pulled out of my body.

Cool air rushed into my center, taking up the space he'd controlled not seconds before, and I felt his loss. Reaching down, he slid his thumb over the wetness between my legs, his and mine, and smirked up at me.

"Fuck, that was amazing."

I nodded, unable to speak just yet, and his eyes softened.

"Say something, Lyla."

But I couldn't. Instead, tears rushed to my eyes and I burst out crying. He backed away from me, fear sweeping into his expression.

"I didn't force you, did I? Lyla, I would never…"

I stopped him with my hand and shook my head.

How could I explain to him how I was feeling? I wanted to tell him that I'd never felt anything so wonderful. My heart broke over the thought that I'd never be able to be with Christopher. Not like a regular couple anyway, and especially not if I wanted to keep my job. It was just another massive push to reveal his innocence.

As if understanding my thoughts, his expression dropped further and he nodded. He knew it, too. He knew that we could never be, and that knowledge burned in my chest like fire.

A sound outside the room brought us back to our situation, and I slid from the bed and got dressed as he adjusted his clothes. His eyes never left my face as if he wanted to take in every thought that crossed my mind.

Outside the curtained space, I could hear Dr. Giles' office door close and I knew it would be seconds before he was checking on me. Again, Christopher entered my space, his eyes devouring me. Reaching up, he ran a finger along the side of my face and leaned in for a quick kiss.

Dr. Giles' footsteps began to echo around us, letting us know our time was up, but before the curtain was ripped back and our passionate moment was taken, darkness consumed his expression. He moved closer, his eyes locked to my lips before he looked me in the eyes.

"This *will* happen again," he promised. "I own nothing in my life. There's nothing but you, and now, you're mine. Mine."

I sighed because I wanted it to happen again and I wanted to be his, only his. As a matter of fact, I wanted it to happen again in that moment. I wanted to take him away from Fulton and let him ravish me in my bed for the rest of the day, but I couldn't.

He pulled away and got back into bed just as Dr. Giles

entered the space, leaving me breathless and flushed with weakened knees and desire thick in my gut.

"You okay, Lyla?" Dr. Giles asked.

Clearing my throat, I nodded before I left the curtained space and escaped to my solitude in the supply closet.

.

CHAPTER 18

X

TWO DAYS IN medical can make someone feel good as new and I was feeling better than ever. Although, I was sure it had more to do with the sex. The release was so fucking raw I thought I'd died and gone to heaven. I'd thought my heart exploded along with my cock, and Lyla was an angel sent down to collect my soul.

She was amazing... her body was like a tight glove that fit me so perfectly I wanted to stay inside her for the rest of my life. Her sweet noises and the fact that I had to cover her mouth was so fucking sexy. Hell, the rushed sex and the thrill of almost getting caught was almost too much. It was one of the best moments of my life.

Two days later, I could still feel her all over my cock. I could still smell her sweetness even after I'd showered. Her taste was a memory on my tongue that sent my cravings into overdrive. I was a kept man mentally and physically by a woman I could never be with. Although, from the second I pulled from her soaking wet channel, I knew I had to have her again. If it was the last thing I ever did with my life, I'd taste her once more.

I felt alive again, as if her essence had enveloped my core and taken over. She'd breathed life into me, and I felt lighter and free as if I weren't surrounded by cinderblock walls of death. I was no longer the shell of a man; I was full of emotion and feelings. I was full of lust and desire. I was full of her.

The following day, through the slit in my curtain, I watched her work. She smiled nicely at the inmates as she administered their medicine and jealously that I wasn't the receiver of her smiles swelled in my stomach. I couldn't get enough of her. I'd never get enough.

As if feeling my eyes on her, she turned my way and bit into her bottom lip, thickening the muscle between my legs and making it tent my pants. I was suddenly upset that they hadn't opted to put me in the usual hospital gown. At least that way, I wouldn't feel so retrained.

She turned, her sweet ass taunting me and telling me how tight and good her asshole would feel wrapped around my dick. Reaching down, I grabbed my hard-on and pumped it. She turned then, and her eyes went from my face to my lap. Lust filled her expression and I smirked, knowing she wanted to fuck me as badly as I wanted to fuck her.

I'd get her alone again, and when I did, she'd never be the same. I'd wreck her, send her reeling the way she had me. Except I wanted to do it in a place where I wouldn't have to cover her screams, in a place where I could hear her beg for it and pant my name in pleasure.

Fuck!

What had she done to me?

When she disappeared from the slit in my curtain, I relaxed in bed and practiced breathing. My head ached, my cocked throbbed, and my heart slammed against my chest in anticipation of being with her again. It was wrong to have hope in a place like Fulton, but all her talk of my innocence and then having her to myself, I couldn't help but think of what my future might hold.

I sat up at the sound of the curtain being pulled back, and

smiled when I saw Lyla step into my space. She closed the curtain, blocking out the tiny slit that I'd used to stare at her, and then she was in my arms. I kissed her fiercely, pulling her body against mine and enjoying the feel of her against me.

The infirmary had grown quiet, and I thanked every God known to humankind for our brief moment together. Her lips moved over mine and I tasted her like the sweat treat that she was, devouring her like a starving man.

"We don't have long," she said between kisses.

Suddenly, she was reaching between us and grabbing my hard dick in her tiny palm. Her fingers flexed around my khaki-covered hardness, and I growled against her lips. She made me crazy, and I wanted her more than my next breath. Once wasn't enough. It would never be enough.

She worked her hand over me, pulling at my muscle and making my balls ache with pleasure. I filled my hands with her breasts, kneading them until I felt her hardened nipples against my palms. Then I moved my hands down, grabbing at her ass and working my hand down into her pants. Once my fingertip reached her wetness, I was done.

Fuck time. Fuck the people outside the curtain. Fuck the hole. Literally. I wanted her, and I wanted her right then and there.

Turning her, I lifted her on the bed and went to work on her pants. She didn't try to stop me. Instead, she kept kissing me, pushing her tongue over mine and filling my mouth with her unique flavor.

"Yes," she hissed. "You're so untamed."

I pulled back, confused by her words. Was I being too rough? Was I forcing her? Did she want me the way I wanted her?

Before I could ask, she pulled me against her and kissed me. "No. Don't stop. Don't hold back on me, X," she said, using my prison-given name. "You're such a dangerous criminal. Show me how dangerous you really are."

I almost laughed at how cute she was. Then again, the tip of my cock moistened and my balls tightened against my body.

She liked it rough. She was begging me to give it to her like the wild man that I was, and I wasn't about to bitch out on her.

Pulling her into a standing position, I turned her and ripped the ribbon holding her hair back out. Her red, silky locks fell against her shoulder and I lost my nose in it, taking in the smell of her shampoo. Her ass molded against my front when I bent her over the bed. Her scrubs fell to the ground at her feet and my khakis followed. Teasing her with my tip, I pressed my cock against her ass and she pressed back.

When I entered her body, it was hard and fast. She stretched around my girth, holding my body in hers and owning me. I pounded into her, gripping at her hip with all of my strength. I was sure I was hurting her, but she just begged for more.

My girl. My sweet nurse. She liked it hard. She liked to be manhandled, and I only wished that I could do it properly. Not stuck behind a curtain where I had to cover her mouth. I wanted to hear her scream my name. Every breath that rushed from her lips, every sound, I wanted to own it.

Wrapping her loose hair around my fingers, I tugged her head back and kissed her hard.

"Is this what you want? You want to get fucked, Lyla?" I whispered in her ear.

She nodded, unable to talk since I had her mouth covered so tightly, and a pleasure tear rolled down the side of her cheek. I licked it from her skin, and the salty liquid melted against my tongue.

I fucked her. Fucked her so good that her legs went weak and she fell onto the bed. I held onto her hips, lifting and pulling her into my thrusts, and she moaned into the bed sheets, biting into white cotton to keep from screaming in pleasure.

Her body gripped at me, the muscles of her inner walls flexing and pulsating. She was close, and I wanted to push her right over the edge. My body pressed into her, my chest to her back, my hips flush with her ass, and I pumped her so hard and so fast that my thigh muscles burned.

"That's right, baby. Give it to me. Come for me. Soak my cock and balls. I want to feel it."

The cotton of the sheets popped as she pulled on them, and I almost didn't cover her mouth fast enough before her cries exploded against my palm. Her body closed in around me, milking me and tugging with sweet, wet longing that sent me spiraling. I unloaded in her, filling her with everything that I was.

I was hers. I'd always be hers.

Pulling out, I shoved a thick finger inside of her. It was sick, but I wanted to know I was there. I wanted to feel our come mixed on my fingertip. She pressed against my hand, moaned sweetly, and I grinned.

She was insatiable, and she was mine. Fucking mine.

I LEFT THE infirmary two days later humming and smiling... fucking humming and smiling like a little bitch on a midnight stroll, which freaked the hell out of Scoop.

"What the fuck's wrong with you, man?"

He was sitting across from me at the chow table, stuffing his face with something that looked like potatoes.

"Nothing's wrong with me," I muttered, focusing on my tray and the shitty food on it.

"Uh-huh. You're so full of shit, man. You've fallen for her, haven't you?" he asked with a conniving smile.

I looked up in shock. Was it that obvious? "Who?" I played dumb, squinting in confusion.

He saw right through it. "Don't try to bullshit me. The nurse... Ms. Evans, she's gotten to you."

His face paled when I continued to ignore him and poke at my food. I wasn't about to feed him any information on Lyla. He knew enough as it was. I trusted Scoop, but my trust only went so far. She wasn't about to be part of anyone's game.

"You don't have to answer, but listen up." He hunkered down and began to whisper so no one around us could hear. "You need to be careful, bro. You know forming attachments in prison is dangerous."

Scanning his face, I sensed that something was up. He met my gaze, probing my brain as if to pass me some secret message that only the two of us would get.

"What's wrong?" I asked, watching his eyes shift back to his food.

He looked around before leaning in once again.

"Don't trust anyone, X. You need to get your girl out of here if you care about her."

A heart I didn't know I still had dropped into my knees, and I felt as if I were suffocating. "Why? She's safe here. No one will touch her as long as I'm here."

As the words left my mouth, the reality of it hit me. I couldn't protect her if I was behind bars all the time. What if something happened in the infirmary and I wasn't in there?

Scoop looked up at me, hesitation across his face.

"What aren't you telling me?" I asked, anger slowly filling me. Something was definitely going on, and he knew it.

"I didn't want to tell you. She's been digging in places she shouldn't, man. It has to do with your case. Some crazy mafia bullshit mixed with murder. I don't know, but she's stirring some shit up and it's pissing the high rankers off." His gaze dipped once more before he met me eye to eye. "She's been green-lighted, man."

My heart slammed into my ribs so hard that it knocked the wind out of me. Being green-lighted meant someone had money on her head, as in the person who took her out was in for a massive payday. "Who knows?"

I tried to remain calm even though my body was so tense I was sure it was ready to snap in two.

"Everyone knows. The first person who succeeds in killing her gets the dough. And X, it's a lot of fucking money, man."

"Who issued the hit?"

I would find them, and I would squeeze the life from their body. They wanted to turn me into a monster? Well, they'd won. I was going to be the biggest, meanest monster they'd ever met, and I'd kill any motherfucker who thought it was okay to mess with what was mine.

"No one knows."

I ground my teeth together so hard that my jaw ached. Scoop had better not be fucking lying to me. As if sensing my thoughts, he held up his hands in defeat.

"I'm serious, bro. I have no fucking clue who did it."

As I stood from the table, my tray slid off and crashed to the floor. I had to do something to stop this. I needed to get to her and warn her before anything happened.

Looking around the cafeteria, I could feel the shift in the environment. Everyone knew what was going on, and everyone wanted that money. I could see the thirst in their eyes—the sick desire to end her life and get paid.

Taking my seat, I waited until the chaos died down. Scoop stared at me like I'd lost my mind. Maybe I had. Once no one was paying me any attention, I stood again, snatching my empty tray from the dirty tile.

I headed straight for Jose, only he had no idea what was about hit him. He was in deep conversation with his thugs, laughing about something they were whispering about. His goon squad saw me as I approached him from behind, but it was too late. I reared the tray back before crashing it over the top of his head.

He fell to the floor like a dead fish, and I dropped the tray to my feet. Standing stock-still, I waited to get pummeled. The only thought that went through my head as the rest of Jose's crew came my way was Lyla. I had to get her out of Fulton. And if getting my ass beaten half to death was the way to do it, then so be it.

CHAPTER 19

LYLA

X WAS A rollercoaster ride—one that turned my stomach inside out and made me fear for my life—and it was amazing, crazy, but so freaking amazing. The terror and excitement of him was intoxicating. Addictive.

One minute you were scared, looking down the length of him and considering backing out, but the next, it was gut wrenching and exhilarating. As the ride ended, you sat there in a euphoric state and you were automatically ready to go again. And again. And again.

What the hell had he done to me?

I hadn't been able to get him out of my head since my first ride. Feeling him inside me, quivering in pleasure, was indescribable. He filled me, swelled and expanded, pushing my walls and stretching me to my limits, and then I'd shatter, effectively ruining me for any other man.

I craved my next dose of him at all times of the day. The desire was palpable, thick in the air all around me, and I feared that the other inmates would see it and react. I feared they would sense my arousal and play on it, but luckily, I was able to tuck that part away from the rest of the world and release it with Christopher.

My shift switch was hard on me, considering I'd spent the day daydreaming about Christopher instead of sleeping. Dragging into Fulton, I cursed the loud bars when they clanked opened and closed, silently praying my night would go by fast. I prayed things would run smoothly.

So much for wishful thinking.

The alarms blared, and I cursed them. Deep-seated hate for the freaking alarms moved through me. I'd come to hate them more than my own alarm clock at home. My body was still fighting me, arguing with my new hours. I'd switched to night shifts for the week, and I wasn't adjusting too well.

Coffee had become my best friend. Even though I had only been at work for an hour, I was ready to go home. As I yawned, I walked around the desk and waited for whoever was going to be dragged through the doors.

The past few days a lot of inmates had been fighting, and it seemed that every inmate who passed through the doors looked at me funny. Some stared at me as if I was a prized pig, while others let their eyes roam over my body as usual. Either way, I wasn't in the mood for any crap. I was exhausted and still half-asleep.

When the alarms finally stopped, I breathed in a sigh. "Thank God," I muttered, massaging my aching temples and sipping my coffee.

Dr. Giles laughed at me. We'd gotten super close since I started at Fulton. In a strange way, he was like a father figure. Giles treated me like a daughter, and I trusted him. I'd even broken down and told him about my instincts when it came to Christopher's innocence and all the details surrounding his case. He didn't ask why I was digging, thankfully, but if I wasn't mistaken, he believed me.

Christopher was innocent. The more I read over his case and the more I dug deep into the history of those involved, it became clearer and clearer. Charlie had even begun to connect the dots in the case, and it was obvious that the mafia had more to do with the death of Sarah Rizzuto and Michael Welch than Christopher did. The closer we got to breaking open the case, the more excited I became.

I couldn't wait until the day he was released from Fulton and we could be together. I wanted him, and it was obvious he wanted me. I didn't just go around having sex with anyone. I cared about him. Emotions I hadn't expected to happen had, and every time he looked me in the eye, I knew he felt the same.

The doors buzzed. Dr. Giles and I stood and waited for the crazy that was sure to come. Five COs entered, dragging Jose Alvarez behind them. It was late and the inmates were at dinner, which was obvious by the splattered spaghetti sauce all over his khakis.

He was cursing and grabbing his blood-soaked head in agony. I shook my head, not feeling any pity for him. After being at the prison for so long, I was slowly losing all my sympathy for the inmates. Thick skin had taken the place of my soft nature. I'd learned I couldn't let these men get the best of me whether it was physical or mental.

I almost turned away since I was sure Giles could handle Jose on his own, but then everything stopped and my heart fluttered when X entered the room. He was bruised and banged up, but I didn't see any blood. His eyes flickered around wildly until they landed on me. He was wide-eyed and panicked. Something was wrong.

The officers took their places. As Dr. Giles went to deal with Jose, he motioned for me to go check X. Going to his side, I asked him with my eyes if he was okay. He shook his head, letting me know he needed to get me alone.

Douglas and Reeves moved from the curtain and took their places by the nurses' desk while I examined him. The moment they were out of earshot, he whispered into my ear. "You need to get out of here."

The words cut through me like a knife. Something in his voice was cold and off-putting. I gazed up at him, taking in the worry on his face. He looked around every few seconds as if waiting for something bad to happen.

"What's wrong with you?" I asked, checking his neck and head before beginning to work down his chest and arms.

My mouth watered as I lifted his shirt over his head and revealed his hard chest. The memories of how he took me hard and fast heated me from within. His muscles rippled with each bit of movement, and I had to resist running my fingers over his chest and down to the small line of hair that escaped into the top of his pants.

Ever since our first time, he was all I could think about. I wanted him. My body craved him even more so now. Tiny twinges of desire lit my insides on fire, making my pussy clench and melt. I took a deep breath, letting my fingers glide over his skin, and his eyes softened.

"Lyla," he said in annoyed pleasure, covering my hand with his own and stopping my exploration.

Loosening his hold, I continued to run my fingers professionally over his back, enjoying the feel of his firm body beneath my touch. My palms slid over his hot flesh, making my stomach tighten with desire. I imagined it was my tongue tasting the saltiness of his skin, and my mouth watered for just a tiny taste of him.

I wanted to drop to my knees and take him in my mouth. Drive him crazy with my tongue until he exploded down the back of my throat. These were thoughts I didn't usually have. Actually, I never thought about giving blow jobs, but I wanted to pleasure him the way he had me so many times already.

Sweat glistened on his skin, making his tattoos look wet. They were strong and bold like the man who wore them. It was a major turn on for me.

"What are you doing?" he asked, his voice strained full of need.

"I'm examining you."

He swallowed hard, his eyes heating with lust and pent-up desire.

"Did you hear what I just said, Lyla?" He turned my way, his eyes begging me.

As I came around the side of him, I examined the bruises that were coming up on his arms and chest again. They were deep and just looking at them made me wince. As I gingerly touched them, he looked at me with tenderness.

"You're in danger. Someone knows you've been digging in my file."

My hands paused, and my heart skipped a beat. I glanced over at Douglas and Reeves to make sure they weren't paying us any attention. Douglas was on the phone behind the desk, but Reeves glanced my way and cocked a knowing brow.

"How do you know?" My breath caught in my throat. Suddenly, the penitentiary felt way too small.

"You've been green-lighted." His jaw was tense, the muscle popping out and throbbing.

The desire to reach up and smooth the tension out moved through me. "What does that even mean?"

"It means there's a bounty on your head. Someone's willing to pay a lot of money to have you killed."

Fear.

It was deep and daunting. It hitched a ride at my heart and rode its way through my veins, filling my body completely until I was sure I was going to pass out.

Charlie was right. I'd stirred up a shit storm and now I was going to pay for it. I wanted to shut it all out and crawl into X's arms. Wanted him to hold me and keep me safe, but he couldn't. He was too busy being locked behind bars for a crime he didn't commit.

Again, my eyes scanned the room, landing on Douglas and Reeves. "I'll be okay. The COs will keep them away from me."

His eyes widened, and his head whipped around at me. "Are

you fucking serious right now?" he hissed. "The COs are just as dangerous, Lyla. They get paid for shit working at Fulton. I'm talking minimum-wage bullshit. You don't think they'll want that money just as bad as the inmates?"

The truth of what he was saying hit me, and I backed away from him. He looked at the officers and made a fist as if to keep himself from touching me and keeping me there.

"Lyla, wait," he said, begging with his eyes for me to stay.

But I couldn't stay. I excused myself, suddenly feeling as if I needed to catch my breath. I retreated behind the door of the storage room, dizzy and disoriented. Someone wanted me dead — paying money to have me killed. I worked with thousands of murderers, and now there were dirty cops to worry about as well?

My mind spun, and I tried to push it aside. My dad's face popped into my head, and I silently wished he were still there with me. He would know what to do. He would protect me no matter what.

Dr. Giles entered a minute later, his face etched in concern. "You okay, Lyla?"

I gave him a smile I didn't feel and nodded. "I'm okay. Just getting some things."

I picked up a batch of gauze and turned to leave to the room, but Giles stopped me with a gentle hand.

He looked over my face as if looking for an explanation, but I couldn't give him one. I couldn't trust anyone anymore. How did I know he wasn't one of the people who wanted me dead? Sure, we had a great working relationship; one that felt more like father and daughter than doctor and nurse, but money was money, and money made the world go 'round.

I went back into the unit, my eyes clashing with X's, and he begged me with his expression to leave. I knew it was what he wanted, but I couldn't. Not yet, at least. There was still so much to do. I had to free him, and I wasn't sure I could do that outside the prison walls.

His eyes followed me and gave me a tiny bit of comfort. At

least I knew there was one person in the room who would protect me. He wouldn't let anyone lay a finger on me. He'd promised me that much.

I avoided getting close to him for the rest of my shift. I knew what I would hear if I did, and I didn't want to have to tell him no. I couldn't quit yet, and he wouldn't understand that. I wanted to be with him. In order for that to happen, I had to clear his name. If that meant sticking around the prison for a little longer, I would. Even if it meant life or death.

When he was finally released to go back to his cell, his eyes consumed my face and I felt sick from the amount of worry and fear I saw in his eyes. He looked like a trapped animal. I wanted to go to him, to soothe his worried brow and kiss him sweetly, but I didn't.

Instead, I watched him go, shackled and cuffed, secretly hating that I couldn't keep him with me. It wasn't until he was out of sight that I felt completely unsafe. He was my safety net, and he'd just been pulled from underneath me.

THE NEXT MORNING as I pulled into my apartment, I made sure to lock my door and the deadbolt. I usually didn't worry about the deadbolt, but I felt better once it was secured. I walked through my apartment and checked all the windows. They were locked, and no one had tampered with them. I took a long, hot shower, enjoying the feel of the steam across my back, and I thought of X and the way his eyes had followed me throughout my entire shift.

He'd watched me like a lion ready to devour his food. It pained me and haunted me, knowing that he was going to spend his day worried about what was happening. I imagined he didn't like to feel helpless, but in a lot of ways, he was.

As I emerged from the bathroom, I relished in the fact that I was on night shift. I liked to think there weren't many killers who were okay with killing in broad daylight, which meant I felt safe alone in my apartment in the middle of the day. I walked to the closet and laid out my nurses' scrubs for that night's shift, pulling on a pair of shorts and a tank to sleep in.

Before I closed my closet door, my eyes landed on the box I kept on the top shelf. I hadn't touched it in years. Reaching up, I pulled it down, feeling the weight of it. I'd forgotten how heavy it was. Laying it on my bed, I flipped open the lock and pulled the top open gently. My fingers moved over my dad's old service revolver, and the cold steel stung my fingertips. It was a thing of beauty and as long as I had it by my side, I felt as safe as if my dad were there with me, too.

He loved his gun almost as much as he loved me. When I closed my eyes, I could still hear him talking about it.

"You have to take care of the things that take care of you, and this gun takes care of me. What happens if I neglect it and I need it? It might not shoot."

His words echoed through my head, irony flooding over me as I smiled.

I needed to take care of the things that took care of me. X took care of me. He protected me, and he had never once neglected me. He had taken a chance warning me, but I couldn't heed that warning. If they were going to kill me, let them. I couldn't hide in fear my whole life, watching over my shoulder. I had to stay and help him.

I picked the gun up and began to clean it the way my dad had taught me many years ago. When I finished, I loaded it and set it in the drawer beside my bed. Having it beside me made me feel more secure and I finally was able to crawl in bed and sleep. Even if my life was being threatened, I had to get some sleep. I had a shift to work, and I had to be on my guard.

CHAPTER 20

LYLA

WORK WAS BORING. There had been a couple of fights and minor injuries, but it was nothing like the past few weeks. As I loaded up my tray with insulin and sharps, I felt a cold sweat breaking out across my neck. I usually never worried about making my rounds through the prison, but now I did. Every eye would be on me, and inmates outnumbered the COs fifty to one. Even if I managed to get a trustworthy escort, he wouldn't be able to hold off someone who wanted to kill me.

Working the nightshift meant taking the medicine to the diabetics and blood pressure patients. I nervously made my rounds, jumping at every sound and scream I heard. The catcalls continued, but most of them just glared at me through their cages. They were plotting. I could see it in their seedy looks and tightened mouths. They wanted the prize money.

Douglas was my escort and I breathed a sigh of relief, knowing he was a good guy. I'd learned firsthand who the dirty ones were, but Douglas was a sweetheart. He smiled and bantered with me, trying to keep my spirits up and make me feel safe. As we finished our rounds, he escorted me back to the medical unit.

"You okay, Lyla?" he asked, his eyes studying me.

"Of course," I lied. "Why do you ask?"

"You just seem jumpier than normal."

How was I supposed to answer that? Of course I was jumpy. Someone was out to kill me—no—not someone, everyone with the exception of a few. It wasn't looking good for me, but I had to stay. At least until I could leave with Christopher.

"Things are just different on nightshift. I guess I'm still adjusting."

Douglas patted my arm and smiled warmly. He reminded me of Santa Claus without a beard—all jolly and smiley—he actually jiggled when he giggled. It was kind of funny.

"I promise you the monsters won't get you while you're here. You have my word." He winked at me as I walked through the doors into medical, making me chuckle and shake my head.

I believed him, and I knew he was one of the few people in the prison I could trust. I felt safe with him, and his words were comforting. He wouldn't let them hurt me. Luckily, we worked a lot of shifts together.

His radio blared and told him to dial a number. He excused himself, walked over to my desk, and picked up the receiver. I turned to Dr. Giles, leaving him to his call. Giles was in his office scribbling notes. The man worked every day. He always looked disheveled and worn out, but somehow had the energy of a five-year-old. He amazed me.

As I entered his office, he glanced up at me quickly before returning to his paperwork.

"How did it go?" he asked.

"They all had really good glucose readings tonight. Brett Caroway was complaining of dizziness, but I think he's just making excuses because his sugar was great."

"Good. You're getting good at predicting who's lying and who's really in need of assistance. It took me a while to pick out the fakers." He smiled up at me, making me feel proud.

I was beginning to feel at home at Fulton, but having a target on my chest wasn't what I had bargained for when I took the job. "Thanks," I mumbled. "I'm going to grab a cup of coffee from the break room. Want a cup?"

He rubbed his eyes and glanced at his watch. "Sounds good. Black. No sugar."

Walking to the door, I waited for control to buzz me out. I didn't normally walk through the prison by myself, but I needed coffee and I knew it was lights out for most of the guys by now. Lights out meant an officer on the catwalk in the cell house gallery. That officer would have a shotgun, and he'd be waiting to fire a warning shot if by some chance an inmate got loose from his cell.

It was the same procedure in the yard. COs weren't allowed to be armed at Fulton. The only ones allowed were the ones in the catwalks, but then again, they could "accidently" mistake me for an inmate and collect. I didn't put anything past someone low on their luck.

My shoulders were tense and my back straight as I made my way toward the break room. As I walked by the cells full of inmates, the COs began to shuffle. Most of them were just coming on for their shift and some were still trying to get the sleep out of their eyes. I relaxed and moved quickly through, smiling at them as I passed. My eyes scanned the shadows at my side, expecting it to be my last breath at any time.

When I reached the break room, I felt relief wash over me. The room was empty. Quickly, I grabbed two Styrofoam cups and poured the freshly brewed coffee. Someone was a lifesaver. They knew I needed the caffeine. As I filled one of the cups, I heard the door open. Douglas poked his head in and took a deep breath, breathing in the delicious scent of the coffee.

"Yes" he said, his smile taking over his face.

I laughed at him and handed him a cup.

"Thanks, doll," he said as he began pouring himself a cup.

Sugar dissolved into the blackness in my cup, and I stirred it, taking in his comedy routine. He took his coffee black, but he ripped open at least ten packets of sugar and emptied them into his cup. As he took his first sip, he moaned.

"That's some damn good coffee."

I chuckled. "Should I leave you alone with your cup, Duggie?"

He smiled at me and winked with a naughty tilt to his lips. "Maybe. It's definitely giving me pleasure. It might get nasty up in here. Does yours need more cream?"

Pretending to gag, I laughed loudly as I left the room.

The darkness swallowed me when I walked the block back to medical. The shadows danced along the edges of the room, taunting and teasing me with death. The COs were spaced out, half asleep in their chairs outside the cells.

As I turned down a row to head back to the unit, a hand grabbed my arm and pulled at me. Gasping, I spun around to face my attacker. I was about to scream when my eyes clashed with a pair of steely blues gazing intently into mine.

He was in his cell, his arms holding me close to the bars.

"X? Oh my God. You scared me," I hissed in a whisper.

"You should be. Why are you still here? I told you to leave. They raised the bounty, Lyla. You need to go."

His words fell on me like cold water. They were offering more money. More money, more problems. More money, more likely to die.

My mind flashed back to the warden and his phone call after I'd left his room.

"Is it the warden?" I whispered.

"Why would the warden green light you?" His brows pulled in.

"I overheard him saying something about me knowing too much to someone on the phone."

A loud sigh escaped his lips, and he rubbed roughly at the back of his neck. "Please, Lyla, you need to leave. Please leave now. I can't protect you behind these bars." His eyes were pleading with me, and it was breaking my heart.

"I can't leave you. You need me. I have to protect you, too."

His eyes softened. Reaching out, he touched my face in the dark. I loved the feel of his hands. They were rough, but so tender. I glanced around quickly, making sure we weren't about to be discovered.

He pulled me closer, the cold steel digging into my stomach and hips, but his hot body soothed the sting. He grabbed my hip with one hand and my shoulder with the other.

"I don't want anything happening to you," he whispered, his breath falling onto my cheek.

I felt myself falling under his trance. His hypnotic eyes danced across my face and I instinctively looked up, waiting for his lips. As he brushed his lips across my cheek and the bridge of my nose, I could feel him quivering. He would've taken me right there if he could've gotten away with it. His soft lips finally found mine and he kissed me savagely, as if he were starving. The kiss only lasted a few seconds, but it left me winded. As I tore myself away, I adjusted the coffees in my hands.

"I have to go," I whispered.

"Yes, you do. Leave, Lyla," he urged, still demanding I quit.

I ignored him and continued to medical. Stopping by a snack machine outside canteen, I grabbed myself a blueberry muffin and held it between my side and arm. As I walked back, I smiled softly, touching my lips gently, wishing his lips were still brushing against mine. When I entered, Dr. Giles glanced up at me, his face angry and dark.

"Lyla, come here please."

My heart sank deep into my stomach. I knew they had seen me. Someone had caught me kissing X, and I was going to get sacked. They'd seen our moment of passion, and I was going to get fired before I even had the chance to free him.

As I approached the desk where he stood, I realized Douglas sat on the other side. His face was forlorn and cold, not like him at all.

"What's wrong?" I asked, already knowing the answer to my question. I was surprised when he held up a tiny wad of toilet paper.

"Care to explain this?" Dr. Giles asked.

Opening the toilet paper, he exposed a few Vicodin. I had

nothing to do with the narcotics. Rarely did I even get close to them.

"I don't understand?" I asked, confused.

"I found these on an inmate earlier," Douglas said, eyeing me suspiciously. "He told me you gave them to him on your way to the break room."

Dr. Giles looked over at Douglas and then back to me, expecting an explanation.

"That's a lie!" I exploded. "I don't do the pain meds; that's Ginger's job," I said, my heart speeding up with their accusations. "I only do the diabetic meds, cholesterol, and blood pressure meds."

Dr. Giles' face softened. He knew I was telling the truth. I could see it in his eyes.

Still, anger pulled at Douglas' lips. "He specifically told me you gave them to him."

"Then he's lying. I don't even have a key for those."

Giles backed me up. "She's telling the truth. She never has the keys to that cabinet. I help her load every tray, making sure that I can take care of any changes in medicine while standing over her. There's no way he got it from her."

Douglas' face shifted to Giles, and then back to mine. "I'm sorry, Lyla, but I have to report this. I don't know what's going to happen when I do." He shrugged apologetically.

He turned away and walked out, leaving Dr. Giles and I staring at each other.

"I didn't," I repeated.

Reaching out, he ran his hand over my shoulder. "Don't worry. We'll get through this.

It was the strangest thing. Not an hour ago, Douglas was smiling and chatting with me, but now he was all business. Now he was accusing me of stealing narcotics and dealing them in the prison. He was accusing me of being a criminal. I didn't like it.

It was upsetting since I liked Douglas so much. He was a nice guy, but then again, being in a penitentiary meant not being able to trust anyone. Just like I was walking around not trusting anyone with my life, he didn't trust me, at least not a hundred percent.

The more I thought about it, the less I could blame him. Fulton was full of criminals. Liars. Cheats. Murderers. Drug dealers. It wasn't a place to make friends. And while I hated to think about it, I was sure everyone in the prison was turning against me. I was green-lighted, which meant I was worth a lot of money. I couldn't trust anyone, not even Douglas. Not anymore.

CHAPTER 21

LYLA

I WAS SUSPENDED the next day as they began an investigation. Reports were filed, but since it was the inmate's word against mine, they let me come back. I later found out it was Evan Moore, aka Scoop, who told Douglas I gave him the narcotics.

It was confusing since Scoop had been nothing but nice to me. Then again, money changed people. I wanted to talk to X about it since he and Scoop were friends, but I couldn't unless he came to me, which he'd suddenly quit doing. I rarely saw him, and I was starting to worry that maybe I was in deeper than he was. Still, if his friend was going to the dark side, he needed to know so he could watch his back.

Dr. Giles was more than excited to see me when I walked in the following evening. He hurried over and threw his around my shoulders. "Glad you are back, kid. It's been one thing after another here. I've had so many inmates through here in the past few hours I almost ran out of beds." He turned me with his hands on my shoulders. "Most have been asking about you, but no one knows," he assured me.

"What about my charges?" I asked, studying his face.

"No charges pressed. Douglas and I went to bat for you. There was no way you could've given him those meds without access to them. I don't know what's going on around here, but something's up." He looked at me suspiciously, and then his face cleared. "I have no idea how the inmate got those drugs, but I smell a rat."

I swallowed hard. I knew how Scoop got the drugs. Dr. Giles was right; there was rat. Someone was setting me up. Still, I wasn't sure who I could trust anymore, and I didn't want to say anything that could reflect poorly on me.

"I'm glad to be back," I said, changing the subject quickly.

Peeling my sweater from my arms, I rested it on the back of my chair. Dr. Giles' office was cooler than the unit when I went inside to put my bag lunch in the mini-fridge. When I turned around, Ginger was standing in the doorway. Her exhausted eyes were devoid of light and her shoulders were slumped. She'd obviously had a bad day.

Her smile was forced as she reached for a Coke. Her jacket hung from her arm and her keys jingled as she waited at the door for command to let her out for the night. I felt bad for her. A cold had ruined her last week at work, but she'd drudged through even though she was miserable. Her nose was red, and she'd spent most of her time at work rubbing it with a deteriorating tissue.

"Hope you feel better," I called after her.

She waved at me, flashing me a half smile. When the door buzzed, she practically leapt out into the shadows of the block. I didn't blame her. Fulton was a dark place, and it had a way of making you feel bad. I imagined that was even worse if you were actually sick.

The night was uneventful again. Nights were usually quiet since all the inmates were in their own cells and asleep. Isolation was key at night, but in the dark, God only knew what could happen.

Other than a few inmates coming in with shortness of breath

and one with possible flu, the night crept by in a slow haze of paperwork. COs were in and out to check on us, occasionally stealing a soda from our fridge. We were known for keeping it well stocked, and the officers knew they could come in and grab water or a soda if they forgot pocket change at home.

With a soda in hand, Douglas sat next to me, setting his booted feet on the desk in front of him. I glanced up from my work and grinned. He was looking around the room, enjoying a rare moment without inmates lurking on the other side of the curtains.

"How's your night been?" he asked.

Things were awkward. In truth, they had been since the moment he accused me of giving narcotics to an inmate, but still, I felt better about our work relationship knowing that he defended me.

"Good. I'm getting a lot of work done tonight." I hesitated, quickly looking over at him. "Thanks by the way," I added.

"Thanks for what?" he asked, puzzled.

"Don't act like you don't know. You help save my job. Giles said you defended me. All I'm saying is I appreciate it."

He grinned sheepishly, taking a sip from his soda to block it.

"He was a liar." He shrugged. "He was probably just trying to throw you under the bus to stir up some shit. These inmates get bored and like to make up their own soap operas. I'm just glad it's been taken care of."

"Me too. It's nice to know I have a friend here to look after me."

Douglas studied me, his eyes swaying over my face, and then he looked away. I wasn't sure what he was looking for. Maybe some deep-set explanation to why things around me had been so crazy lately. Then another question came to mind.

Did Douglas know I'd been green-lighted?

I was sure the COs weren't as clueless as they seemed. They probably knew all about the shady stuff that went down at Fulton, but they had to have some secret code that said they couldn't talk about it with anyone who wasn't a corrections officer or something.

Pushing it from my mind, I went back to work. I still had

digging to do when it came to Christopher's case, plus a mountain of paperwork that needed to be filled out and filed.

Just when I thought the conversation was over, Douglas reached out and laid a hand over mine.

"Don't worry, Lyla, I got your back." At that, he stood and left to do whatever it was the officers did outside the infirmary.

The unit settled into a deep silence… one that left me humming songs and working as if I weren't in a max pen. Briefly, I forgot about the world outside the infirmary. I forgot about the murders that were longing for my blood and the paycheck that was posed on top of my head. It was just my paperwork and me.

The buzzing of the doors cut through the silence, and Reeves was coming in with X shackled at his side.

There were no alarms. There were no codes called. There was only X and Reeves, walking in like they were out for a stroll around Fulton.

"What's going on?" I asked, standing and directing them toward a bed.

"He said he's dizzy. I figured I'd better bring him in here since he's still healing from his head injury." Reeves grinned openly at Christopher. "That's what you get when you fall down the stairs around Fulton."

It was a direct dig. Everyone knew that Christopher hadn't fallen down any stairs. It was common knowledge there had been retaliation for his attack on the COs, but no one talked about. No one ever talked about it.

Christopher raked Reeves with a sinister stare, a promise that one day he'd get the last say, and I could feel the temperature drop around us.

Once I had him settled into a curtained space, he pulled me to him, his lips landing on mine so roughly that it hurt. I didn't stop him. I wanted it. I always wanted him. Reaching up, I wrapped my arms around his wide shoulders, and he lifted me from the floor like I weighed nothing.

"Don't stop," I whispered, going in for another kiss when he pulled away.

He chuckled darkly and ran a single finger down my cheek.

"My little wild thing," he said, capturing my lips once more. "One day you'll be mine, and I'll spend the entire might making you come over and over again."

My body heated instantly, and I wrapped my leg around his hip to bring my center closer to him. Again, he chuckled, the sound of his deep voice striking deep in my overly sensitive core.

"I can be quiet." I smirked.

"Yeah, right." He tapped my nose and set me back to the floor. "As much as I'd love to bury myself inside you, we need to talk."

I rolled my eyes. "Not this again. I already told you that I couldn't quit. Not yet anyway. I have bills to pay for one, and for two, I need to be here for you."

He looked down, his eyes turning sad.

"What's wrong?" I asked. "What did I say?"

Again, his steely blues captured my eyes, and he reached up to cup my cheek with a roughened palm. "Nothing. It's just I wish I could take care of you. I wish we could have what other people have, but we can't." My body went cold when he pulled away from me. "Lyla, if you don't leave, they're going to kill you. I can't stop it. I can't protect you here. I can take care of myself. Please, just go."

I shook my head. I couldn't leave. There was still so much left to do.

"If you go, I'll send you money every month to help with your bills," he said, shocking me.

"What? You're not doing that. How the hell would you do that anyway?"

"There's a fight club," he started.

"No," I hissed when I wanted to yell.

I didn't even let him finish. I'd heard about the fight club. I'd stitched up boys who fought in it, and there was no way I was going to let him do that. No freaking way. Especially not for me, and especially considering he'd just recently healed from a head injury.

"Lyla, just listen," he started.

"No. There's nothing to listen to. I'm not quitting yet, and you're not fighting in any stupid fight club."

Without letting him talk again, I turned to leave. His fingers dug into my arm when he pulled me back, his hand going straight to my ass and squeezing. He was hot and cold—on and off—my own personal rollercoaster ride.

"You're so fucking hot when you're angry," he growled against the side of neck.

His teeth grazed my skin, sending chills down my side. Then he was kissing me, his tongue plunging into my mouth roughly as he tasted me. I kissed him back, enjoying the feel of being manhandled. He was so big—so strong—so freaking sexy.

Oxygen flooded my lungs when he finally pulled away, and my hand flew to my swollen lips, feeling the tingly heat from him.

"Think about it," he said, and then he turned away and sat on the bed just in time for Reeves to pull back to curtain.

"Everything okay in here?" he asked, his eyes moving from X to me.

"Everything's just peachy," X responded in his usual gritty tone.

He was taken back to his cell an hour later, and it wasn't long before I was finishing up my paperwork and biting the tip of my pen thinking of him and the way his hands and mouth felt all over my body. My skin flushed and I smiled to myself, knowing that one day soon, he'd be all mine.

THE NEXT MORNING, Dr Giles and I were walking out. We'd just finished our shift and while he still had tons of energy, I felt as though I was seconds away from passing out. Sleep tickled the edges of my conscious, and I was worried that maybe it wasn't safe for me to drive home.

Tossing my bag onto the counter for the officers to look through, I stepped through the metal detector just like I did every day. I stepped through coming in and I stepped through going out, never had there been a problem, except for this time.

The alarm beeped, warning the officers that something metal was on my person. There wasn't. I knew that. I'd taken the time to put everything in my bag. I'd learned the rules, the way things worked, and I also knew what to do to get myself out of Fulton and into my bed quicker. I was prepared for the metal detector.

Jumping at its loud beeping, I rolled my eyes as I turned around to go back through. I stepped through a second time, sure that the first alarm was a fluke, but again, the alarm beeped.

"What the—?" I started. Looking down, I made sure my badge was taken off. I didn't have pockets in my scrubs. There was no metal on me.

The alarmed beeped again the third time I stepped through, and I sighed in aggravation. I was tired. Stressed. And every other word that meant I really just wanted to go home and get in my bed.

Officer Mitts stepped my way with a smile. "It's procedure," he said.

I held my arms out to my sides and shook my head. "Yeah, yeah, yeah."

His waved the hand-held metal detector my way, running it up and down my legs and around my hips. When it didn't beep, he moved it up over my stomach and then down my left arm. Bringing it across my body, the alarm beeped when he waved it across my chest. My shirt had a tiny pocket that I never used, and that seemed to be the spot that was drawing out the metal detector's attention.

Mitts reached into the tiny pocket and pull out a small, thin knife. The switchblade popped out with a click when he pressed a tiny button on its side. Shock moved through me. I'd never seen the tiny knife before.

How did it get in my pocket?

"That's not mine," I said adamantly. I looked around with wild eyes, and everyone was looking back at me. "I swear. It's not mine."

Giles had gone out before me. Douglas was already in bed with his wife, I was sure. I had no champion to come to my defense.

"I'm sorry, Ms. Evans, but I have to report this," Mitts said.

Reports. There was always something to freaking report. It was like they were grown men turned toddler tattletales. It was annoying, but at the same time, I understood why they had to do it. It was to keep everyone safe.

So instead of going on the defensive, I simply nodded my head and attempted to smile.

That day I slept for shit. I lay in bed trying to figure out how the hell I'd gotten a tiny knife in my pocket, but nothing was coming to me. By the time dinnertime rolled around, I was sleepy and starving. I was being switched back to day shift so I had the next day off, but I knew when I got back to Fulton, there would be hell to pay over the tiny knife that was found in my pocket.

ON MY NEXT shift, I was taken straight to the warden's office. There was no pass go. There was no collect two hundred dollars. It was just a metal detector and then the warden's office.

I sat in the tiny waiting room, smiling at his secretary and secretly hating her for having an easy job. Then again, while I was sure it was easy to sit around and answer phones all day, I knew I would get bored out of my mind within the first hour.

Twenty minutes later, I was being ushered into his office. My eyes went straight to the warden and Douglas when I walked in, but it wasn't until the door closed behind me that I noticed Dr. Giles standing across the room.

I was in deep shit. It was like an intervention. They were going to try to talk me out of giving the inmates narcotics and bringing knives into the prison. Both of which I didn't do. Then it hit me. They were all gathered, standing tall in their suits and uniforms.

I was getting canned.

"I'm fired, aren't I?" I asked, sure that the tiny knife had done the trick.

The warden sat down at his desk, his face serious and his brows pulled down deep. "Have a seat, Ms. Evans," he demanded.

I did as I was told, not taking my eyes away from his.

"How am I supposed to believe you didn't give drugs to an inmate when only the next day you're found carrying a knife in your pocket?" he asked with a deadly growl. "A knife! In my prison!" His desk shook when he slammed his hand down on top of it.

"I didn't..." I started.

He held a hand up to stop me. "Don't. Am I supposed to believe you didn't bring a weapon into my prison?"

My mouth went dry. I didn't want to be in his office. I didn't trust him. Something about him made me want to crawl under a rock and hide. Douglas and Giles were sitting there, however, and somehow it felt as though that shifted things in my favor.

"Yes, sir, you are." I swallowed my nerves and continued. "I didn't do those things. I've never seen that knife in my life. If you check it for fingerprints, I can guarantee you mine aren't on it."

"Are you telling me how to do my job, young lady?" he asked, his eyebrow lifting.

"No, sir, of course not. I'm just trying to make sure I get my named cleared."

"You seem to be trying to get a lot of names cleared lately." I didn't miss the underlying sarcasm in his voice.

He sat straighter and cleared his throat. Douglas looked at him sharply as if trying to figure out what he meant. Dr. Giles shook his head as if he was aggravated with the lies that were being spun against me.

The warden leaned onto his elbows, his fingers crossed under his chin. "If I catch anything else going on... if I even suspect that you might be involved with anything or anyone, you're gone.

Understand?"

I bit my tongue, words that begged to be said pressing against the back of my teeth. "Yes, sir." I nodded.

Relief rushed through me when I stepped out of his office. I felt lightheaded with happiness knowing that I'd be able to keep my job a little longer. But it was for the wrong reason. It wasn't about the money anymore. It was about Christopher Jacobs. I wasn't ready to walk away from him without knowing for sure I'd see him on the outside.

CHAPTER 22
LYLA

SOMEONE OBVIOUSLY WANTED me gone. It made me uneasy and on edge. I went to work and wrapped my head around intake screenings and blood work. It was obvious I needed help with my situation. People were out to get me, and I found myself watching my back at every turn.

I thought about calling Diana, but I wasn't ready to hear her bitching. She'd be more pissed about that fact that I hadn't come to her sooner, and then she'd tell me to quit. I didn't need to hear that right now. What I did need was someone higher up... someone with some pull, and I had an idea of where I might find that.

The boys in the police station patted me on the back with smiles and a few even gave me hugs. I was always welcomed there since my dad was somewhat of a legend in their ranks. Charlie looked up with a smile when I stepped into his office. That smile melted from his face when I began to tell him about all the crap that was going down at Fulton.

"Do you know what it means to be green-lighted, Lyla? Do you have any idea how much shit you're into?"

The vein throbbed on the side of his neck with his anger. It was then that I thought that maybe going to Charlie wasn't such a great idea.

"I want you out of there," he said in a rage. "And I'm posting armed officers outside your house."

I put my hands up, trying to stop him, but he kept going.

"I can't believe the shit storm this has stirred up. The case has been opened all of three days and look what's happening. I knew this was a bad idea." He sat down, his face red with fury. Sinking his face into his hands, he sighed. "Your father would haunt me if anything ever happened to you." His voice softened, and he leaned back in his chair. "No arguments, Lyla. You're quitting."

Listening intently, I sat silent. Going to Charlie was a terrible idea.

I left his office feeling worse than I did before. Nothing was accomplished, and when I crawled into bed, I passed out knowing the following day at work was going to be hell. I'd never been someone who gave up easily. I wasn't about to start now.

THE LAST DAY before my four-day break always seemed to stretch on. A minute felt like an hour, an hour felt like a day. Every time I looked at the clock, it seemed as if it were taunting me, the hands playing tricks on my mind and never actually moving. It dragged to the point of madness.

Every time the door buzzed, I held my breath and hoped that it was Christopher coming to see me. After all, he was the main reason I was still working at Fulton in the first place. But no matter how many times I looked for him, he never came. I supposed that was a good thing since that last thing I wanted was for him to get hurt, but still, I wanted to see his face.

I brought my lunch in a Ziploc bag and allowed the guards to search me. I made them search my pockets, too, just in case someone tried to pull some shit. I was careful. After eating my lunch, I threw away the plastic. I checked my pockets every hour to make sure nothing had been slipped into them. I felt crazy, but working at a max pen would do that to you, I supposed.

By the time afternoon rolled around, I was done with intake, doses, and paperwork and left with nothing to do but read a few of the magazines that were lying around medical. Instead, I found myself staring into space and watching Douglas pout from the other side of the room. He seemed fidgety and on edge.

"A penny for your thoughts," I offered as I noticed he was daydreaming.

"Hmm?" He smiled and stood up straighter.

"Are you okay?" I asked, worried.

"Yeah, I just have a lot on my mind." He shrugged. "Family stuff."

"Oh. Sorry."

He grinned at me and nodded. "Are you okay here? I need to take a leak."

I didn't even respond. Instead, I waved him away. There were no inmates in the infirmary, and Dr. Giles had left early for once. I'd noticed him slowing down a bit, but I didn't say anything. More than likely it was because he worked all the freaking time.

I read over my magazine, letting the rest of my shift go by. Yawning loudly, I stretched my arms above my head and adjusted in my seat. As I was putting my arms down, something went around my neck, jerking me back and cutting off my oxygen.

My fingers flew to my throat, grasping for whatever it was choking me, but it was so tight I couldn't even get my finger in between what felt like plastic tubing and my skin. Choking sounds spewed past my lips, and then I was pulled to the ground and staring up at my culprit.

Miguel Cortez.

He was Jose Alvarez's right-hand man. I'd taken care of him a few times, patching up his cuts and bruises.

He stared down at me, his dark hair falling into his face and covering the single tear drop tattooed beneath his eyes. Sweat glistened above his brow, and he licked at his lips as his face turned colors with his struggle to choke me.

I looked up at him, darkness dancing around the edges of my vision, and begged him with my eyes to let me live, but apparently, the money was more important. He jerked, the plastic tube cutting into neck, and I knew I had seconds left.

Suddenly, the pressure around my neck was gone.

Air rushed into windpipe, and I gasped, sucking in as much as I could and making my lungs burn. Grabbing for my neck, I looked up into the eyes of my savior. My stomach tightened with joy when I saw officer Reeves standing above Miguel's limp body.

Douglas lifted me from the floor, and I latched onto him with a death grip. The fear that consumed me was raw, and it cut deep. Deeper than the plastic tubing, or what I now knew was IV tubing, that had cut into my neck.

One thing was for sure, I was done with Fulton. X had been pushing me to quit for a while now, but it was obvious I wasn't safe there anymore. I packed my bags, called Dr. Giles, and put in my resignation all within the hour.

I drove home that afternoon with the pressure of an elephant on my chest. I left without saying goodbye to X, which I knew I could remedy with a visit, and I left without knowing where my next paycheck was going to come from. It was a scary thing, not knowing what the future held, but I knew I could do it. After all, I'd worked in a maximum-security prison, and I'd fallen in love with an alleged murderer.

I was no longer the girl I used to be. Fulton was famous for transforming their inmates—turning boys to men—and the innocent into criminals. No one ever talked about how it changed the staff. And after working there, I could honestly say I was a different person... a stronger person.

CHAPTER 23

X

I'D TRIED EVERYTHING to get her fired. I'd had Scoop set her up with the pills, and I'd even tried to set her up by slipping a knife in her pocket, yet she was still working at Fulton. I spent every day thinking it would be the last time I'd ever see Lyla, worrying every moment that I wouldn't be there to protect her when some lunatic finally caved and went for the kill. It was enough to drive a sane man crazy.

Then again, I wasn't all that sane.

I stayed away from the infirmary as much as I could, but I couldn't deny it any longer, I missed Lyla when I wasn't around her. Lying about my head bothering me got me a trip to medical, but I must have had her schedule backward because she wasn't there. It was too early in the afternoon for her to be gone already, which meant she was either off or working the night shift.

I waited, pretending to have a headache I didn't have, until finally it was obvious she wasn't coming to work. I'd missed chow time, so I ate in my cell and fell asleep worried that something might have happened to Lyla.

The next morning when we were lining up for breakfast, Scoop grabbed at my arm roughly trying to get my attention. I almost decked him until I realized it was him.

"What the fuck, Scoop?? I asked, yanking my arm away and taking in his wide-eyed expression full of panic.

"Lyla got attacked yesterday," he said in a rushed whisper.

His news came to me in a hushed tone, but it felt as if he'd hit me with thunder and lightning. It slammed me in the chest, sending icy cold into my bones. "Is she okay?"

I knew when I asked how desperate I sounded, but I didn't give a fuck. I needed to know Lyla was still on this earth. Needed to know that there was still something good in my world. I wasn't sure I could go on without her now that she was mine. Already I could feel myself breaking apart into tiny pieces just thinking about losing her.

"She's okay."

The tension in my shoulders loosened at those words, but still, the anger simmered in my stomach to a dangerous level.

"What happened?" I asked, not sure if I wanted to know. My jaw ached from grounding my teeth so hard.

"It was Miguel, one of Jose's boys. The Mexican Mafia is coming in hot on this green light, man. They're hard up for that cash. I think Jose might have put him up to it." He gripped the back of his neck, obviously uncomfortable with telling me the rest.

"Tell me."

"I don't know how he got in, but he wasn't there for medical. He tried to strangle her to death with IV tubing. She was blue by the time Reeves and Douglas got to her. He's in solitary now, but the talk is he won't be in there long."

We were in the cafeteria, but instead of getting food, I went to a table to sit. Scoop sat beside me, his eyes moving over the room, making sure no one was listening to our conversation. Some inmates watched in interest, but I didn't care. Fuck them. I fucking dared them to come at me.

I hated the idea of anyone touching her, but maybe this would be the push she needed to finally quit. Over my dead body would she continue to work at Fulton. I hoped now she understood how serious I was about her leaving.

I hated to think about what my life in Fulton would be like without her, but I knew it would be worse if she was murdered. Plus, my case had been reopened, and there was always that chance that I'd be released.

I looked up just as Jose and his boys came into the room, and my blood started to boil. My skin felt as if it was melting from my body, and I was being transformed into a completely different kind of monster. One who really could rip limbs from a person because in that moment, it was all I could think about doing.

I pumped my fists and moved to stand from my seat. His eyes clashed with mine, and he lifted a brow as if to tell me to *bring it*. He had no idea how bad it was going to be for him.

Scoop touched my shoulder, stopping me. "If you're in the hole, you can't do anything. Remember that."

I growled, knowing he was right. I wanted to kill him. I wanted to choke the life from him, feel his heart stop against my fingers. Better yet, I wanted to shove him into the dryer and turn it on the highest setting. I was being accused of killing Carlos; why not actually commit the crime?

My mind spun back to the day I found Carlos in the dryer. I smiled darkly, and the sick desire to see Jose in the same predicament swam in my gut. My stomach churned at the idea, and I shook my head to rid myself of those thoughts. I was a lot of things, but a sick fuck wasn't one of them.

Regardless of popular belief, I wasn't a killer, but that didn't mean I wouldn't want to beat him until he was almost dead.

"Anyway, there's good news, too."

I scanned his face to see if he was full of shit, but he grinned. "She finally quit."

And just like that, things felt lighter. Sure, I was going to miss being able to see her every time I went to the infirmary, but at least this way, she was still alive and she was safe.

I didn't respond. Instead, I nodded.

Skipping breakfast, I spent my time in the yard, staring off into the skyline. Freedom had never been so important to me, but knowing who I had out there waiting for me made it vital. The knowledge that I had a shot at a real life, it was worth more than gold.

I spent the morning alone, and I think even Scoop understood the importance of my solitude since he didn't speak to me again until we were lining up for lunch.

"Hey, man." He eyed me, feeling out my mood.

"What now?" I asked, sure that he was bringing me more bad news. "Let me guess, someone died?"

"Actually, yeah, Miguel's dead. They found him in the hall outside solitary. He'd been choked to death."

His words moved over me, and strangely, I didn't feel as happy about it as I thought I would.

"Do they know who did it?"

"Nope, but I bet you can guess who's getting all the blame." He shrugged, shoving a still-frozen fry into his mouth.

Me.

Of course they thought it was me. Fuck, it was always me. I'd killed my girlfriend Sarah and her high school friend Michael. I'd killed Carlos, and now, I'd killed Miguel, too. I was fucking lethal apparently. Motherfuckers died just by looking at me.

Fuck them!

"Let them think what they want. Maybe now they won't fuck with me anymore."

We ate lunch in silence, and I could feel the eyes of the room drilling me on the top of my head and my back. I fucking hated having so much attention on me, but it came with the territory when everyone in the building thought you were a killer.

LATER, AFTER WORK detail, it was visitation time. Usually, I hung out in the rec room and watched TV, but when the COs called out the names of those who had visitors, this time my name was called.

I looked over at Reeves, sure he'd called the wrong name.

"Are you going to sit there and stare at my ass all day or are you going to get up?"

I stood and lined up with the rest of the guys. In the back of my mind, I knew it was Lyla who was visiting me, but I still hoped it wasn't. As badly as I wanted to see her, it wasn't safe for her to visit me. Not to mention, what we had going on was no one else's business. Her coming to visit me lit up a red light that flashed, *We are fucking.*

I guessed in a way it didn't matter since she didn't work at Fulton anymore, but still, I didn't want people to think badly of her because she was fucking with an inmate. They didn't know our story. They didn't understand us.

The visitation room was all gray. Gray walls. Gray tables. Gray chairs. It was the most depressing place in Fulton, but it was the only place where people really smiled. That was exactly what I did when I stepped into the room and saw Lyla sitting at a table waiting for me.

She was in a light green top and a pair of jeans. Her hair was down and had a bit of curl to the tips. She'd even put a little color on her face, not that she needed it. She looked fucking amazing. No. Better than amazing.

"Hey, you," she said when I sat at the table in front of her.

The cuffs on my hands rattled when I placed them on top of the table, and my fingers flinched with the desire to touch her. She looked up at me under dark lashes and smiled, making my heart beat funny, but I knew I couldn't soften in front of these people. As happy as I was to see her, I knew people were watching. They were always watching.

"This wasn't safe," I said, my eyes scanning the room and

landing on Jose.

The side of his mouth lifted in a knowing smirk, and it took all the strength I had to remain seated.

"I know, but I wanted to see you. I quit without saying goodbye."

Her fingers twitched, and she moved her hand a little closer to mine. Closing my eyes, I imagined she was holding my hands. I pictured her soft skin touching my rough and her sweetness pouring into me.

"I'm glad you quit," I said, my eyes moving over her face and taking in as much of her as I could. I was hoping she would never come back to Fulton. I'd hoped to see her again on the outside maybe, but never inside of Fulton.

"Miguel's dead."

Her eyes widened, and she licked nervously at her lips. "Did you?"

I shook my head and chuckled sarcastically. "You know, everyone in Fulton thinks I did it. I guess it was stupid of me to think you'd know better."

At my words, she reached out and covered my hands. "I'm sorry. I just know how protective you are of those you care about. After he attacked me, I just figured..."

I squeezed her fingers, stopping her and relishing in the feel of her skin against mine.

"I didn't kill him, but I would've. I'm so sorry I wasn't there for you."

"Stop, Christopher. All that matters now is I quit. Our next step is getting the charges dropped against you. Give me time, and I'll have you out."

"And then we can be together?" I asked, intertwining our fingers together and not caring who saw.

She grinned, her face lighting up the room and making the gray in the room feel happy. "Yes."

I smiled, and then my eyes met Reeves from across the room. The look he gave me was full of hate and accusation. The proverbial cat was out of the bag, and everyone in the room could look at Lyla and me and know we were more than just nurse and inmate.

I pulled away, not sure if they could still file charges against her or not since she no longer worked at Fulton, and her face dropped.

"I didn't think I'd ever get you out of here," I said, turning my head and taking in the rest of the room.

As long as I wasn't looking her in the eye, I didn't feel like I was falling. When I had the feeling I was falling, I wanted to hold on to her. Touch her and imagine she was the anchor that kept me rooted to the earth.

"Oh, you begged me to quit every day, but I guess I didn't realize how serious the situation was."

"I did a hell of a lot more than beg. Scoop placed the narcotic blame on you for me, and I slipped the knife in your pocket."

Her face darkened with anger. I knew there was about to be hell to pay, but suddenly, she burst into laughter.

"I can't believe you."

We spent the rest of our visit going over things about my case. The insider she was dealing with inside the police department had asked her to let him take care of it, and I agreed. It wasn't safe for her, and I could tell there was a lot more about my case that she wasn't telling me.

Maybe the real killers were still a danger?

Something told me that whatever she was holding back was something that would push me over the edge.

"So there's going to be a lawyer stopping by next week to talk things over with you. So far, everything is looking good for you. I think this might actually happen."

I'd heard her, but I was too busy watching her lips move. I couldn't wait to get her alone and be able to kiss her. Sitting across from her and smelling the scent of her hair and her skin was making me wild with want.

We didn't touch each other again during her visit, but when it was time for her to go, we stood and hugged. My eyes went across the room to Reeves, and his eyes burrowed holes in the back of her head.

If anyone asked, she'd visited about the case. No one needed to know there was more.

While I held her close, I whispered to her so only she could hear me.

"God, I've missed you, Lyla, but you can't come back here. I'll see you on the outside, baby."

She pulled back with a frown.

"Just trust me. Do you trust me?"

She nodded.

"Good. As much as I loved seeing you today, I need you to stay away from Fulton. Promise me you'll stay away."

Her eyes moved across my face, sadness seeping in and transforming her expression. "I promise."

"Okay, everyone, visitation is over," Reeves' voice echoed throughout the room.

I wasn't ready to let her go, but I couldn't keep her there. I couldn't leave with her either. It was goodbye until things were smoothed over... until my case was taken care of and I was a free man. It was going to be hell without her, but I knew it was for the best.

She smiled as we prepared to say our goodbyes, but instead of saying bye and turning to leave, she threw herself into my arms, not caring who was watching.

"Stay safe in here, X. Come home to me."

Her words soothed every scar on my body, every broken part of me, and I couldn't resist. I lost my hands in the hair at the side of her face and looked into her eyes.

"I love you, Lyla," I whispered for only her.

Her eyes filled with tears and she opened her mouth to speak, but before she could respond, I was being pulled away from her and lined up with the rest of the criminals.

From across the room, she smiled sadly back at me. Then she mouthed the words that would make the remainder of my stay at Fulton bearable.

I love you too.

CHAPTER 24

X

"**COME ON, X**, get your shit together, man. It's time for work detail, and you need to work. You're starting to look a little flabby."

"Fuck you."

"No thanks, big boy, your tits aren't big enough for me. Not yet anyway. You keep this lazy shit up, and they might be soon."

I hadn't come out and said how badly I missed Lyla, but Scoop wasn't stupid. He could tell I was more miserable than usual. It had been a week, and I was feigning for her like a crack addict needing another hit. I dreamed about her at night and woke up to my nightmare every morning. It was pure hell.

The walls of Fulton felt closer, more depressing, and I couldn't shake the depression no matter how bad I tried. Things were going downhill fast around me, and even the COs had taken to treating me like shit ever since Lyla had showed up for visitation. Scoop was the only good left in Fulton, and I hated to think about leaving him behind when I was hopefully released.

I was obsessed with the thoughts of leaving Fulton and being with Lyla forever. There were no other words to describe the deep ache that had planted itself in my center. It was obsession—dark and deep—and it felt good.

As usual, Scoop was right. Working helped me focus and clear my head. Heaps of dirty linens, pillowcases, and uniforms lined the room in their respective bins. Having over five hundred inmates in all the blocks made for long days of washing, drying, and folding. Thankfully, we had some hardworking guys in the laundry. It wasn't the manliest job, but it was strenuous work.

The day stretched on, and we worked fast and hard, hoping to earn ourselves a little more time in the yard by finishing early. My back was to the door, and I was folding blankets when I was jerked away from my table by a pair of strong hands. Spinning, I came face to face with Jose. His face twisted into an evil grin.

Three of his largest guys had caught me off guard, and because of that, they had a tight hold on me. Conveniently, the room had been cleared, but behind Jose stood Scoop, who was also being held by one of the Mexican Mafia boys.

With a paper blade to his throat, Scoop's face paled.

"You're making a big mistake, motherfucker," I growled at Jose.

He put his fingers to his lips, daring me to speak again.

"I lost out on a lot of money because of you, Pendejo. If it wasn't for you, our little redhead wouldn't have flown the coop." He sucked at his teeth and shook his head. "I'm tired of waiting and watching. I know your weaknesses."

My mouth dried and my teeth grinded together so hard my jaw ached. My biggest weakness was Lyla, and I'd kill him before he even had the chance to try to hurt her again. It didn't matter if my case was under review or I was being close to be released. All that mattered was keeping her safe, and if I had to kill to do that, then so be it. I'd lived in prison for the last ten years of my life. I'd do it again until the day I died for Lyla.

I lunged at him, his men holding me back and digging their fingers into my flesh. I lunged again, and this time, one kicked me in the back of my knee, making me bend to them. A towel came around my neck like a leash, tightly choking me into submission.

"Are you finished?" Jose asked with a chuckle.

Again, I growled and lunged toward him, the air being choked from my body as the men holding me tightened their grip.

"What's wrong, X? Can't stand being helpless?" He stepped toward me and lifted my face to him. "I know where your allegiance lies, and I'm tired of certain people putting their noses where they don't belong. I think it's time to put an end to that."

He left me and went to Scoop before running a single finger over Scoop's swollen cheek. Apparently, one of the motherfuckers had hit him already.

In that moment, seeing him touch Scoop so softly, I knew exactly what he was up to. He wasn't talking about Lyla being my weakness, he was talking about Scoop.

My eyes moved over Scoop's helpless face, and I could see how afraid he was by the tightness in his eyes and lips. Scoop had balls to be so small, but I'd never seen him so afraid. Worry etched his brow, forcing a few wrinkles across his forehead. His muscles were tense as he waited for the attack that we both knew was coming his way.

"Don't," I said, earning another tug on the towel around my neck.

Jose ignored me. Instead, he motioned to the two men standing behind Scoop, and they quickly stripped his uniform from his small frame.

"Jose, come on, bro," Scoop said, trying to save himself.

Instead of responding, Jose backhanded him across the face and blood flew from Scoop's lips.

"I'm not your fucking bro."

They slung him across the table, his bare ass shining to the room around us, and my stomach turned. Scoop was looking at me, begging me with his eyes to help him, but I couldn't. I'd fought and won against more men than this before, but they'd gotten the jump on me and I was as helpless as Scoop in that moment.

Jose stepped up behind Scoop and started to unzip his khakis.

"No! You fucking touch him and I'll kill you!" Spittle flew from my lips, and I felt like a rabid animal foaming at the mouth.

Jose's head flew back as he laughed, his hand frozen on his hard cock. "You're going to what? You're going to kill me like you killed Carlos? I don't think so. You take from us, we take from you."

He grabbed a fistful of Scoop's hair, tugging his head back and forcing him to look me in the eye. I wanted to look away, but the men holding me forced me to watch. Their grimy fingers dug into my face, keeping my head straight.

The man at Scoop's side pressed the knife into the side of his neck, and a trickle of blood dripped to the table beneath him. There was nothing I could do. I couldn't stop this. I shook my head at Scoop and tried to relay my sorrow with my eyes.

Again, I lunged, and I felt my own blood beginning to soak into the towel around my neck.

Jose pumped his dick a few times and stepped in between Scoop's thighs. With a tense jaw and his eyes locked on mine, he pressed into Scoop with a quick, rough pump, making him scream out.

With a jerk, Scoop tried with one last feeble attempt to get away, but it only pushed the blade deeper into his skin.

I was forced to watch as the two holding him down banged his head into the table and his blood spilled down the side of his face. They slammed him down, pinning him to the table as Jose continuously shoved his cock into his ass.

When Scoop opened his mouth to scream out, they shoved a dirty washcloth in his mouth, shutting him up. His eyes bulged from their sockets, and his face turned three shades of red as he lay there, helpless and unable to fight back, while Jose brutally raped him.

I watched as the light in his eyes slowly dimmed. The boy he was slowly moved away from him until he was gone. I'd seen it before. He was trying to survive by removing himself from the situation, but by looking at his bland expression on his face as

Jose stuffed his body repeatedly, I wasn't sure he'd ever come back. He slumped against the table, all his fight gone completely, and sweat beaded across his face until he finally closed his eyes.

I was going to kill them. There was no question in my mind. I wanted out, but in that moment, I wanted them dead more. Anger seethed in every pore of my body. When I got loose, there was going to be hell to pay.

Finally, Jose finished with a groan before moving to the side and letting the others get their go. My eyes burned his face, and he grinned as he shoved his flaccid dick in his pants and zipped them up.

The room filled with the erotic sounds of bodies beating into Scoop—the sounds of their heavy breaths as they took a piece of him one by one. They weren't killing him, but still, when he opened his eyes, the spirit behind them was dead.

Jose reached over, pulling Scoop's head from the table and forcing him to look at him.

"Keep your nose out everyone's business or the next place I'll shove my cock is in your mouth. Got it?"

He dropped Scoop's head back onto the table and again, Scoop clenched his eyes closed, blocking out the room around him.

In that moment, something inside me snapped. The room around me took on a red haze, and I felt myself shutting down. I was slipping into something dangerous. Something unknown or unseen, and I became afraid of myself. I was afraid of what I'd do when they finally let me loose, and at some point, they'd have to.

The towel cut into my neck and the floor beneath me was covered in my blood. I wasn't sure how badly I was bleeding. I was numb. There was no pain. There was no ache. There was only the raw hate and anger that was rotting in my stomach.

Finally, the towel loosened enough for me to get away. I snatched the bloody towel from my capturers and turned on them, tearing into their faces with my fist in a way I never had before. I screamed with my attack like a madman, and my screams echoed through the room and out into the walkway outside the laundry.

I lunged toward Jose, but just as I moved, officers filled the room. They piled in with pepper spray and calling out codes. The alarms sounded, and more COs came pouring in. Soon, they had us all pinned to the floor with their knees in our backs. My eyes met Jose's from across the room and I promised him without even speaking that as soon as I was loose, I was going to kill him.

I watched as they led Jose and his two half-naked men to the hole. Afterwards, they transported Scoop to the infirmary. His dead eyes flashed my way before he disappeared with the guards out of the laundry room. He'd pulled his pants back up, but they were covered in his blood, showing how badly Jose and his men had ripped him apart. They had violated him in the worse way possible, and I wasn't sure Scoop was ever going to be able to come back from that.

SCOOP WAS IN the infirmary for three days following their attack. I was more worried about his mental status, though. Not many men could come back from that, and I prayed he'd overcome.

On the third day, I stood at the bars and watched as Reeves and Douglas returned him to his cell. He didn't look my way. He didn't blink. He just disappeared behind the cinderblock wall that separated us. The bars to his room clanked as they closed and slammed into place, locking him in.

For days he didn't speak, not even to me. His eyes became shifty as he walked in the chow line with his head down and his shoulders hunched. He quit eating, spending breakfast, lunch, and dinner poking at his food rather than consuming it.

My friend became a shell of himself, hollow and void of even a glimmer of the old Scoop. I stayed beside him, guarding him and hoping he'd be able to shake it, but every day, there was the same silence.

At night, I'd lay awake and listen to him crying from his cell. He never slept anymore, and it showed. His eyes grew darker and more lifeless, his lids getting heavier as time went by.

As the week after the attack stretched on, I silently planned my attack on Jose and his men when they were finally released from the hole. When I wasn't planning, I was worrying about Scoop and Lyla. It was a never-ending cycle that I couldn't manage to break.

Finally, on the fifth night after his attack, Scoop spoke.

"Hey, X," he whispered from the side of his cell.

"Yeah?"

"I want you promise me something," he muttered, sadness etched deep in his voice.

I swallowed, not liking the way he sounded. "Anything." I rolled over, facing the cinderblock wall as if I could see him through it.

"Promise no matter what you'll take care of yourself. I don't want anything happening to you."

I sat up, my eyes scanning the darkness around me. "Come on, bro, you know you don't have to worry about me," I said playfully, trying my hardest to sound like him.

He chuckled darkly from his cell, and the weight on my chest lifted a bit. A hush settled over the room, and I assumed he'd fallen asleep.

"X," he said again.

"Yeah?"

"I miss my family. I miss my wife and my daughter. You know they quit coming to see me?"

"No. I didn't know that. I'm sorry to hear that."

"Yeah, I'm sorry, too."

I'd forgotten that Scoop had a family outside. He knew so much about everyone else, but he rarely mentioned anything about himself.

I smiled at the thought of him getting out and hugging his

baby girl. He would get to see them again. Unlike me, he wasn't serving a life sentence.

"You're halfway there, man. Halfway." I yawned.

There was silence after that. I drifted to sleep, dreaming of Lyla and her sweet smile.

God, I missed her.

CHAPTER 25

X

SCOOP HUNG HIMSELF with his bed sheets with the words *Daddy will always love you* painted on the wall in his blood. I guessed it was too much for him to handle. Hell, it was too much for anyone. Rape was rape, and Scoop's had been brutal.

I stood at my bars and watched as Scoop's death scene unraveled. The sounds of the camera clicks filled my room as they took pictures of his body. The COs laughed and chatted about their day as if a human being wasn't hanging dead from his cell window.

They didn't know him, and they didn't care. He was nothing but an empty cell now. He was a statistic in some file... a name to be blotted from roll call. Soon, there would be another inmate in his cell. They moved them out and moved them in just as fast.

The coroner came and made a few inquiries. I listen from my cell as he asked questions and took more pictures. He emerged with Scoop in a body bag some time later. I stood at the bars and watched as they rolled him down the block on a stretcher.

Would his family ever find out the reason why he'd taken his own life?

I hated myself for not fighting harder. I should've fought harder.

The urge to cry was strong when his body disappeared from sight, but I'd always known the number-one rule of prison.

Never get attached.

It'd gotten attached to Scoop. I trusted him. He was my friend in a friendless place and the only brother I ever knew. And now, because I'd grown weak over time, he was gone. He'd opted out of this life, taking the easy way out rather than reliving the heinous crimes against him over and over.

I was angry with him, but I understood. I'd known from the moment the rape was over that he'd never come back from it, and he hadn't, not really. Scoop had died on the table in the laundry room a week before he hung himself. I'd seen the light go out in his eyes. I'd watched him leave us.

Everyone left. My mom left. Lyla left, and now Scoop. There was no one. There was no one left.

Even I was gone. I didn't know who I was anymore. Was I X or had I become Christopher Jacobs again?

I didn't know much, but I knew the agony that laced my nervous system after Scoop's death quickly turned into revenge. The monster I'd kept at bay for so long was begging to be released.

I had nothing left to lose, so I let him out.

THE DINING HALL was silent when I entered the following day. Every eye was on me as I strode across the room and got in line for what looked like chicken and rice. I sat down at a table alone and stared off into space as I ate.

The days after Scoop's death became a blur, and I drifted in and out of a strange state of mind. Hours would go by and I wouldn't realize it. I would drift into my moments of emptiness and wake up in another part of the prison, unsure of how I got there. Things became dark for me, and I could feel myself shutting down completely.

Jose Alvarez and his boys were found murdered a week later, hanging from the showers. It couldn't be tied to me, but again, everyone assumed it was me murdering everyone. It just so happened that everyone who was being killed at Fulton was somehow linked to me. I didn't understand it, but I quit questioning it. Someone out there was doing my dirty work, and while I missed the thrill of watching the life leave Jose's eyes, I appreciated whoever was committing the murders.

Another week went by, and I heard nothing else about my case. Things moved slowly in my world, which meant it could years before I was released. I wasn't sure I would last that long. Taking the easy way out was starting to sound appealing, but every time I considered it, I'd close my eyes and see Lyla's face.

She loved me. She was waiting for me. I couldn't leave her. I wouldn't leave her.

A few weeks after Scoop's death, I began to hear the rumors. Whispers of Lyla's name would skim past my ears, making me think that maybe I'd missed her so much I was hearing people say her name, but that wasn't the case.

Sitting at the table, shoving an overcooked piece of pork down my throat, I heard an inmate behind me say her name. I spun around and before I realized what I was doing, I had him jerked up by his collar.

"What was that?" I asked through my teeth.

"I didn't say nothing," he lied.

He was scrawny. In his late forties, he had patchy facial hair and rotting teeth. And to top it off, he stunk like he hadn't washed in months.

"Don't fucking lie to me. I heard you say her name. You said Lyla Evans. What about her?" I hissed in his face, my fist tightening in his collar.

"She's been green-lighted," he said around my chokehold.

My fist loosened. "That's old news. She doesn't work here anymore anyway."

"No. The green-light's been extended past the prison walls. She's fair game no matter where she is. Some mob boss wants her pretty little head on a plate."

I dropped him to the ground with a thump.

Was he telling the truth?

What the fuck was going on, and was the mob involved somehow?

There had been a lot of deaths lately. Starting with Carlos and ending with Jose and his boys. Maybe the Mexican Mafia was affiliated somehow?

Ideas flowed through my head like water, but nothing stuck. Nothing made sense.

The dynamics of Fulton had shifted once again, and I had a feeling that an outside source was to blame. People were acting afraid. Gangs stuck closely to themselves, and everyone was being quiet. It was totally fucked up, but something was definitely going down.

FIRST THING, I needed to get the fuck out of Fulton. If the green-light had been extended past the prison walls, then she was no longer safe. I couldn't sit there and wait without knowing what was happening to her.

I'd already lost Scoop; I wasn't about to lose Lyla, too. I couldn't make it without her. Wouldn't even try to make without her. I had to get to her before anyone else did, and I needed to do that fast.

I paced my cell for two days before an idea struck me. Without hesitation, I slammed my fist as hard as I could into the cinderblock wall. My knuckles cracked against the cement, sending my blood splattering to the floor by my feet. Pain shot up my air, but I held it in, gripping my fist until I could get an officer's attention and get hauled off to the infirmary.

Once my escort came and the doors to the infirmary were opening, I knew there was no going back. Something inside me shifted, and instinct had me looking around for her face. I closed my eyes, wishing I could see her, touch her soft skin and kiss her sweet lips.

Dr. Giles came in, his eyes dropping to my hands as he pulled on a pair of latex gloves. He shook his head and sighed. "Put him in there." He motioned to an open bed.

He followed me into a curtained space and then shook his head again. "What did you do this time?" he asked as he began to clean my battered hand. He eyed my suspiciously.

"I got mad," I said honestly.

"Mad about what?"

"Scoop," I muttered. His name burned my tongue like hot sauce.

Giles lowered his eyes and glanced over his shoulder to see if the COs were watching from across the room. They stood, leaning against the desk and talking among themselves. "I'm sorry for your loss. I know he was your friend."

I jerked and hissed as he poured straight alcohol over my knuckles.

"I also know you two were trying to set up Lyla."

His eyes found mine, and I didn't even try to hide my surprise. How had he found out?

He grinned as I searched his face for an answer to my unasked question.

"I'm not stupid, son. I've been around long enough to know what you guys were up to. I knew about her being green-lighted, and I actually was relieved when she quit. It was getting way too dangerous around here for her."

"Agreed," I said through gritted teeth.

Dr. Giles had no qualms about bringing the pain. It was more than obvious he was getting off on it since he kept pouring alcohol into my cut.

"She's still in danger," I said, finally putting my plan into place. His eyes moved from my knuckles and searched my face. "I'm telling the truth. Someone on the outside is trying to get to her now."

His face paled. "How do you know?" he asked while he bandaged my knuckles.

"I shook it out of another inmate. I need to get to her, Doc.

"Leave it to the authorities."

I shook my head. Surely, he wasn't serious. The authorities couldn't protect their own. What the fuck could they do for Lyla now? Especially since half the cops were in the pockets of someone.

"Seriously?" I looked at him incredulously. He couldn't be that daft.

He sighed deeply, coming to the same conclusion I had this whole time.

"Can you help me get out of here?" I took a risk and asked.

Asking someone to help break you out of prison was a huge violation. It meant permanent isolation, but I was willing to risk it.

"I know you care about her, too, Giles. She's like a daughter to you. Please, let me save her. You know I'm right about this. You know it."

Reluctantly, he nodded, his eyes studying me intensely. "You're allergic to Penicillin, right?"

I nodded, knowing exactly where he was going with his question.

"I think those knuckles are deep. I'm worried about infection. I think you might need a dose of Penicillin."

He winked at me before he left my side, coming back shortly with a syringe. Pulling the curtain, his eyes moved over my face once more.

"You're sure about this?" he asked.

I set my jaw and closed my eyes. Lyla's face popped into my

memory. "Yes. Just do it."

He pulled the cap off the syringe and injected it into me. Within minutes, its effects began closing up my throat. As I began to swing into full anaphylaxis, Giles leaned over me and grinned.

"Remember, X, I had nothing to do with this."

I nodded and shut my eyes, focusing on my shallow breathing. Dr. Giles waited a few seconds before finally calling out for help.

"Call for an emergency transport!"

He ran from the room. The COs jumped to attention, pulling at the phones and speaking into their walkies. My mind was spinning, but I could make out Giles filling them in and letting them know I was having an allergic reaction.

Soon, he ran back into my space, plunging another needle into my arm. Immediately, I could feel relief. My throat was scratchy, but I could breathe again.

Minutes later, I was loaded into an ambulance. Dr. Giles followed me out and pressed a hand into my shoulder to reassure me. As his hand slipped away, he pushed something into my palm and I closed my fist around it.

My symptoms were slowly diminishing, and I was beginning to feel strong again. I knew I only had one shot at my escape, and for the sake of Lyla, I had to make it good.

Reeves sat in the seat beside me, jotting down something on a clipboard, and my eyes roamed over his body, landing on the gun at his side. COs weren't allowed to be armed until they were transporting an inmate.

Feeling what Giles had pressed into my palm, I felt the coldness of a paperclip. I pulled at it, careful to not draw attention to myself, and I slowly worked at the lock on my handcuffs.

Once they were loose, I quietly began unbuckling my seatbelts, letting the last one click to the floor. Both the medic and Reeves looked up at me, but before he could pull his weapon, I lunged at him. Knocking him to the floor, I went for his gun and pulled it from his side.

I had the upper hand then.

"What's going on back there?" the driver called to the back.

"Nobody move," I whispered, holding the gun up and directly at Reeves.

With pinched lips and angry, red cheeks, he stared up at me from his place on the floor.

The ambulance began to slow. I quickly snatched the key from Reeves and unlocked my leg shackles.

Once the ambulance came to a stop, I didn't waste any time. I slung the back door open and hopped out into the middle of traffic. Making a run for the tree line, I held the gun at my side. I ran until my legs ached, until I was sure there was no one following me.

I didn't stop until I was swallowed by the darkness with only the moon to light my way. Tilting my head back, I breathed in the air of the free. It was then I remembered that Giles had put two things in my hand. Opening my fist, I stared down at the sweaty piece of paper sticking to my palm.

Opening it, I read it. It was an address—Lyla's address to be exact. I knew where I was, having grown up only a few blocks away, and I knew I wasn't far from her place. Gathering my bearings, I turned and started in her direction. I needed to get to her as soon as possible, and I could only hope I wasn't too late.

CHAPTER 26

LYLA

HAVING SPENT THE night out with Diana, I was more than happy to finally be home. I didn't have the money to go out, since I was only working part time at a doctor's office close to my apartment, so instead, we'd stayed in at her place, watching movies and drinking wine.

I put my key in the door, turned the lock, and stepped into my dark apartment. Patting at the wall to my side, I tried to find the light switch until finally I found it and flipped it. My living room lit up and I sighed, tossing my purse onto the couch.

I turned to shut the door, making sure to lock the deadbolt, but before I turned back around, a hand landed over my mouth, trapping my scream.

"Shhh…" a deep voice hushed me.

The hand lifted from my lips and I turned, finding X standing there.

He was really there, standing in my apartment. I'd missed him so much. It had taken everything I had not to go to him on visitation day, but I'd promised and I didn't want to break a promise to him. No matter how badly I missed him.

For weeks, I'd gone back and forth with the lawyers, trying to get his case going, but it was like no one cared but me. It was aggravating and annoying, and I hated feeling helpless.

His dark blue eyes moved over my face, taking me in inch by inch, and relief coursed through my veins. Having him close to me felt amazing.

I threw myself into him without hesitation. He wrapped me in his thick arms, pulling me into his large chest and making me feel safer than I had in a long time.

He massaged my cheek with his thumb, touching me everywhere and nowhere all at once. And then reality set in, and I knew something wasn't right.

I pulled away, and he looked down at me longingly. "You're here. How are you here right now?" I asked.

"I had to, Lyla. I did it for you."

"Wait, what did you do, Christopher?" Panic rushed down my spine.

"I escaped."

I couldn't believe my ears. How? Fulton had COs posted everywhere, and everything ran like clockwork.

He pulled me to him again, my face burrowed into his chest. "I had to, Lyla. You're not safe. I had to make sure you were safe."

"What are you talking about? I'm so confused right now." I was beyond happy to see him, but the pieces weren't fitting together.

"The green-light was extended past the prison walls. Whoever they are, they want you dead no matter what."

Cold struck me deep, moving through my veins and freezing me from within.

"I don't care what I have to do, I'll keep you safe. I've already lost one person; I can't lose you, too."

Cupping his cheek in my hand, I ran my thumb beneath his eyes and enjoyed the feel of him. "What do you mean? Who did you lose?"

His expression dropped and sadness filled his eyes. "Scoop.

He hung himself.

"Why would he do that?" I whispered, my mind going back to the happy-go-lucky guy I remembered.

"Jose. He and his gang held me down and raped him in front of me. He wasn't the same after that."

His voice trailed off, and I could hear a twinge of sadness and guilt in it. It tore my soul to pieces. I pulled his face to mine and made him look into my eyes.

"Christopher, it wasn't your fault." I watched his face darken, and I couldn't bear it anymore.

I ran my finger across the arch of his brow and down his rugged jaw line. His teeth clenched beneath my touch, making his jaw muscle pop against my fingertip. His eyes softened and he closed them gently, turning his face into my palm.

When he opened them, strong emotions swirled in the depth of his blue irises, consuming my soul and pulling me under with him. Calloused fingers slipped around my waist beneath my shirt, and chills lifted my skin. I moaned when his lips found mine, sucking and tasting. It was slow and erotic, temptation at its finest.

He kissed me tenderly, his hands moving up and down my back beneath my shirt, until he finally lifted it, breaking our kiss to pull my top over my head. He tossed it to the floor, and his eyes moved over my flesh like it was the first time he'd ever seen a naked woman.

"So fucking beautiful," he said as his finger whispered across my cleavage.

Leaning down, he pressed heated kisses along the side of my neck, working his way down to just above my bra. He sucked softly at the flesh billowing over the top of my C cups, and his fingers worked deftly at the latches on the back. Once he freed me completely, he moved lower, sucking my nipple between his lips and lavishing it will gently licks.

I panted loudly, pressing my palms into the back of his head to hold him to me. His mouth felt amazing, feeding on my body

SLAMMER

like I was a delicious morsel and pushing me to the brink of madness.

Things picked up. His kisses became more hurried, our passion a flurry of hands and mouths. Clothes fell to the floor as we uncovered each other like we'd never been able to before. Our eyes moved over each other's bodies, taking in every dip and curve. I'd never felt more beautiful in my life. The way Christopher looked at me—it was as though he was worshipping me. And when he dropped to his knees in front of me, pushed my panties to the side, and buried his face into my wet heat, he did exactly that. He worshiped me.

My hands roamed across his head, his wide, muscled shoulders, and anything I could reach, feeling his naked skin in a way I never got a chance to before. The sounds of my wetness and him tasting it filled my living room, followed by my loud moans. It was erotic before when we had to be quiet. I enjoyed the feel of his hand over my mouth, holding in my pleasured noises, but this was different. Hearing myself was turning me on even more.

Finally, I crumbled. My knees weakened and my back fell against the door, keeping me from falling to the floor. He continued, licking and sucking my juices as they flowed from my body until I was shaking and begging him to stop.

I slumped against the door as he licked his way back up my body. Once we were face to face, he kissed me hard, filling my mouth with my own personal flavor, and lifted me, wrapping my legs around his waist.

"Bed," he growled against my lips, making me chuckle.

I pointed in the direction of my bedroom and held on tightly around his neck while he walked us through my apartment to my bedroom. My mattress creaked under me when he tossed me to the bed, and then I stared at him openly as he peeled his pants from his body and stood before me completely naked.

He was magnificent. Tall and lean. Dark and sexy. His cock stood tall for me, letting me know how badly he wanted me, and I moved toward him. My knees dug into the mattress when I went

209

to him. He stood still, letting me kiss him everywhere, sucking on his hot skin and marking him as mine.

He bit into his bottom lip and tangled his fingers in my hair. "Lyla." His voice broke.

I moved lower, licking him from his navel to his pelvic bone. He growled in pleasure, his fingers tightening in my hair and tugging. The tip of his cock glistened, his want for me already spilling from his body. I licked at the salty goodness, making his body go tense, and then I wrapped my lips around him, pulling him into my mouth and releasing him with a loud pop.

"Fuck, Lyla." He let his head fall back, and his mouth fell open in pleasure.

It made me feel good to make him feel good. So I sucked him hard, the head of his cock rubbing the back of my throat. His fingers pressed into the back of my head as he thrust his hips to get deeper.

His salty flavor coated my tongue, and my mouth watered for more. He swelled in my mouth, filling it to the brink, but before I could suck at him again, he tugged my hair roughly, pulling my mouth away from him.

"I can't, baby. It's been too long. If you don't stop, I'll unload before I even get to feel you."

He pushed me back on the bed, and my eyes took in his chiseled body as he crawled across the bed toward me. He was all predator, stalking his prey and readying himself to eat me alive. I wanted him to devour me, to take every bit of me into his mouth and leave me torn and destroyed. His eyes flashed with excitement, and I knew he felt the same way.

His mouth found mine, and I lost myself in his kiss. His tongue teased me, playing in my mouth and making me crazy. I lifted my hips, rubbing myself against his hardness and silently wishing he'd rip my panties from my body. They were the only thing left between us, and I wanted them gone.

His hand teased my neck, working down my body until his hand was full of my breast. His finger moved over my nipple, sending raw sensations through my core. As he teased my erect flesh, his mouth moved over mine, catching my moans and swallowing them.

Breaking our kiss, his moved to my neck, driving me crazy. Again, I lifted my hips, rubbing myself against him.

"Please, baby, give it to me," I begged.

"That's right. Beg me for it. I fucking love it when you beg."

His hand slid down my body, his fingertips skimming the inside of my thigh, and my breathing accelerated.

"Yes. Please touch me." My voice cracked like a woman in need. I didn't sound like myself. I sounded weak and wanting. That was what he did to me. He weakened me so completely, and it felt good to let go of control.

"Here?" he asked, his finger dipping into the side of my panties and running along just the outside of my center.

Again, I thrust my hips. He was so close to the point of insanity—the part of me that throbbed for him—and I wanted to cry from wanting him so badly.

I cried out when his finger penetrated me. Bending it at the knuckle, he rubbed my inner walls before pulling it out with a wet pop and thrusting it in again.

"Did you miss me, Lyla?" he asked in a husky voice.

"Yes," I panted.

"Did you miss this?" he asked, adding a second finger and reaching for my soft spot within.

I cried out louder. "Yes. God, yes, I missed everything."

His fingers worked me until I was close to breaking, and then they were gone. He tugged at the soaked scrap of fabric between my legs, and it gave with a loud snap. Moving between my thighs, he grasped his hard cock in his palm. He pumped it, rubbing the wet tip against my swollen nub.

My leg stretched around his hard waist, and he lifted it, lining himself up with my center. With one quick thrust, he entered me, hard and fast, filling me so deeply that I didn't know where he started and where I ended.

Again, I cried out, the sensation so pleasing that my eyes rolled back in my head. A gentle smile crept across his face as he lifted my leg high and slid even deeper.

"That's feels so fucking good, Christopher," I said loudly, enjoying the feel of being able to express myself.

He moved, pounding his rigid flesh into me fast and hard. "Say my name again," he demanded.

"Christopher," I moaned.

"Louder!" he growled, his body picking up the pace and slamming into me.

The room filled with the sounds of our sex. Our bodies coming together so roughly that our skin echoed off each other. His musty scent filled my nostrils, mixed with the sweat of our lovemaking and the moisture of our bodies. It was potent... strong just like his thrusts.

"Christopher," I screamed. My orgasm climbed up my skin, making me go tense.

"This is mine," he grunted. "You're mine." With each word, he thrust deeper and deeper into me, pulling loud groans of pleasure from my lips.

My fingers twisted into the blanket at my side as I braced myself for the onslaught of pleasure that was teetering on the edge.

And then I shattered.

He pumped me, pulling my orgasm out of me loudly. The slide of his body in mine slickened as my inner muscles tightened around him, holding him inside me. My legs cramped and my toes curled into the mattress.

He didn't stop. Reaching under my shoulders, his fingers tangled into the hair on the back of my head, putting his chest flat against my own. His hips bucked, the only part of his body that was still moving, and he pushed me directly into another fall.

My cries filled the room as I begged. Happy tears sprang to my eyes, rolling down the sides of my face and escaping into my hairline.

He panted against my lips, trying to kiss me but not having enough breath to do so.

His body going rigid, he came long and hard, his growl of pleasure filling my room and vibrating against my chest. Resting his forehead against my shoulder, his hot breath bathed my skin.

His weight lifted from me, and he fell to my side, pulling me into his arms. He pushed my sweat-soaked hair from my face and planted a soft kiss against my cheek. "I love you so much, Lyla," he whispered, brushing another curl from my face.

His eyes devoured mine, making me his own personal prisoner. His tenderness was different this time. It wasn't raw and untapped passion. It was gentle, timid, and reassuring.

Palming his cheek, my finger glided along the stubble on his jaw. "I love you, too, Christopher."

And I did. So much. It was unexpected. I hadn't walked into Fulton knowing I'd fall in love with an inmate, but I had. Now I was lying in bed with him, knowing he was an escaped convict, but also knowing with all my heart that he was innocent of everything but loving me.

He reached behind him and grabbed my blanket, covering us and enveloping me in the warmth of his body. I'd never felt more safe. I'd never felt more loved.

I closed my eyes and drifted off to sleep, knowing that things were about to change for me. Knowing that I'd do whatever it took to keep him, even if I had to run away with him.

CHAPTER 27

X

THE SUN SLID through the blinds, cutting the room into lines of light. That was what life was when I was with Lyla... light. Everything glowed. Everything was brandished in happiness. It made me sad to think that once I knew she was safe, I'd have to return to Fulton.

I wasn't a runner, and even though I knew it was going to kill me to leave Lyla, I had to go back. I had to face my responsibilities. Escaping meant there was probably no way I was going to get off, even if they did find me innocent. But after spending time with Lyla outside the cinderblock walls, facing life in prison seemed so much harder than before.

I'd already survived ten years, but I wasn't sure I could continue inside. It was different knowing what was waiting for me outside. And who was to say she'd even wait. She deserved a life, and sitting around waiting for me wasn't living. She deserved a family—kids and the white picket fence. I couldn't give her those things. No matter how badly I wanted to, I just couldn't:

She rolled into me, a soft smile on her plump lips. For just a second, I debated taking her and running. We could do it. We could leave and never look back. She'd do that for me. I could see in her eyes every time she looked at me, but again, what kind of life was that for her?

Could I be that selfish?

I smiled down at her, letting my fingers slide over her perfect skin. She was magnificent. Her disheveled hair was spread over her pillow and across my arm, tickling my skin. Last night's eyeliner was smeared on the sides of her eyes, reminding me of the pleasure tears she'd shed the night before.

We'd made love practically all night. Once I'd even woken up inside her as she rode me, my fingers digging unconsciously into her hips. The best moments of my life included her. They were condensed into a few months that I knew I'd have to keep alive in my memories for the rest of my life.

It wasn't healthy, my obsession with her, but it felt amazing. I never wanted to be apart from her. I wanted to live in her. Breathe her into me every second of every day, but reality was real, and that wasn't something I could do.

She sighed in her sleep, her lips opening with a breath I felt against my chest. I didn't want to move. I wanted to stay in bed with her forever, but my stomach growled loudly, reminding me that if I didn't eat soon, I'd never be able to pull off round ten with her.

Her eyes popped open and she chuckled, her voice scratchy and sexy. "Was that your stomach?"

Twisting a strand of her hair between my fingers, I nodded with a grin.

"But didn't I feed you enough last night?"

I laughed like I hadn't since I was a boy. My stomach rumbled and tightened with my laughter. It felt good.

She traced the smile on my lips with her fingers, and I kissed them. She was perfection.

As she stretched in my grasp, I let her wiggle free.

"Then I supposed we better shower and get some food in your

belly."

She pulled the blanket off, and I admired her naked back. A few freckles dotted her shoulders and I leaned up, kissing them briefly. Her back was flawless, her skin soft and milky. I ran a finger down her spine, and she practically purred.

Stretching her neck from side to side, she stood, and her perky ass moved straight into my eye line. I wanted to nibble on it, but again, my stomach growled, reminding me how hungry I was for something more than Lyla. I watched as she walked across the room totally naked, giving me the perfect view of all my favorite physical attributes. Stopping in the doorway of the bathroom, she motioned for me to follow her.

Like the lovesick puppy I was, I stood on shaking legs and followed behind her. Leaning against the doorway, I watched her body flex as she leaned to turn on the shower water. A heated cloud moved across the room, fogging the bathroom mirror and blocking out our reflections.

She got in, the water running over her body and wetting the tips of her hair, and I followed her in. Her back met my chest, and I kissed the side of her neck before licking the hot water from her shoulder. There was no such thing as enough.

Forgetting about my growling stomach, we had round ten against the shower tile. Her nails dug into my shoulder, mixing pleasure with pain. I exploded for her, shattered into a million pieces, and I was sure that I'd never be able to put myself back together again.

SOMETHING WASN'T RIGHT. One minute, I was in the shower with Lyla, pounding into her sweet body, and the sounds of our lovemaking filled the steamy bathroom with echoes of pleasure. The next, I was standing in her living room, staring at her open front door.

The sound of the clock on the wall was magnified, my senses honed in on everything around me. Chills from the unknown moved up my spine, leaving me feeling cold and unsure. I gripped my fists at my side, realizing then that my hands were wet. Moisture ran down my arms in a ticklish line and dripped to the carpet at my feet.

I should've dried off better after our shower.

Lyla's name was setting on my tongue, but instead of calling out to her, I let my eyes roam around the room, sure that something was definitely off. I could sense him... the murderer. He'd come to kill Lyla. He'd come to get the job done so he could collect his reward, but why couldn't I remember opening the door and letting him in?

Then again, why would I have opened the door in the first place? I was fugitive on the run. My face was plastered across the TV screens, warning the people of the neighborhood that I was armed and dangerous. It didn't make sense for me to be seen.

Then I remembered.

I got out of the shower before Lyla, and I'd gone into her kitchen to make us something to eat. She stayed in afterwards to do her womanly stuff—shaving legs and washing hair. Standing at the kitchen counter with a knife in my hand, I tensed when the doorbell chimed out.

There wasn't much after that.

Shaking my head, I couldn't believe how foggy and disoriented I was. Reaching up, I ran a wet hand across my cheek, but when I pulled it back, it wasn't water that was on my hands. It was blood.

So much blood.

Quickly, I checked my naked chest for any cuts, but there were none.

Where had all the blood come from?

Lyla.

Her name rushed through my brain. Slamming the front door, I turned to run toward her bathroom, but when I did, I came face to face with Officer Douglas.

He was lying on the carpet in the middle of Lyla's living room, his eyes wide open in death, staring accusingly back at me. His mouth was wide as if he'd screamed his final breath. His neck and chest were sliced open, his blood still spilling from the fresh wound.

I backed away so quickly that I slammed into the door and the knob dug into my spine.

Again, Lyla's name rushed through my head. Panic gripped my heart, squeezing and pushing my blood through my veins faster than a freight train. My head started to pound. It hurt as if someone was stabbing me in my temple. Reaching up, I smoothed my palm over the side of my head. It was then that the images came. They smacked into me with the force of a hurricane, making my stomach turn and my breath seize.

Sarah's face moved through my mind. Her expression was contorted, full of shock and fear. It was the way she looked when I walked in Michael Welch's apartment and discovered her fucking him.

They jumped out of bed, throwing their clothes on like there was a fire, and then I remembered her trying to calm me down, but there was nothing… only the loud buzzing in my ears and pain in my heart.

Michael came my way. "Hey, man, listen, let's talk about this."

But I stopped him when I lodged a knife I hadn't realized I was holding into the side of his neck. Sarah followed. My hands burned as I cut them into pieces, and blood soaked me and everything around me. As I passed a mirror in Michael's hallway, I looked at myself and smiled sadistically.

But there was unknown DNA under my fingernails. Someone else had been there. It wasn't me.

Then the memory of waiting outside Michael's apartment building came back to me. I remembered waiting until I felt close to exploding. I remembered knowing what she was in there doing and finally breaking. I moved across the parking lot, accidently running into a teenager on a skateboard. I caught him before he fell to the ground, and my nails sank into his arm

"Hey, watch it, dude," he called out as he rode away.

I gripped at my head as the memories kept moving through.

And then there was Carlos. The memories of fighting him in the laundry room —of smashing his head under the laundry press until I heard his skull cracking —of shoving his lifeless body into the dryer, setting the temperature at its highest setting, and walking away, leaving him to tumble and burn.

Those memories were followed by the ones of Miguel begging me to live, and Jose and his boys and how they'd cried like bitches when death was near. The way I'd choked them to death with my bare hands, and then strung them up to let them hang the way Scoop had.

The images attacked me over and over; beating into my brain until my stomach soured and nausea filled me. I'd done those things. I was the monster everyone said I was. I'd murdered Sarah and Michael; there was no mafia conspiracy. I'd never been set up. Then I'd murdered members of the Mexican Mafia like it was nothing.

I'd killed over a broken heart —over the death of my friend — and over Lyla. And even though I'd somehow blocked out the memories of those murders, I knew if it came down to it, I'd do it again for Lyla. Over and over again. I'd wear the blood of anyone who tried to hurt her on my hands proudly, and that thought made me feel even sicker.

But why had I killed Douglas?

He was never a threat to Lyla or me, yet there he was, lying on the floor like a piece of dead trash.

My hands shook when I looked down at them.

What was wrong with me?

I was obviously a very sick man.

I was totally unaware of my crimes. The monster in me had taken over completely in those moments. I was Jekyll and Hyde, and my darker side liked to come out and commit crimes I was clueless about. Those memories were buried deep inside of myself, and I wasn't sure why they were starting to spill out of me like water.

Why now?

Why in that moment of complete and total happiness?

I'd decided when I was inside of Lyla in the shower that we were going to run away together. I knew that I couldn't leave her—that I'd rather live life on the run with her. But that wasn't possible now. I was dangerous. It wasn't safe for even Lyla to be around me since I no longer trusted myself—I no longer even knew who I was.

"You're X," a deep voice whispered at my side.

Turning, I was ready to attack, but there was no one there. I rubbed at my face with bloody hands, sure that I was losing my mind. The voice continued to whisper—my alter ego—telling me what my next move should be. He told me to get rid of Lyla. He told me to cut her perfect flesh into tiny pieces and then to run, but I couldn't listen to him anymore.

I had to protect Lyla.

As if I'd somehow summoned her, she was there. She gasped at the scene before her as she stood in the doorway of her living room. Her eyes moved over Douglas' dead body, and then down at my hands. Her face was pale and twisted in shock and fear.

Her fear cut through me like a hot knife. I loved Lyla with all that I was. I would never hurt her. She had to know I'd never hurt her.

Without my permission, the darker side of me crept in, and the desire to sink my knife into her milky skin moved over me, taking away my breath and my will.

CHAPTER 28

LYLA

I WAS SEEING things. This couldn't be right. Christopher Jacobs was innocent. He was the love of my life, and he was innocent. He didn't do the things everyone said he did. He didn't kill Sarah and Michael. He didn't kill Carlos and the rest of the boys in the Mexican Mafia the way the inmates thought. And he definitely hadn't sliced Douglas open and bled him out in the middle of my living room.

He couldn't have. Especially since not thirty minutes before he was touching me sweetly and telling me how much he loved me. Not when he'd made love to me all night, holding me like I was his life and bringing me to the edge of everything over and over again.

He was my protector—my savior—he was the man I wanted to spend the rest of my life with. He wasn't the bad guy or the criminal. He wasn't the monster.

Then again, if he were so innocent, then why was he standing over Douglas' dead body in the middle of my living room? Why was he covered in blood and looking down at Douglas with a smile?

"You're X," he whispered to no one, his shoulders tense.

My eyes moved over his body, taking in the blood on the khakis he'd put on after his shower and the red smeared all over his hands and face.

"She's next."

His voice was a sinister whisper. I'd never heard him speak that way before, and the hairs on the back of my neck stood on end.

"No. Not Lyla," he begged.

It was confusing. It was like watching two different men speak.

At that moment, it hit me. Christopher Jacobs and X *were* two different men. My brain spun, and everything I learned in Psychology class rushed through my memory. Dissociative Identity Disorder was the medical term. Christopher had multiple personalities. I wasn't a doctor so I couldn't officially diagnose him with that, but it was obvious from where I stood that he was a very sick man.

"We don't hurt Lyla; we protect her. We love her."

My heart squeezed in my chest, being squished tightly between the love I had for Christopher and the pain of finding out that he was sick and a murderer.

His madness unraveled in front of me as he had a conversation with himself… as he debated on whether or not to kill me. He wanted me dead, and he wanted to protect me all at the same time.

His eyes moved my way and latched onto me. Pain moved over his expression, and his shoulders dropped.

"Lyla." My name rushed from his lips in a whisper. "I'm sick. I don't know what's wrong with me"

He dropped to his knees and the urge to go to him—to hold him—was overwhelming.

As he shook his head in disbelief, his eyes glazed over and filled with heated tears. He looked so lost—so afraid. The big, fearless man he'd always been was gone. In his place was the scared nineteen-year-old boy I'd seen in the pictures. I didn't understand it.

The path of my tears cooled on my skin and I sniffled, wiping my nose with the back of my hand. I hadn't even realized I was crying. It was all too much to take in. The man I was in love with was a murderer—a monster—a sick person in need of mental health professionals immediately.

The knowledge of what was going on trickled through my brain and down my spine until it reached the pit of my stomach, making me nauseated.

"I think I killed him."

He looked up at me in desperation, his eyes full of trust, and I had to close my eyes and look away when a single tear dripped down his cheek.

"Please, Lyla. Please help me," he begged.

My legs moved on their own, stepping around Douglas until I was standing before Christopher. Tucked away in the back of my mind was fear. I was putting myself in the path of a brutal murderer, but I loved him so much. I couldn't stand by and watch as he begged for my help. Not after all he'd done for me. Not after all we'd been through together. And if by some chance he turned on me and took my life, then so be it.

He fell forward, his bloodied face buried in my stomach, and I couldn't help myself, I wrapped my arms around his shoulders. His body shook as he cried, his deep, manly voice breaking over his tears as he tried to talk with his face smashed into my stomach.

"Shhh," I soothed him with closed eyes. "It's going to be okay. We'll get you some help."

My heart flipped in my chest, breaking into hundreds of irreparable pieces. My breath was stolen, and I couldn't breathe. No air would move into my lungs. I was slowly suffocating as I held the man I loved against me.

He stopped crying and looked up at me with a tearstained face. There were lines in the blood on his cheeks where his tears had fallen, a trail of sadness mixed with a trail of murder.

My fingers moved over the mixture, feeling his skin and

wishing that things could have been different—wishing that I'd met him under different circumstances—wishing he wasn't sick.

In the distance, the sound of police sirens echoed. They were coming for him, and as badly as I wanted to keep him forever, I knew I couldn't. I knew he belonged behind bars, but not at Fulton. I'd still get him out of that place. I'd still save him from prison, but in return, he'd spend the rest of his days in a mental institution. It was where he belonged.

He tensed when the sirens grew louder. Their flashing lights skimmed my curtains and even in the middle of the day, they lit up the white lace with red and blue.

The soft overgrowth of Christopher's hair tickled my palm as I ran my fingers over his face and head. Perhaps I was sick for still showing him emotion knowing he'd killed a man not minutes before. Maybe that made me a terrible person, but I couldn't help it. I loved him.

"I'm a monster, Lyla."

"Shhh," I continued to soothe him. "You're not a monster; you're just sick. I promise we'll get you help. I promise I'll get you out of Fulton."

His eyes grew wide and he stood, backing away from me like I was the dangerous one.

"No." He shook his head. "I'm dangerous. I can't be trusted. I belong at Fulton. I belong away from you."

Again, tears filled his eyes and escaped down his cheeks. He closed his eyes and turned his head. He was in pain. I was in pain. And there was nothing we could do to make it go away.

"No. You belong in a facility, but not one like Fulton. I'll take care of you, Christopher. I love you so much."

Again, his eyes widened. "Don't love me, Lyla!" he shouted, making me jump.

Seeing my distress, his voice softened. "I'm sorry. I didn't mean to yell at you. It's just that it's not save to love me."

I moved. When I went to him and wrapped my arms around his center, he didn't stop me. He didn't touch me either. Instead, he held his palms up as if he'd kill me with a single touch.

"I'm protecting you, Lyla. Let me protect you from me, please," he begged.

I hugged him tighter, sure that I, too, was losing my mind. "I'll be fine. We'll make this work." I couldn't believe the words that were coming from my mouth. What kind of person was I?

Grasping my shoulders, he set me away from him. The sadness in his eyes cleared and instead, I only saw resolve.

"No. I'm not doing this to you. I won't ruin your life this way."

He wasn't making any sense, but before I could ask him what he meant, a policeman called out to us over the loudspeaker.

"Christopher Jacobs, we know you're in there. Come out with your hands up."

Looking down at me, he ran his thumb over my cheek and the sadness returned to his eyes. "Thank you, Lyla, for giving me greatness."

I swallowed the lump in my throat and nodded. "No, thank you."

Standing on my tiptoes, I pressed my lips to his. He kissed me back briefly before pulling away and clenching his eyes closed.

"I'm going to do whatever it takes to keep you safe. I love you more than anything in this world." His words struck me in the chest and again, a wave of fresh tears rushed down my cheeks.

"I love you, too, Christopher."

His somber eyes devoured my face as if it were the last time he'd ever seen me. It wasn't. I was going to fix this, even if fixing this meant having him committed for life. I'd rather him live the rest of his days in a mental facility than Fulton.

"You're not going to give me up, are you?" he asked.

I shook my head. "No. You're mine, and I'm yours. That's all that matters. We'll deal with the rest as it comes."

Leaning in once more, he kissed me hard, weakening my knees and sending my mind twirling, but when he pulled away, he pushed me to the wall and pinned me there. Fear flooded my veins, but I didn't flinch. He loved me. Regardless of how sick he was, I had faith that he would never hurt me.

"What are you doing?"

"I'm saving you from me." He pressed his forehead to mine and breathed me in. "I want you to live your life, Lyla. Get married. Have beautiful babies with your red hair and beautiful green eyes. I want you to forget about me."

"Never," I said desperately.

"Then you leave me no choice."

Turning me, he handcuffed me with Douglas' handcuffs. I pulled against the restraints, trying to figure out when he took them from Douglas' body.

Afterwards, he turned me to face him once again.

In the distance, I heard the police officers outside issue another warning. If he didn't go out, they were coming in. Either way, my gut told me this wasn't going to end well.

"Are you going to kill me now?" I asked. The cuffs behind my back clacked against the wall as I struggled to get free.

His rough finger moved across my cheek and his eyes moved over my face, taking me in and devouring me whole.

"I love you more than life, Lyla... more than my next breath. I love you in an impossible way that burns my skin and scrambles my soul. It's you. It will always be you."

Stepping away from me, he moved to Douglas' body once more. Bending, he reached for the revolver clipped to his side and plucked it from its holder.

I closed my eyes, my fear, hurt, and love combining to make me feel sick to my stomach. Mentally, I prepared myself for the end. He was going to shoot me. Sure, he was saying words of love, but he was sick... he was disturbed and unhinged.

He moved toward me once more, the gun heavy at his side, and I held my head high, looking death in the face. "I love you, Christopher. No matter what you do to me, I love you. I know you're sick. I understand you can't help it." I meant my words.

Pain flashed across his eyes once more. "No. You still don't get it. I'd never hurt you. Not ever. It's you, Lyla. You're everything to me."

Moving in, he kissed me again, his warm lips marking my memory. He moaned against my mouth, and I could taste the tears on his tongue.

When he pulled away, I sucked in my breath.

He backed away from me and toward the front door with his eyes locked on mine.

"What are you going to do?" I asked.

He didn't respond. Instead, he smiled and mouthed the words *I love you* once more.

It wasn't until he was pulling open the front door that I realized what he was doing, but by then, it was too late. I moved away from the wall, tripping over my own feet to get to him, but he slammed the door behind him in a loud crash.

Silence swallowed me whole for a few seconds, and then the loudspeaker sounded once more.

"Put the gun down or we'll shoot."

A moment of silence and then a single gunshot echoed loudly, making me jump, and that single gunshot was followed by many more.

Chaos ensued once the silence settled in. Officers rushed my apartment, finding me handcuffed on my knees in front of the door. Tears streamed uncontrollably down my face, and the screams of a desperate woman lit up my living room.

I glanced up just as Charlie filled my doorway, and that was all it took. I broke like a priceless vase — like a doll that had been laid on the floor and stomped on. I would never be the same again. I was altered so deeply that I was sure I could feel the cracks as they formed on my soul.

CHRISTOPHER JACOBS LEFT this world in a blaze of glory. At least, that was how the news reporters said it. They liked to add that extra bit of drama for ratings. I watched the news on Diana's flat screen and cried while the reporters went off about what a terrible criminal he was and how the world was safer without him.

Little did they know he was only doing what he did best... he was protecting me. Sure, it was from himself, but he'd loved me too much to let the monster that hid within him get me.

Charlie and the boys helped me pack up my apartment. I couldn't stay there knowing what happened in there. I couldn't close my eyes without seeing Douglas dead on the floor or Christopher saying goodbye. It was too much.

Instead, I put all my stuff in a storage, packed what I needed until I got back on my feet, and crashed on Diana's couch, which wasn't as comfortable as I'd hoped it would be seeing that she was dating a new guy who liked to come over all the time.

Still, anything was better than the shadows that crept through my apartment, filling my sleep with nightmares, or the memories that hid in the walls, waiting to haunt me. Not to mention the terrible stained floor that was just beneath the new carpeting. I knew in the back of my mind that I was being unreasonable, but it didn't matter.

Nothing much mattered anymore. I didn't have much to look forward to since I wasn't sure I'd ever be as happy as I was when I was with Christopher ever again.

The news on Fulton Rhodes Penitentiary broke days later. The warden was arrested for his crimes against the inmates, and a few COs went down with him. Apparently, he'd become a very rich man thanks to the fight club that no one talked about. Stories filled the TV screen. Ones about corruption and crime—about cover-ups and murder—stories about Christopher.

I watched even though it broke my heart. I watched because they'd occasionally show a picture of him, and I'd get to see him once more.

Charlie posted armed officers outside Diana's house until the crap with the Rizuttos and the Lanzas died down. The green-light on me seemed to expire the second I stopped digging into

Christopher's case—the second he died and the family's secrets were no longer at risk. They hadn't set him up, but they still had things to hide. My digging for his sake had put those secrets in danger.

It all made sense now. The puzzle pieces of Fulton and everyone involved in Christopher's life fell into place. I didn't like the image it was painting, and when the puzzle was completely done, I stared at a portrait of a very sad future. One without the man I loved. One that I wasn't sure I wanted to live to see.

Depression was real.

Monsters were real, too. They didn't live in our closets or hide under our beds. They squatted within us—coming out occasionally to destroy the things we loved—coming out to destroy us.

EPILOGUE

"**LOOK, MOMMY, I'M** a monster!" Christopher called out as he ran across the park toward me.

He held his arms above his head and clawed his fingers like he was going to get me.

I laughed and pretended to be afraid. "You are! You're a *scary* monster," I played along.

He growled at me, reminding me so much of his father, before he ran away, laughing on his short, three-year-old legs. His brown hair flapped in the breeze, and his smile lit up the park like the sun above us.

I'd never seen anything so beautiful in my life.

Who knew that two people were capable of producing something so wonderful?

I liked to think that if Christopher knew what he was leaving behind, he would've stayed for me, but then again, I thought he knew how unstable he was. Deep down, I know that it wouldn't have mattered how he left or when he left, he was always bound to leave. He was sick and had he not taken the route he did that day outside my apartment, he would've done so at a later point.

Just thinking about him still hurt, but I had to move on.

Especially once I found out that a tiny part of Christopher was growing inside me.

Some days when I looked at my son, my heart ached. It was so full of love for him for one, and two, because his eyes were an exact match to his father's, royal blue and so dark and mysterious that I could never figure out what he was thinking.

His smile reminded me of my final night with Christopher and how happy he'd looked. How free he was in the moment. Little things, like taking longer in the shower or sleeping in a comfortable bed, had meant the world to him. But more than that, I felt happy knowing that his final night on Earth, he was at peace.

Sometimes when I closed my eyes in a silent room, I could still hear his laughter. I'd only heard it a few times, but it stuck with me always. Occasionally before I fell asleep and my tiny, two-bedroom house was quiet, I could still hear his voice. I could almost make out the words *I love you*, and I'd fall asleep with a smile on my face.

I wasn't lonely, though. I had Christopher—my little man—my reason for everything I did in my life, and he was more than enough for me. He was all I needed.

"Christopher!" I called out.

We'd been at the park for over an hour, and the southern heat was starting to bake the top of my head. I stood, waiting for him to run back to me, but he was nowhere to be found. I moved across the sandy space, checking behind the equipment and dodging playing children.

"Christopher, where are you?" I called out loudly.

Panic moved in, but it dissolved immediately the second I spotted my son playing in the sandbox beneath the slide. I moved up behind him, listening as he talked to no one. It was kind of cute.

I moved closer, ready to tap his shoulder and playfully pull him into my arms, but I stopped when I heard exactly what it was he was saying. My heart slammed against my ribs. Surely, I was hearing him wrong. He was only three. Three years olds didn't think like that.

"No," Christopher said adamantly. "I don't want to hurt Mommy. It's my job to protect her."

I gasped, earning his attention. He turned my way with worried eyes before he smiled at me. The corners of his mouth lifted and his cheeks puffed out, but the smile never really reached his eyes.

"Oh hi, Mommy, are we leaving now?" he asked.

I swallowed over the sandpaper in my throat and nodded. "Yeah, baby. It's time to go home."

He stood, shaking the sand from his shorts. "Good, because I don't want to play with the monster anymore."

I felt dizzy. He words were so close to the last ones his father had spoken minutes before he basically took his own life.

"What monster, baby? I don't see anyone."

Christopher laughed, his baby soft cheeks reddening and his dark blue eyes glistening. "You can't see him, silly. He's inside of me, Mommy."

If you or someone you love has been a victim of
rape or any other form of abuse, please seek help at
http://www.joyfulheartfoundation.org

If you or anyone you love suffers from a mental disorder and
you feel like that person might be a danger to themselves
or the people around them, please seek help at
your local mental health institution.

COMING OCTOBER 27TH

SACKED

When Sawyer Reed wants something, he gets it.

And I WANT her.

She doesn't know it yet, but she's already mine.

Her resistance is futile because once I start a play, I always follow through. And I ALWAYS win.

Nothing, not even the deep-seated hate I have for my rival, Jacob Byrd, is going to keep me from my end game.

And my end game is Gretchen Cole.

But I have to keep my head in the game. Everyone knows what happens to a quarterback when he loses focus. He gets SACKED.

ALSO BY TABATHA VARGO

THE CHUBBY GIRL CHRONICLES

On the Plus Side
Hot and Heavy — Coming in 2016!

THE BLOW HOLE BOYS

Playing Patience (Zeke)
Perfecting Patience 1.5 (Zeke)
Finding Faith (Finn)
Convincing Constance (Tiny)
Having Hope (Chet) — Coming in 2016!

CO-WRTTEN WITH MELISSA ANDREA

Little Black Book
The Wrath of Sin
The Procedure
Jack Hammer

STALK TABATHA VARGO

www.tabathavargo.blogspot.com
www.facebook.com/tabathadvargo
www.twitter.com/tabathavargo
Sign up for updates: http://eepurl.com/R29_5

ACKNOWLEDGEMENTS

Thank you. Yes, you, the reader. Without you I would still be writing in notebooks and hiding my stories under my mattress. You're awesome and I can't thank you enough for taking the time out of your life to read my work.

A massive THANK YOU to R.D. Douglas for giving me a hand with Slammer. The storyline for Slammer has been stuck in my head for almost two years. It was nice to finally get it out and R.D. was there for the whole ride. So thank you for being an amazing and supportive friend.

To the lifer who wished to remain nameless: thank you for your hardcore honesty and attention to detail. You've lived the prison life for many years and your knowledge was needed. May the rest of your life be easier and may you finally get a decent piece of chocolate cake. You're not an innocent man, but being locked behind the cinderblock walls of prison has made you an honest man. Thank you for taking time out of your life to help me with this book.

To the correctional officers, who also wished to remain nameless: thank you for your help with Slammer and also for having the balls to do your job. You boys make the world a safer place and for that, you kick so much ass. Thank you.

To my beta readers: Melissa Skoog, Paula Kaesberg, Michele Wiegert, and Tonia Cardenas. Thank you. You girls got it rough, which is fine since I know y'all secretly like it rough. Hehehe

To my fabulous author friends, M.S. Brannon, J.M. LaRocca, and Vanessa Booke, who took Slammer for a spin and gave me honesty… THANK YOU!

Regina Wamba, the designing genius behind the dark and sexy cover for Slammer, you're amazing and I love you. Thank you.

To Nadege Richards, my formatter and adorable friend: I love you. That is all. Every time I see your face I smile and that means so much. You're freaking amazing and genuine. That's rare. I'm happy to call you my friend.

To my kick ass street team: you girls ROCK my face off. I love each of you for taking time out of your life to pimp me. I can't thank y'all enough for everything you do for me.

To Cassie Chapman and Danielle Linhart: thank you for always hooking me up with gorgeous swag. You girls are effing awesome. That is all.

Finally, to my hubby and my daughter: thank you for being understanding when I shut the world out to finish a book. You are the reason behind everything I do. I love you more than words and I'm so blessed to have you in my life. Mini, mommy loves you more than love.

Made in the USA
Lexington, KY
22 May 2016